BENTLEY BROWNE WINS THE DAY

BY HUGH E. COATES

CHAPTER 1

A Wave Goodbye

It was late June. Many weeks of endless drizzle and dense cloud had conspired to banish all good humour and tolerance from the Browne residence situated in close proximity to the picturesque village of Barton-on-the-Green, Hampshire, England.

The house, an early Victorian extravagance recently purchased by ageing musician and actor of some note, Bentley Browne, stood at the far edge of the village green opposite the church, conceived and built during the mid-18th century by local MP and government adviser Sir William Wiggins, considered by many at the time to be one of Hampshire's finest country homes, and was much desired by the local gentry. Set down in many acres of rural Hampshire close to the B2017 on its run to Portsmouth, adorned with chimneys of such ornate splendour as to rival Hampton Court Palace, it gazed down in comforting benevolence upon many aspects of rural life, its presence dominating all that lay before it.

The entrance to Barton Manor House lay just beyond cast iron gates recently restored to their original Victorian splendour, firm and in place, open and welcoming to all. A porter's lodge stood close by.

Long neglected, with windows boarded, a sad reflection on better days long gone. Continuing its journey, the driveway meandered for some distance between well-tended grassland before broadening out in front of the manor. A secondary driveway ran past the house to greet a partly restored barn and several outhouses, finally coming to rest before a neglected stable yard now sadly empty, bereft of both horse and carriage. At the rear of the house, a recently renovated terrace ran the considerable length of the building at either end of this expansive display of York stone. Broad steps reached down to sweeping lawns and herbaceous borders that ran away into the distance to embrace an impressive display of Victorian glasshouses encased within high walls of cherry red brickwork.

Up close to the entrance a motor coach, old in years, waited in silent anticipation. Its classic colours of county cream and maroon at one with the soft Hampshire stonework and dark cladding that adorned the front porch. A young man, tall and of shabby appearance, was seated upon the highest step in the open doorway of the coach out of the rain, dolefully drawing upon a cigarette, eyes purposely averted from a couple surrounded by suitcases standing in the porch. The woman pointed towards the coach displaying obvious dismay. "You expect me to travel in this thing?"

The man pulled upon his earlobe, a clear sign of discomfort. "Ah, a mistake, somewhat down the line," came the confession.

"A mistake?"

"Yes, it would appear so," he murmured.

"Explain your mistake please, Bentley."

"Well, I asked for a big old bus on account of the volume of luggage involved."

"Meaning?"

"Well, you must agree with me sweetheart that you do travel with a somewhat large accompaniment of suitcases wherever you go."

"What nonsense you do talk Bentley, and even if that were so I would not travel on this. It's more suitable for one of your awful English WI excursions to Bognor," she shuddered. "Tell me, Bentley," her anger growing by the second, "Is this a publicity stunt? I can only conclude that you wish for a return to the limelight."

"Good God no, most certainly not," Bentley assured her.

The driver, meantime, having finished his cigarette had left his perch and appeared at the front of the coach to begin polishing the headlights with conspicuous vigour. Pausing in his work, he approached Mrs Browne.

"If you will forgive my intrusion, madam, this coach is a Bedford O.B. 29 seater circa. 1949, one of the few remaining in service to the public." He reached for another cigarette. "I personally supervised every aspect of the restoration from start to finish. It's a delight, runs as good as new, and it will motor for many more years to come," he concluded proudly.

Mrs Browne was clearly unimpressed. "Yes, yes, I'm sure. Tell me, did my husband request this specific vehicle to drive me to Southampton?"

Receiving nodded encouragement from Bentley the driver answered without hesitation. "No madam, if truth be told, Mr Browne requested pretty much as he said, a big old buggy with plenty of room. It was my uncle's idea, him being a close friend of your husband and all that." He moved to the other headlight teasing it with the duster.

"Your uncle. Would that be Mr Rudd from the village?"

"Yes Mrs Browne, Chuffer Rudd is my uncle. Is that

a problem?"

"Of course it's a problem," she snapped, "one of many, but if my husband is unable to drive his wife to Southampton due to losing his licence, then I must put trust in you, Chuffer Rudd and a 1960 Bedford coach."

"A 1949 Bedford coach," said the driver correcting her.

"Oh yes, 1949, sorry," she sighed wearily, resigned to her fate.

"You could do worse, Mrs Browne," the driver persisted. "For a start there is a stack of room for all of your luggage, you can sit where you wish and," the driver added encouragingly, "you can see over the top of the hedges and glimpse another world."

"Yes, yes, I can see that as a mode of transport it has its advantages." Grabbing Bentley's arm his wife pulled him to one side, away from the driver. "Look Bentley, I'm not completely without a sense of humour, and should it get me to the cruise ship on time, I shall say no more; anything to get me away from this dreadful weather. Sometimes Bentley, I swear you are best appreciated from the back end of a departing taxi, or in this unfortunate occasion, a coach," she added wearily.

"I shouldn't be too eager to get away Christina, they say a heatwave is imminent, coming in from the Azores."

"Bentley, even if this English weather were to improve a hundred per cent it would not encourage me to stay. A few days of sunshine does not constitute a summer to me, so please spare me. And to add to my misery, in a week or two that awful village fete will be upon us again. A week of unremitting noise, irritating whistles, poop poops, growls, and unmentionable smells. Not for me Bentley, last year was enough. Vulgarity abounds in this country." She grabbed him by the arm. "Come out and join us in Bermuda Bentley. Have a holiday, have a break," she urged.

"Christina, I am far too busy for foreign jaunts. We've been through all this many times. There is much work on the manor to complete."

She glanced across at the driver who was showing signs of impatience. "Must go Bentley," she said, "the rain is starting to ease, wonder upon wonder." She stood on tiptoe and kissed him warmly on the lips. "I do love you, Bentley."

"Me too."

"If you change your mind…." She prodded him

playfully in the stomach. "It has to be said Bentley, you're going to seed. You need more exercise."

"Thank you, most kind."

"Bentley, my love. At the risk of repeating myself, you have to get rid of this monstrosity on the courtyard, people are talking."

"What people?"

"Village people. That nice Mr Patel from the corner shop said it confirmed his view on western decadence. You are aware that it can be seen from the church spire?"

"Well the solution to that would appear to be not to go up there my love," Bentley retorted flatly.

"Has to be said Bentley, you've become a spiv, what folk in Italy call, no, I won't say, I won't demean myself. How a man such as yourself having been so successful in life can become involved with such a man as Chuffer Rudd is beyond me. The name Chuffer, what kind of name is that for a grown man?"

"I have it on good authority that it is a nickname. As a child, he loved steam trains. His father was station master at Horsham before Beeching closed the line."

"What nonsense are you talking now, Bentley. Who's

Beeching? You spend every hour working on this place or in the public house engaged in deals with that man Rudd," Mrs Browne persisted.

"Shady deals? Hours in the pub? Really Christina, you do exaggerate on occasions. Sunday lunchtime, light conversation over a beer or two. What's the harm in that? I have precious little social life as it is."

"You should come on holiday with us then, shouldn't you?" came the sharp reply.

"Not again. Please." Bentley groaned. However, her caustic remarks regarding Chuffer Rudd reminded Bentley of sleepless nights during completion of the stoneworks and a recent conversation with the man during payment for work completed.

"There you are Mr Browne, the largest area of natural stonework me and my boys have ever set down in one spot. There may be a few extra shillings involved but that it is to be expected, what with all the cutting and that, that's what takes the time, the cutting, pushes up the price. Mind you, I threw in a good-looking statue for virtually nothing. Looks a treat on your drive," he added proudly. Bentley had paid up in full without protest despite serious misgivings over the providence of the Portland stone as it was always arriving at weekends under the cover of darkness and in an unmarked pick up. His wife's wise words had re-awakened many unwelcome misgivings.

"Bentley, Bentley, are you listening to me? What is wrong with you, pay attention please."

"Sorry, daydreaming."

"Promise me Bentley that you will remove that statue on the drive before I return. If I ever should return," she added darkly.

"I will ignore that threat. Anyway, it would not be easy, it weighs a ton," he conceded ruefully.

"You should have considered that before accepting the damn thing. Cover it up with something Bentley, please. Please, promise me."

"I promise."

"Today?"

"Oh steady on!"

"Today, please," she implored, "make your wife happy, please."

"Ok. Today," Bentley agreed reluctantly.

"One more thing Bentley."

"Eh, you mean there's more?"

"Yes, there's more. May I remind you of Mrs Clemspon our housekeeper, you may remember her, she runs around after you all the time. She will not be here for a few weeks. She is having her veins done." Bentley winced at the very thought. "She has arranged for a replacement to take care of your needs whilst I am away."

Bentley protested strongly. "Hang on! Not necessary, I can look after myself thank you."

"That's just it Bentley, it is necessary, you can hardly boil a kettle without setting fire to something. The lady will present herself to you on Monday morning. She comes highly recommended. She is the new vicar's wife."

Bentley groaned. "Vicar's wife? God help me."

"Her name is Mrs Jameson. I have not met her personally. Mrs Clemspon has done all the arrangements. She was a local girl apparently. Her family emigrated to Australia some years ago. She's back here on an exchange visit accompanied by her husband, a man of the cloth, for some six months or so. Christian integration and harmony apparently. Time to pause and reflect on Christian values and encourage further understanding between God's flock. Something like that or so I'm led to believe, should be right up your street Bentley."

"Mmm, you seem to be very well informed Mrs Browne. Very impressive. So you are to leave your husband in the hands of a vicar's wife. Thank you my love, very kind."

"Bentley, be nice to her. You can be nice when you try," squeezing his arm affectionately. "You may also catch a glimpse of our gardener Mr Rawlings and his boy, he comes in every day."

"I am aware of Rawlings, my dear, I'm not in a complete vacuum you know."

"Good, that means you will recognise him when it comes to payment. He doesn't say much but he expects to be paid in cash Friday dinnertime." She looked up at him forgivingly. "Have you got all that Bentley? I will phone when I get there, keep your mobile on."

"No, damn thing, you'll have to use the landline," came the firm reply.

"Really Bentley, you test the patience of a saint. Look I must go, help me with the luggage darling will you?"

Within seconds, all luggage aboard with fond farewells completed, a reluctant Mrs Browne joined the driver on the coach. A surprisingly robust engine burst into life and with a crunch of the gravel and a turn of the wheel, the ageing coach was away up the drive. A final wave and then out of view onto the open road, past the green, turning right at the church heading towards the A30 and Winchester. Trailing behind, an ever-increasing spiral of toxic smoke to be seen for many miles around.

Within the hour, just outside Winchester, the long predicted change in the weather came to fruition. Skies above southern England miraculously cleared, temperatures soared and with it, the nation's spirits. An uninterrupted afternoon's play at Lord's between England and Australia was keenly anticipated. Coastal roads were solid and donkeys ventured onto the sands at Margate. Several ice-cream cornets were sold in quick succession on Brighton pier and Mrs Browne, upon reaching Winchester bypass seriously considered returning home.

CHAPTER 2

A Constable Calls

Meantime, back at The Gables, Bentley, having dutifully covered the offending statue in bubble wrap was seated upon the terrace, glass in hand, when he received a visit from the local bobby, Norman Willoughby, a recent graduate from Hendon Police College, now working out of Petersfield. He had been successful in securing lodgings at Mrs Bishop's semi in Lower Barton for the duration of a six-month probationary period. A tall lad of high nervous energy, narrow in the head and hip, he was in no mood to take prisoners. After an almost incoherent introduction lasting several minutes a bemused Bentley gleaned from the young man that after a night out with several colleagues at a Real Ale Appreciation Society held fortnightly in the Coach and Horses public house in Havant near Portsmouth, he had been drawn from his bed much earlier than anticipated that morning to answer an excited phone call from God knows where, he shrugged, reporting on a dangerous level of toxic smoke in the vicinity of the Barton Manor, perhaps indicating a fire. Although officially off duty this weekend, Bentley was informed by the constable he had risen from his bed regardless determined to do his duty.

"Did the call come from this property, sir?"

"No, most certainly not young man, if you ask me I..." The constable raised a hand, irritation evident.

"Before you continue sir, I feel I must point out to you that any investigation I undertake I shall insist on being addressed as Police Constable Willoughby, never ever young man. It indicates a lack of respect for the force sir. Furthermore, should we ever find ourselves in a social gathering, I wish to be addressed as Norman, never ever under any circumstances, Norm!"

"Whatever you wish constable, I'm with you all the way. I must say it is rare indeed in these days of loose morals and the sad decline in social behaviour to encounter such leadership from one so young. I am impressed." Bentley reached upon the table for the wine bottle. "In the interests of hospitality constable, help yourself to a glass. You look rather under the weather, if I may say so, perhaps an aspirin, I am sure I could find one or two somewhere if you give me a minute." Dismissing both offers and with a deep frown and a firm shake of the head the young man took a brief stroll along the stonework, sniffing the air with gusto for several minutes. Finally, finding little of interest the constable returned to Bentley's side.

"Slight touch of toxic in the air sir, recent barbecue perhaps but perhaps not," he shrugged, "as for your kind offer of a pick me up, not for me, and as for the aspirin sir, I am in fine form, thank you. Now to business. You are the present owner of this property I deduce, am I correct sir?"

"You are constable, yes, very astute of you."
"Your name sir, would it be Mr Browne, with an e, Bentley Browne?"

"Yes constable, correct."

"You must forgive my ignorance Mr Browne, I am new to this area, yet to find my feet."

"I understand constable"

"Now sir, my reason for being here and not tucked up in my bed. Toxic smoke sir, a phone call suggesting a fire."

"I know nothing of such a nature constable, I can assure you."

The constable looked around him displaying undeniable disapproval as to his palatial surroundings. "You do display an extravagant lifestyle during this period of government cutbacks affecting most of the country if I may say so sir."

"You may constable, yes, I have no problem with your assessment of my lifestyle."

"Are you a merchant banker, perhaps, or a politician maybe."

"No constable, neither, not so fortunate I'm afraid."

"You are married sir I imagine."

"I am constable, for the umpteenth time if I am truthful."

"In that case then may I speak to the present Mrs Browne sir?"

"Not today constable I'm afraid."

"And why would that be sir may I ask?"

"Well may I ask as to why you would wish to speak to my wife constable?"

"To confirm I am not the victim of a hoax sir, wasting police time."

"I know nothing of a fire constable, nor a hoax, as for my good lady, she is away for six weeks cruising in the Caribbean."

"Mmm, how the other half lives eh sir?"
"Yes I am very fortunate constable, now if you don't mind I have things to attend to."

"Such as sir?"

"Every day living constable, every day living."

"Er, are there others I can converse with Mr Browne? Family, household staff, a butler perhaps?" the constable persisted.

"No constable, no staff, no Jeeves to call upon at this moment in time, I am on my own and glad to be so at the moment. Now if you are finished." Bentley rose from beneath the parasol. "If I may say so once again constable, you look rather unwell, I am concerned, we don't want you throwing up all over the stone work do we constable?"

The constable nodded in agreement. "No sir, you have a point, I do feel rather wishy washy. I shall continue this investigation another day. Perhaps a sudden rise in temperature has got to me somewhat." Plainly unwell, the young man rubbed upon his stomach somewhat gingerly. "I shall return to my lodgings forthwith sir."

"Very sensible constable. Have you means of transport?"

"No transport sir, it would not be prudent of me to get behind the wheel after a night out with my colleagues."

"Very sensible constable. I could offer you a lift but as you are aware, I have had a drop or two myself this lunchtime. It would not be prudent of me to invite trouble upon myself, you being a policeman of such honest conviction. However, let me escort you to the green."

"No sir, I am Hendon trained, thank you, my radar level is spot on."

"I insist constable."

Following Bentley to the front of the house the young constable paused along the way to point out a top heavy fig tree standing high in a large terracotta container, suggesting as he passed that the container could, if hit by a strong wind overturn and injure a passing child. Bentley to his great credit listened intently before pointing out in a reassuring manner that children were unlikely to visit The Gables at the moment and any such intruders, however young, would be severely dealt with.

"Nevertheless," the constable insisted, "such things should be considered in the interests of health and safety, sir." That said, the lad hurried along the driveway followed closely by Bentley. Reaching the lodge house, the constable turned to face Bentley.
"Before I go sir, may I comment on a few matters?"

"If you're up to it constable, of course."

"Well sir, the gates here, wide open, rather surprisingly an easy entrance to property of such opulence if I may say so, a delight to criminal opportunists, don't you think sir?"

"Yes constable, I am aware of such possibilities. I have further work to do to them and given time, I plan to restore the house and surroundings to original Victorian splendour, that is my wish. Now I shall say goodbye constable. Many thanks for your concern regarding Barton Manor but I can assure you there has been no incident here."

"As you say sir, as you say. However, I must point out I am proud of my reaction to this morning's incident. I have displayed pride in my uniform and responded rapidly to an emergency above and beyond the call of duty. I rest my case, but be assured sir, this matter is not closed, I shall return."

"Yes, constable, a bit like Superman eh?"

"Sorry sir, I didn't catch that."

"I said I'm a super fan constable."

"Thank you sir."

That said, the constable hurried across the green in the direction of Lower Barton. Bentley, in the meantime, returned to his sun lounger.

CHAPTER 3

Help From Above

"Hello! Excuse the intrusion, may I come over?" The request, apologetic in tone came from behind the high laurel hedge that ran the length of the grand conservatory. Momentarily denied a planned afternoon's indulging, Bentley rose reluctantly from beneath the parasol to beckon his latest visitor closer with a wave of the hand.

"Yes, yes of course, all are welcome at the manor, open all hours here." Shielding his eyes from the explosive sunshine gripping southern England that afternoon, Bentley watched her skip lightly across the stonework. Standing beside him, a vision of autumnal delight, she offered a hand in greeting.

"Pleased to meet you, Mr Browne. I have heard much about you, some good, some bad," she added followed by a mischievous chuckle. "My name's Melody."

Bentley shook her hand with increasing enthusiasm. "Pleased to meet you Melody. Interesting name. Cue for a song perhaps?"

Hands on hips radiating ill-concealed excitement she

looked around. "All as I remember," she signed contentedly. "Save this perhaps." She tapped upon the stone veranda with her toe. "This is all new. In Major Newgent's reign, this was all long neglected herbaceous border. Not a man for home improvements was our major. Anywhere you looked, the property back then was falling into disrepair. Mind you it was many years ago, it looks wonderful now. An absolute delight to the eye."

"So are you young lady, if I may be so bold." Bentley reached for a second sun lounger, drawing it into the shade under the parasol. "Join me and tell me who you are and what it is you want with me." Without hesitation, she accepted the offer.

"My dear man, I am so sorry, I was given to understand you were expecting me, forgive me."

"Nothing to forgive, I assure you. But at this moment in time I am drowning in a pool of uncertainty as to who you are." She reached out upon the table in front of her to draw a half-empty bottle of wine closer.

"Could this be the cause of your amnesia?" she teased. "May I?" Reaching for his glass, she took a quick sip returning the wine to the table with a triumphant smile. "Just as I thought, peach wine, 14% in strength. One of the major's favourites. Where on earth did you come by it after all this time?" She removed the cork from the neck of the bottle. "May I keep it as a memento, the bottle is almost empty, it won't affect the taste," she giggled.

"Be my guest," Bentley replied, overcome with good intent, "whatever makes you happy Melody."

She moved her chair closer to him under the parasol. "Bentley. I may call you Bentley may I?"

"You may madam, you may indeed."

"In answer to your question as to why I am here, I am responding to a cry for help from a Mrs Clemspon, your housekeeper I am given to understand. She has approached me with a request, that being, to keep an eye on your good self over the coming six weeks or so while your wife is away re-charging her batteries, while she herself is in recovery from a recent operation on her varicose veins. So it was decided that I, being a curate's wife may have the necessary experience and patience to handle such a person as yourself. That Mr Browne is why I am here."

Momentarily unbalanced but still on his toes Bentley forced a weary half smile. "My apologies, I should have realised. Most reassuring to be placed in the hands of one so qualified to handle my often erratic and outlandish behaviour. I shall be forever grateful."

She rebuked his remarks with a playful wag of the finger. "Don't be so difficult, Mr Browne, you're a man, that says it all, I shall say no more except I will be honest and admit the prospect of spending some little time back at Barton House where I spent many of my formative years sufficient compensation for running around after you for a few hours a week. I have such fond memories of this grand house; it could prove to be a pleasure." She stretched out on the recliner, hands behind her head, eyes closed contentment evident. "Do you know Mr Browne, this is the first time since my return to England I have experienced sunshine, my idea of heaven. Strange comment from a vicar's other half perhaps, but true."

Reaching beneath the table Bentley produced a further bottle of peach wine. "Would madam join me in a toast to the major?" he asked.

"She would indeed Mr Browne."

"Good, then whilst you relax Melody, tell me how come you came by such a name? And I would be more than interested to know a little more of your time with the Major."

She laughed. "I have been asked this many times and the answer is very simple but says much more about my father really. He was ten years old at the end of World War II, grew up with big band music, loved it, never took to pop music, etc. When I was born in 1970 big bands had had their day really, sadly in decline, and he missed the melody, hence the name, a reminder of better days for him."

"Sounds a decent chap," Bentley concluded.
"Yes, he is still alive and with us at 83, still loves big bands and melody," she laughed.

"And you, young lady, what's your taste in music?"

"Oh anything and everything, as long as I can dance to it," she giggled.

"And the major?"

"I should think he is rather past dancing now Bentley, I am sure the major received his wings in heaven many, many years ago, sadly. I worked for him during my teenage years before my family emigrated to Australia. I believe at the time he made some bad investments and he lost a great deal of money in the mid 70's and in an effort to keep the manor house he turned to making authentic country wines, a hobby he turned into a business, did very well, Barton Country Wine, quite a demand for the label I believe. During the school holidays and weekends I would label and date, cork etc, dogsbody really, but he was a lovely man and it helped that I was seeing his younger son, Charles at the time, very innocent it was, too innocent perhaps," she laughed. "He started seeing someone else but I wasn't too concerned, I was off to a new life and this," she picked the cork out of her pocket, "is a memento of my teenage days at Barton Manor. Happy days. But that's enough of me, let's talk of you Bentley Browne. I know of you of course, I remember your music and your reputation and of course your appearance on a long running television series as an officer of the law, what was his name?" she drummed upon the table, "Detective Inspector..."

"Jack Dawkins," Bentley answered finally.

"That's it. It was terrific, still very popular in Australia, repeated all the time on the box."

"Really, I never realised." Bentley raised his glass. "Here's to Inspector Dawkins, I must have a word with my agent, there might be some outstanding royalties in the pipeline somewhere. Could contribute towards the upkeep of the manor somewhat."

She smiled. "I'm glad to bring a little sunshine into your life Mr Browne. Now changing the subject, how long have you been here exactly?"

Bentley thought hard. "Mmmm, just under three years I think, the first year was a nightmare, builders in month after month, it was a complete...well, cost a small fortune, but much accomplished in a short time.

Next in line is the lodge house and then I will concentrate upon the greenhouses. Much to do but I shall do it in my own time, perhaps with a little help from a local builder. Now I have retired from showbusiness I have time on my hands."

"Do you miss it, showbusiness?"

"Yes I do, I must admit, but I needed a break for a while, age catches up with you young lady." She nodded sympathetically.

"Which begs the question, why didn't you accompany your wife on the cruise? A six week Caribbean cruise, oh bliss, I would have moved heaven and earth for just the chance."

"Yes, I understand your point but in truth, having travelled the world many times I've seen much of it and enjoyed it immensely at the time, but now I find I get a little restless after a few days and I need to focus my mind on some project or another, otherwise I spend much of the day on a bar stool drinking I'm afraid, much to my wife's annoyance. But I must point out that my wife is not alone, she is accompanied by her two sisters and if I know the three of them, they will enjoy themselves far more without me around, hopefully to return to England full of fun and good humour," adding wistfully, "one can only pray."

For the next hour or so, the two remained beneath the parasol engaged in easy conversation. She, reminiscing with much fondness about her early days in Barton and subsequent life in Australia. Bentley likewise suitably engaging with choice anecdotes recalling his life on the road as a musician, TV actor and his subsequent retirement. Finally, late afternoon as the sun slipped behind a trio of mature horse chestnut trees she called it a day. "I really must go, Bentley, my poor husband will wonder where I am. Nice to have met you." Bentley struggled gamely to his feet.

"You must let me escort you to the vicarage, I insist madam." She turned.

"My dear chap, you are in no condition to put one foot in front of the other let alone cross the green unaided," she giggled, "besides, I came by bicycle, it's resting alongside your lodge house." Retrieving her straw hat and dark glasses from the tabletop, she turned to go.

"Er Melody, before you go what is your decision?"

"Decision?"

"Yes, decision. Regarding working at The Gables. What do you say?"

She turned to face him, her face adopting a serious pose. "Well I shall have to speak to my dear husband first," came the reply.

"Oh yes, yes, of course," Bentley conceded. She laughed delightedly.

"I'm teasing you. Yes of course I will, it will be a pleasure."

"It will? Aah wonderful, when shall you begin?"
"Well I have a busy schedule at present; it will be next week, perhaps on Thursday morning at 9 o'clockish. Will you be up by that time?"

"Mmm, I'll make sure I am madam."

"Good, good. Now Mr Browne, I really must move on but before I do tell me, where did you find this wine exactly?"

"The boilers in the greenhouse, full of wine bottles, hundreds and hundreds of them. I came across them quite by chance. And now I know how they got there, bequeathed by Major Nugent, I would like to know more of his life."

She stopped mid-stride. "I may be of some help there. I suggest you visit the corner shop on the green and seek out a copy of…" she paused a moment deep in thought. "Mmm that's it," she continued knowingly, "a history of Barton on the Green written by local historian Elizabeth Standing if my memory serves me correctly. A whole chapter is devoted to Barton Village. You may ask how I am so well informed, well, before we emigrated to Australia, my dear old dad purchased a copy to take with us to remind us of home and our English heritage should we ever feel the need in moments of homesickness of course. I must confess, I reached for it on occasions and it gave me comfort, but I soon came to love my new life and have no regrets whatsoever. Mum and Dad are still fit and well over there, thank the Lord. However, I digress, there may be a copy somewhere in the far corner of the shop gathering dust, and it will tell you everything you wish to know concerning Barton Manor."

"The corner shop you say, Mr Patel?"

"Yes, that's him. You've met him of course?"

"Well I can't say I have, but my wife mentions him from time to time. I have never ventured into his store."

"Oh, he's the most charming man Bentley, born salesman. I must tell you this before I go. Upon our arrival at the vicarage after a 24 hour journey from Australia plus a subsequent trip from Heathrow, my husband and I, upon reaching the vicarage by taxi and ready for bed, were confronted by a van parked up outside, heavily laden with everything from fresh vegetables to toothpaste and toilet rolls, all on offer at discounted prices, presented by who do you think? He wouldn't take no for an answer and we ended up buying half that he had on offer, quite a killing he made. However, most charming man, I liked him. And you say you've never visited the shop, you've lived in Barton for two years and never popped in there?"

"No, I've never had cause to, my wife takes care of much of that sort of thing."

"Mmm, as I first reasoned Mr Browne, like most men you are spoilt. Women run after you all the time no doubt. Well, I'm afraid Bentley I have better things to do, I certainly will not be at your beck and call, we understand each other I hope," she laughed waving a finger.

"Oh yes, yes of course, fully understood, fully understood Melody."

"Right, I'll be off. By the way, have you visited the local pub on occasion since you've been here, I would say that you are a regular?"

"Well yes, pop in occasionally," came the wary reply.

"Have you met my husband yet?"

"Your husband?"

"Yes, the vicar, my husband."

"Oh yes, no, not that I am aware, mind you my visits to The Mariners are usually early evening to avoid the crowds, perhaps our paths have never crossed."

"Mmm, you rather surprise me, I'm sure they will at some point however. He is very fond of company my husband. All in the pursuit of Christian harmony and togetherness, you understand?" she laughed.

Bentley nodded in agreement. "Oh yes, yes, I fully understand, rest assured."

"Right, now I am really going. Bye Mr Browne. See you on the ice."

Early evening Bentley decided to retire to bed. Throwing the bedroom windows wide-open Bentley lay upon the marital bed listening to crows circling adjacent fields and woodland in noisy agitation having been disturbed by gentleman farmer Nigel Smethurst's insatiable quest for a bumper harvest. Despite the disturbance, Bentley was soon fast asleep blissfully ignorant of events that had unfolded outside Southampton that afternoon.

Alice Turner, an up and coming reporter for BBC Southern News, had gone on air to report that a vintage coach en route to Southampton was causing serious delay on the M3. Toxic amounts of exhaust gases from said vehicle had according to several eyewitnesses been wholly responsible for adverse visual conditions making overtaking virtually impossible. A later report suggested traffic stretched all the way back to the Winchester bypass. A man and a woman were detained by Sussex Police. A police spokesman later suggested the pair were possibly illegal immigrants. An investigation was in progress.

The following day, a slightly hungover Bentley answered a bedside phone call.

"Mr Browne. Is this Barton Manor House sir?"

"As far as I'm aware, yes."

"Are you Mr Browne sir?"

"Mmm it's possible, I'm not sure."

"Ah I see, let's try again, shall we? I left my depot at 6.30am this morning, travelled 30 miles on a congested motorway to arrive at a stately mansion, where, fortunately with gates wide open, offering easy entry. Once inside I manoeuvred a long winding driveway with some difficulty to arrive upon a large courtyard, here to sit for almost twenty minutes trying to contact someone within the building, finally receiving attention I am told you're not quite sure who you are, should I believe this sir?"

The musician suppressed a heavy sigh, "Not completely, no."

"Well then, can we start again sir, if you are Mr Browne and my information is correct, this is Barton Manor. Now I have a busy schedule ahead of me today sir, so if you would be kind enough to send a housemaid to open the door or perhaps even better still open the door personally, that way we could perhaps make some progress."

Within several minutes, Bentley answered the door to a man dressed in green overalls carrying a clipboard. "Ah, you would be Mr Browne, sir, am I correct?"

"Yes, you are, very astute young man, how do you know that?"

"You're wearing pyjamas sir, hardly appropriate for a servant, don't you agree."

"Ah yes of course, how can I help you?"

"Well, I work for JJ Plant Hire Basingstoke, and you are my first call this morning, so I hope we can get this over and done with rather quickly." The driver turned and pointed toward a formidable forklift truck secured upon a trailer and large cab dominating all surroundings. Bentley followed his gaze expressing solemn approval.

"Yes, very impressive, why is it here?"

A slightly bemused driver addressed the musician with some irritation and concern. "Well, I would have thought you would have been the first to know sir. A phone call was received at head office requesting the hiring for one day only of a forklift truck sir, and here it is, top of the range sir, we were informed a large object was prohibiting easy movement within the courtyard, that'll be it sir, would it?"

Stepping forward the driver lifted the corner of the bubble wrap. "My word, a bit cheeky, even in these so called enlightened times."

"It is considered a work of art in many quarters," Bentley contested rather weakly.

"Ah I don't think it would go down too well in Guildford sir."

"Do you live in Guildford?" Bentley asked expressing genuine interest, his father having been employed for many years as head salesman for Willis & Sons, a renowned garage situated on the Hogs Back roadway running between Farnham and Guildford, a business well renowned for its import and export of luxury cars, hence his insistence upon the name Bentley for his first born later to evolve as famed musician Bentley Browne.

"No sir, I do not live in Guildford, but I have visited there many times, a very conservative area, Guildford."

Upon this very irrelevant observation of a Surrey town, Bentley stepped back inside the doorway disinterest evident. "Look, I've had a very unusual weekend and I'm feeling, to be honest, a little under the weather. Could you give me an hour or so to get myself together, perhaps you could take yourself to a café somewhere."

"No, no I am self-sufficient thank you, you have to be these days, you never know what the day will bring," the driver said pointedly. "A flask, plenty of fruit, nuts, mint tea, a key to a healthy lifestyle, sir."

"Fair enough, fair enough, I'll leave you to it."

"Very well Mr Browne, I shall unload, as I've said, I have a very busy schedule ahead of me."

Bentley stiffened. "Well you can't leave that thing

here, it has nothing to do with me," the musician insisted.

"It's on my docket here sir," the driver tapped his clipboard, "Mr Browne, Barton Manor, as clear as day."

"Let me repeat, I have no recollection of ordering a forklift truck."

"Well it's a puzzle Mr Browne, but there you are," said the driver "these are my instructions."
"Why don't you ring head office and request some clarification," Bentley suggested.

"I have sir and I am at the right address."

"You may be at the right address young fella, but not at my request, so I shall say goodbye."

"Well do as you will sir, but it cannot end here, I shall return to the depot and report your denial of ever such a request of the forklift truck. Their response could either be apologetic or hostile, who's to know sir, only time will tell. Right, I'll be on my way, but before I do may I ask, have you ever been on TV, only you remind me of a bent copper I recall watching on TV during my teenage days. Could that have been you sir?"

"No, it was not me," came a flat reply.

"Truly?"

Bentley nodded gravely. "Truly."

The driver's disappointment was plain to see. "Shame, the wife will be disappointed, I don't meet many celebrities."

"Sorry young man, you've got two issues wrong here, I am not the bent copper as you suggest and I did not order a forklift truck so I shall say goodbye." Closing the door, Bentley allowed himself a small smile. Price of fame eh, a bent copper.

After two pieces of toast, a shower and shave, a slightly repentant Bentley opened the door to be greeted by an empty driveway and two spent teabags upon the porch floorway.

CHAPTER 4

A Brief Hello

After a brief tidy up in the main areas of use within the manor and disposal of the tea bags, Bentley left the stately pile earlier than planned that morning, circumstances dictating a trip across the green to visit the corner shop. On many occasions during Bentley's late afternoon visits to The Three Mariners, a young Labrador with a friendly disposition would appear out of nowhere and accompany him to his destination, often to remain seated outside, awaiting Bentley's re-emergence sometime later with a warm welcome. After a rewarding handful of crisps, the pair would cross the green once more, always parting outside a row of cottages close to the village church leaving Bentley to complete the further half mile to Barton Manor alone. Large areas of village green were roped off that morning by council workmen, grass cutting in progress, preparations for the forthcoming cricket match to be held that coming Sunday. Wishing to avoid such high levels of activity Bentley took the longer route and circled the village pond. A large dog, engaged in noisy disagreement with several ducks, spotting Bentley's approach instantly suspending hostility, bounded to his side.

Warm greetings completed, the pair headed towards the corner shop once again in close harmony.

Albert Jugg, landlord of The Three Mariners perched precariously upon a wooden crate watering numerous hanging baskets displayed in every conceivable position possible upon the Victorian frontage of the building waved a hand in recognition. "See you later Bentley?"

"You will, Albert, you will."

Outside the store, many baskets piled high with an abundance of fruit and veg restricted easy entry. Parting ways with his companion Bentley entered the shop for the first time ever. Pushing hard against the door to gain admittance, somewhere above his head a bell on a spring registered his presence. Once inside, a celebration of commercial exuberance greeted him. A VE day of special offers, with aisle upon aisle of cut-price delights festooned with bunting running from wall to wall. Beyond the cornflakes and baked beans next to the fresh rolls an Asian man, Bentley rightly perceived to be Mr Patel, was addressing a man clothed only in a singlet and shorts in a somewhat aggressive manner. The victim, a post office employee, was pressed up against the soft drink dispenser unable to escape his aggressor.

"In my country, we dress accordingly, a mark of respect, both given and received. There is little respect in your manner of dress to suggest a working relationship of any standing worth consideration."

The postman, finally slipping beneath Mr Patel's outstretched arms made for the door, grabbing his satchel from the counter as he rushed by. "You deliver Royal Mail, your patron is Her Majesty the Queen, her likeness on every stamp, you show little respect, in my country your casual dress would not be tolerated, your boots would shine with pride."

The man stopped at the door and turned to face his tormenter. "I can assure you Mr Patel, I am wearing approved post office attire for hot weather."

"You call this hot," Mr Patel snorted. "You should experience Calcutta during high summer, that I consider hot."

"Mr Patel, I would welcome such a year in Calcutta if it were to guarantee a few hours away from a man such as yourself. As the door opened offering escape, he turned. "May I add that Gandhi was generally considered by many to be a man totally without any dress sense whatsoever."

Mr Patel approached the postman with anger and flayed his arms in the air furiously. "I find your words deeply offensive, please leave my premises now, go."

"I'm going and I shall report your aggressive behaviour to my shop steward forthwith, I can assure you."

"Go, go," ordered Mr Patel resisting a strong urge to follow and remonstrate further. Mr Patel finally returned behind the sweet counter shaking his head sadly. "Such insolence, no respect." Finally, he addressed the awaiting Bentley. "My apologies sir, so unfortunate, how can I help you?"

Bentley hesitated slightly, not wishing the wrath of the shopkeeper to descend upon him. "It's of little consequence but my daily newspaper did not arrive this morning."

With a heavy sigh, Mr Patel reached below the counter producing a ledger. "The house?" he enquired sharply.

"Pardon?"

"Your name, sir, your residence?"

"Oh yes, I see of course, yes. I live across the green, Barton Manor, my name is Browne, Bentley Browne, with an 'e' by the way."

Mr Patel immediately returned the ledger behind the counter grasping his hands joyfully. "Of course, Mr Browne with an 'e'. Barton Manor, a fine house sir, wondrous architecture, magnificent chimneystacks. My apologies sir, the paperboy never arrived for work this morning, a common occurrence in this country.

Sadly, you have been neglected sir, I feel such dismay. In my country this would not occur."

Wisely, Bentley nodded gravely in agreement. "Yes, yes, so I believe, the work ethic amongst paperboys in your home country has been well documented." Bentley reached for a copy of 'Golfing Monthly'. "However, it is not a problem, good excuse to get out of the house if I am honest."

"Hardly a house Mr Browne," replied Mr Patel, "a palace, a wonderful property, you have made many improvements I believe." He leant across the counter in confidence. "Tell me sir," his voice dropping to a whisper, "may I enquire as to the nature of the damage sustained yesterday, damage to the house sir?"

"Damage, I have no damage to the manor Mr Patel."

Mr Patel persisted. "Yesterday I was concerned to observe clouds of dense smoke emitting from the direction of your fine house sir and I felt obliged to inform the emergency services, I was very, very concerned."

Bentley looked upon the shopkeeper with some dismay. "Aah, it was you that informed the constable, Mr Patel. Well, thank you for your concern but it was nothing, I can assure you."

"As you say sir, as you say, it shall remain our secret. You wish to take these newspapers Mr Browne?" Mr Patel indicated the Golfing Monthly and Daily News tucked under Bentley's arm.

"Yes I will," Bentley nodded adding "but no petrol today."

"Petrol Mr Browne, we do not sell petrol."

"Just trying to inject a little humour Mr Patel."

"Ah yes, a joke of course, you English, er, you are happy with such a newspaper Mr Browne?" He indicated the newspaper tucked under Bentley's arm.

"For an extra 20p sir you can purchase this wonderful source of information." He reached down beneath the counter to re-appear with a copy of the Calcutta Monthly News and held it high. "A fine read Mr Browne, a fine read."

"I am sure it is Mr Patel, but no thank you, one paper is enough for me."

"As you wish sir, as you wish."

Bentley searched his pockets. "Aah, I seem to have come without any money Mr Patel, I do apologise."

"No problem, no problem, I can assure you. Your wife is on a voyage of spiritual discovery I believe Mr Browne? She will return in good spirits I am sure. Convey my best wishes to her whenever you speak to her again."

"I shall indeed Mr Patel. A cruise and plenty of sunshine will do her well."

"Ah sunshine, plentiful in my country Mr Browne."

"Yes, so I believe Mr Patel, sometimes too much?"

"Oh no sir, never too much, sunshine is God's heartbeat sir. You had no desire to be with your wife on the cruise, sir? In my homeland, a wife would have no wish to be apart from her husband for any length of time I assure you sir." From within her cubbyhole across the way seated behind the post office counter Mrs Patel rolled her eyes in amusement. Suppressing a wry smile, Bentley offered a firm opinion.

"Yes very commendable I am sure Mr Patel, but in this country, for some couples it can be a very desirable situation."

Mr Patel sniffed disapprovingly. "Certainly that is true sir, sadly. Tell me Mr Browne, I understand that for some years you have been recognised as something of a celebrity throughout the western world. Do you miss the adoration of the masses sir?"

"No, no not at all," Bentley answered somewhat unconvincingly.

"But you have always travelled first class in life with a full back pocket I imagine," Mr Patel insisted.

"I have been very fortunate, yes," Bentley conceded.

"You are familiar with the Indian rail system Mr Browne?"

"A little yes," replied Bentley somewhat bemused by the line of questioning.

"Ah wonderful, you have paid a visit to my country sir." A delighted Mr Patel raised his arms in joy.

"Well, no I'm afraid not, snippets on television mostly, Michael Palin, TV chappy."

"Television, not always as it seems I fear," said Mr Patel "You would not wish to experience the railway system in India, rather other than first class Mr Browne, I can assure you."

"Mmm, so I believe, rather a dangerous mode of travel seated upon the roof of a steam train travelling at 100 miles per hour, still, life is a gamble at the best of times eh, Mr Patel." Bentley turned to go. "Er, before I leave can you help me?"

"In any way sir, just say the word."

"Er, well I believe you may have a publication relating to this village in times over the past century and a half, written by a local lady, Elizabeth Standing?"

Mr Patel reached for his glasses. "It strikes a chord sir, strikes a chord, stay there, I shall consult Mrs Patel, articles of such serious nature are kept under lock and key by my dear wife." After several moments of serious discussion, Mrs Patel released a copy of Mrs Standing's publication to her husband, returning to the counter. Mr Patel beckoned Bentley closer to him, his voice dropping to a whisper, confiding in Bentley that his wife was fearful that such a publication may fall into the wrong hands. "My wife's fears are profound and understandable sir, observe the cover if you will." Mr Patel placed the book onto the counter top stabbing fiercely at the cover with his forefinger. "A man sporting a handlebar moustache with top hat and cane standing proudly beside a vintage vehicle. The picture, dating 1912, had been taken outside the entrance to the manor house before years of tree and shrub growth had hidden much of the house and surrounding area from view.

Bentley was puzzled. "I fail to see an issue here," he

said.

Mr Patel stabbed the book even more forcefully. "The man sir, pure evil. His look, his stance, it defines a time, many, many years ago which my wife and I would like to forget. British Rule. Our homeland in India, I wish to put it behind us. You must understand Mr Browne, grim times sir."

"Well yes, I understand your wish to forget such a time. I shall ensure that such a book will reside on the top most shelf of my home, well out of the way of inquisitive eyes, rest assured Mr Patel."

Mr Patel nodded his thanks. "Very considerate Mr Browne, very considerate, we thank you. Now sir, before you depart, on your pilgrimage across the green this morning, did you encounter a wild dog sir, full of unsavoury behaviour?"

"Not that I am aware, Mr Patel, why do you ask?"

"Because such a dog is God's curse sir. It relieves himself upon my prize fruit and veg sir. I shall require the authorities to do their duty, have it put down sir."

"Well I can't say I am aware of such an animal Mr Patel, but should I ever come across such a pest I shall inform the police immediately."

"Very sound, Mr Browne, very sound. Perhaps they will do their duty." Bentley allowed himself a small smile.

"If I may say so Mr Patel, I have felt for some time that England is going to the dogs."

"You have lost me somewhat Mr Browne, going to the dogs? I fail to understand sir."

"Just a saying Mr Patel. British humour."

"Oh yes, quite Mr Browne, British humour."

"Before I depart Mr Patel, may I purchase a packet of plain crisps?"

"You may indeed sir." The delighted shop owner pointed across the way. "Two for the price of one, sir. Patel's special offer, very popular. Mind you, that will be a further £2.10 sir."

"No problem Mr Patel, put it on Mrs Browne's bill, I'd be much obliged."

Mr Patel opened the door. "It has been an honour to meet you Mr Browne, I wish you well sir."

"Very kind Mr Patel, thank you. I shall say goodbye." Closing the door as quickly as possible behind him,

Bentley breathed a sigh of relief. All was quiet, the dog mercifully having left his post to return to the pond.

Outside the store, Bentley encountered the banished postman seated upon an upturned banana crate speaking excitedly into a mobile phone. Pausing to offer condolence to the poor man as he passed, Bentley gathered from him that under no circumstances whatsoever would he, a postman, return to this store to be treated in such a manner again until the wearing of singlet and shorts by post office workers in hot weather be sorted and confirmed in writing.

Entering the manor, Bentley was greeted by a phone call from within the library. "Hello, Norman Willoughby's Garden Centre, how can I help?" With a curse from the other end, the line went dead. A minute later, it rang again.

"Hello, is that you Bentley?"

"Yes, it could be."

"Bentley, is that you playing the bloody fool?" Christina Browne was clearly angry.

"Sorry sweetheart, I should have realised it was you, how are things, where are you? Enjoying yourself, you girls?"

"Yes we are, but no thanks to you."
"Sorry my love, I didn't catch what you said, the line is very poor, speak up my sweetness, what did you say?"

"I said yes, we are enjoying ourselves, but no thanks to you. I rang home many times yesterday, where were you?"

"Here of course, at the manor. I had a visit from the vicar's wife, nice woman. What's the weather like on board ship? It's glorious here."

"Never mind the weather, Bentley. Have you any idea what I've been through these past 24 hours, sending me off in a battered old coach?"

"Speak up my love, it's just crackle and pop at this end, you'll have to speak up, can't hear a word."

"I shall say goodbye Bentley, I shall see you in the divorce courts."

"What did you say my love, can't hear a damn word you're saying, I am losing you."

"You're right there, Bentley Browne, sooner than you think."

"Sorry Christina, you've gone completely now, can't hear a word, hello...hello..."

Aboard the SS Stargaze Christina Browne joined her sisters at the captain's table, the three ladies having received an invitation to join the captain for evening cocktails that very afternoon.

CHAPTER 5
A Look into the Past

Confident that the relationship with his wife would improve given time, Bentley headed for the sun lounger with Mrs Standing's well-appointed book tucked under his arm. Once settled he turned immediately to page 32, the history of Barton Manor. To read as follows:

The building was constructed between 1868 and 1870, built under the instructions of Mr William Wiggins who had returned to England after the abolishment of the East India Company in 1857. Paid off with a handsome remuneration he landed at Poole in mid-September 1858 with the promise of future work with the Admiralty. Heading immediately to London, he stopped overnight at the Bull and Butcher near Barton-on-the-Green, Hampshire. Immediately falling in love with the area he vowed to return some day. Once settled in London, the place of work and good lodgings in place, he invested his payments from The East India Company into Great Western Rail and as the rail company grew, so did his investment. Soon to become a wealthy man he returned to Barton within the decade buying twenty acres of farmland off the village green. There he built Barton Manor. Relinquishing his job at the Admiralty, he entered politics becoming Tory MP for Petersfield and surrounding area, in total serving for some 35 years. Offered a directorship on the board of Great Western Railway in 1880, he was therefore often referred to in parliamentary circles as Puffin Billy. His life ending in 1910 due to a bout of influenza. His obituary in the London Gazette took note of his hedonistic lifestyle. Summing up his life, he was described as a lucky chancer who made good. Survived by wife, Edith, the parson's daughter from Godalming and two sons, Charles and Cecil. Edith passed away in her sleep some six months after his death leaving the manor house and surrounding land to eldest son, Charles. Considered by many to be a chip of the old block, Charles lived life to the full. The photo on page 34 shows him in full finery, off to Henley on that fateful day in June 1913. Plainly in poor health, as the photo would suggest and subsequent autopsy confirmed. At Henley that afternoon Charles was purported to have overindulged in fine claret, having spent much of the day with a wine salesman from Munich. Unable to stay the course he collapsed in the hospitality tent next to the bandstand. Rushed home by his loyal chauffeur Henry Goodhall, also included in the photo on page 34, proved to be an ill-considered move. In a drunken stupor propped upright with many cushions in the back of the open Rolls he was unable to find refuge from the chilly northeast wind that developed unexpectedly that evening, enveloping him as his car sped along at suicidal speeds of up to 60mph. The coroner's report some weeks later decreed that he had died that night of a heart seizure somewhere between Henley and Farnham, brought on by excessive drink and extreme cold.

Remaining son, Cecil, inherited everything and now of independent means he relinquished his post with the local solicitors, Bracket & Co and embraced religion. A portly chap of small stature he took to preaching across the country astride a huge shire horse of some 17.5 hands high by the name of Hugo. He would spout his religious teaching from the back of his beloved horse where he often said he felt closer to God. However, the few that gathered to listen to his preaching about the countryside often grew impatient, feeling he lacked that killer punch. This invariably led to unruly and disruptive behaviour by way of spooking poor old Hugo. A nervous and highly-strung animal at the best of times, he would take flight at the slightest provocation, much to the merriment of onlookers. This repeated unseemly behaviour left Cecil with little alternative than to take his Christian philosophy abroad selling Hugo for a paltry five guineas. He shut The Gables and engaged in missionary work in West Africa. Nothing is recorded of his time abroad, returning to England a short 8 months later a changed man and in a somewhat sorry state. Stopping for just one night at Barton Manor for a bath and change of clothing, he headed to London, much as his father had done before him. Once settled, he frequented the infamous

Red Lion Public House in the Elephant and Castle area. Embracing the gin and tonic sect to the manor born he discovered an appetite for many things, among them music halls, particularly fond of The Hackney Empire. Here he made a name as comedian Big Billy Hatto, a contemporary of Marie Law. He shared top billing with her many times and in 1916 was voted top box office attraction in the country, excluding Scotland. However, his irrational behaviour always at the forefront of his life, he tired of superficial public acclaim, re-embracing Christian values and teachings, swearing off the gin he returned to sobriety. On many occasions, pausing mid-song during his widely acclaimed signature tune, The Vicar's Lament, to berate his audience for their coarse language, bad behaviour and love of a tipple. Lampooned in Punch Magazine in June 1917, a cartoon depicted him preaching from a pulpit dressed as a bishop holding a Bible in one hand and a gin bottle in the other. This proved to be the undoing of Big Billy Hatto. By the end of the war, he was finished, returning to Barton Manor as plain Cecil Wiggins.

Sadly unable to settle, overwhelmed by a return of a religious fervour he left Barton Manor once again, this time heading for India to pursue his beloved missionary work. Within hours of his arrival upon the outskirts of Bombay, availing himself upon a small gathering of goat herders enjoying a tea break by the roadside, he was crushed underfoot by a terrified crowd fleeing a rampaging elephant. Unable to secure a Christian burial due to the hysteria and hostility of many locals blaming him for provoking the animal with wild hand gestures thus causing the carnage he was soon on his way home again, sadly for the last time. Aboard Naval dreadnought HMS Accomplish stuffed head first into a barrel containing ginger roots and fennel in the hope that it worked well as a preservative it proved a disaster for on arrival at Gibraltar for supplies he was well gone off. The captain, a fearsome man, mindful of unrest due to the stench among the ship's crew, had the barrel containing Wiggins dumped overboard, an incident fiercely denied by all present that night for many years, until in 1931 Junior Petty Officer David 'Nobby' Funnell, mentioned in an article printed in the Portsmouth Echo had confessed to being present at the deed. An Admiralty enquiry later that year decided, with much reluctance, that to consider a search for the said barrel after such a length of time would be pointless. However, Petty Officer Funnell, still a serving officer, was severely reprimanded. His captain at the time, now retired Rear Admiral Percy Ginger O'Shea denied all knowledge, saying under oath. "I was far too busy looking for loose mines bobbing about the sea to find time or desire to countenance such a foul deed." The timing of the accident, coming just after the armistice with the oceans still full of unchartered dangers etc, Ginger

O'Shea's evidence was received with relief and a sterling determination to put a lid on the whole sorry episode. It was also accepted that Cecil Wiggins i.e. Billy Hatto had indeed died in India in 1918 with numerous broken bones and being dumped at sea was merely an unnecessary appendage to his rich and varied lifestyle. After much legal wrangling and tooing and froing, Barton Manor re-opened in 1919 under the ownership of distant relative Gwyneth Adams. Little is known of her save for a footnote in the Hampshire Record suggesting she was from a theatrical family well known in the Hackney area. However, soon tiring of country life, she sold up within months returning to London, the house being purchased by the government for use as a military nursing home.

Much engrossed in Elizabeth Standing's history of Barton on the Green, Bentley was startled by gardener Rawlings emergence from behind a sizable clump of azalea bushes accompanied by his young assistant. Sweating profusely dressed in a dirty grey singlet and corduroy trousers held up with the obligatory length of string the gardener approached Bentley.

"Nearly 2.30pm. Me and the boy are off in a tick."

"Oh, ok. In tomorrow?"

"Might be," came the curt reply.

Bentley looked up. "Something wrong?"

"Might be."

"Come on Rawlings, out with it. What's the problem?"

"No problem."

"Good. So I'll see you tomorrow then." Bentley returned to his book.

The horticulturalist stood his ground belligerence evident. "How is she?"

"How is who?"

"The Mrs, your Mrs," he snapped.

"The Mrs. What are you on about?"

"Your wife, Mrs Browne. The traffic snarled up yesterday at Winchester and your poor lady was at the centre of it. Blimey, don't you know, it was in all the papers, look." Rawlings waved a newspaper in the air, finally searching through it hurriedly thrusting it in Bentley's face. "There, there, centre pages look, poor woman, plainly suffering." The full report with accompanying photo courtesy of a Mr Gordon Harrison from Hayes, Middlesex, showed a familiar coach on the hard shoulder of the M3 surrounded by a group of men from the emergency services. On the grass verge sat Mrs Browne obviously distressed surrounded by many suitcases, the driver, hands deep in pockets, had a look of resigned indifference. Rawlings pointed at the photo. "That's that old bugger Rudd and his coach, he wants locking up, what fool would send his wife away on a clapped out old time capsule like that, no respect." He flicked his cigarette butt into the lily pond. "She's a fine woman your Mrs Browne."

"Yes, yes thank you Rawlings."

"Bloody disgrace."

"Yes thank you, that will do, thank you Rawlings. If you excuse me for a moment I must make a phone call." Leaving the terrace and Rawlings behind him, Bentley hurried inside the manor quickly to the nearest phone. "Hello, Rudd residence, this is Bentley Browne, can I speak to Mr Rudd please?"

"Oh Mr Browne, nice to speak to you at last, my father in law is always on about you, says what good friends the two of you are."

"Does he indeed."

"Yes, he does. My name's Annie, I married Ted, his eldest son."

"Nice to speak to you Annie. Is he at home?"

"No I'm sorry Mr Browne, he's away on business I'm afraid, my husband and his brother have taken him to Southampton for the day to collect a vehicle or something and I don't know an awful lot about it. He should be home any time, can I take a message?"

"No, no that's ok, I'll catch up with him some time. Perhaps he's at The Mariners."

"Could be any pub at all," she laughed, "he knows so many, chance you take I suppose."

"Ok, thanks for your time Annie, I'll say goodbye."

"Rather an honour to speak to you Mr Browne, you're the first celebrity I've ever spoken to," she giggled. "In future, can I call you Bentley?"

"Whatever you like Annie, bye."

Returning to the terrace, the musician was witness to Rawlings and his lad, each with respective cycle in tow, both making use of the abundance of high rise herbaceous borders to keep a low profile across the far reaching grassland surrounding the rear of the manor house pursuing a short cut to the lodge house and easy exit from the grounds. Standing at the foremost area of commanding stonework Bentley addressed the two from a distance. "Wait, hold it chaps, can I see you for a minute Rawlings please?" Visibly aware of the musician standing high upon the terrace the pair changed direction approaching Bentley with much reluctance. "Tell me lads, are you finished for the day. Must I remind you that your working hours are 8.30am until 2.30pm, five days a week and at this exact moment in time according to my timepiece it is 2.17pm so you are still under my command for a further thirteen minutes, is that correct?"

"Ah gov," Rawlings protested "it's 80 degrees, we've been outside all day, give us a break please, what's the matter of ten minutes in life."

"Well, it's enough time for you Rawlings to collect a sit on mower for me and getting it here."

The gardener reached for his tobacco pouch. "Oh yeah, you got a private job on gov have you, need the readies do you?" Rawlings sniggered.

"Yes, something like that Rawlings, now do as I say please, leave your bike here and make your way to the barn and get me the mower."

Rawlings raised his arms in exasperation. "Which one do you want, there's the turbo charged red one, the quiet battery driven one with the trailer attached, there's the one......"

"Yes alright Rawlings, thank you. Bring back the first one you come across please, now hurry along."

Without further comment, the pair headed towards the barn. Returning within the working fifteen minutes the pair pulled up close to the terrace seated upon the Pathfinder, a high tech monster of a grass cutter, bright red in colour, renowned for his grand design and accomplishment. Seated upon the machine, Rawlings looked down upon Bentley with some amusement. "There you go governor, that'll get you to Bournemouth and back in no time."

"Yes I'm sure it would Rawlings, I need it now for a trip across the green. I am sure you're aware I am denied the use of a car at present due to my licence being revoked."

"I am yes, your good wife has told me many times governor."

"Yes I'm sure she has Rawlings." Bentley approached the impressive machine. "Right, get off the seat Rawlings, let me have a look."

"Well if you think you are crossing the village green governor may I suggest you borrow my hat, don't want you getting sunstroke out there in the open do we, eh boy."

"Yes, yes, thank you for your concern Rawlings but I shan't be long. Now then, let's have a look."
Bentley addressed the machine with some concern. "Good God, big isn't it, is there enough petrol in it Rawlings to cut across the green?"

"Might be, I don't know, might a bit tricky getting back though, might need to find a hotel for the night," he laughed.

"Yes, very droll Rawlings, very droll, thank you. Remove yourself from the seat please."

"Very well squire, there you are sir."

"Right, how does it work?"

"Well you sit on the seat for a start."

"Yes, I gathered that Rawlings."

"Show him boy." The boy leaned forward pressing a button and the mower burst into action.

"It's a blue button governor, it says 'to start' on it,

next to the steering wheel, can't miss it." Both man and boy suppressed a snigger.

Bentley engaged first gear. "Are you two going to follow me out?"

Rawlings pursed his lips. "Are we on overtime?"

"You are most certainly not."

"Then the answer is no governor, we are not following you out."

"Fair enough, fair enough, no problem, stand aside please, I'm on my way."

"Hold up, hold up." Rawlings reached forward. "Oh show him again boy."

The boy engaged the gear leaver. "You're in the wrong gear gaffer, you need to go forwards, not backwards."

"How many gears are there Rawlings as a matter of interest?"

"How many do you want skipper? It's not Formula 1. We're not talking Brands Hatch here, are we boy? Just forward and reverse, Oh blimey!"

"Alright, thank you Rawlings. Thank you for your help. Move aside now please, I'm on my way."

Watching Bentley's departure up the driveway Rawlings nudged the boy. "Silly sod he is, loses his licence for speeding and such like so he can't drive his good wife to her destination causing much eternal strife within the manor I wouldn't doubt. Pop star royalty he was. Could play a good tune on the piano, I give him that. At the height of his fame you know, he turned down a guest appearance in 'Carry on Cabby' starring Sid James. Bad mistake, it would have done his acting career a lot of good. Any association with the Carry On team and Sid James would have broadened his appeal throughout the country I reckon. Of course, all of it before your time boy, you wouldn't know anything about it." Rawlings drew heavily upon his butt end. "Mind you," he said thoughtfully, "I could have been big in the music scene m'self if I followed the right path. We are both the same age you know. I played a mean whistle and flute when I were at school, boy."

"Yeah, but he's got a lot more hair than you have Grandad."

"Well yes, he has been fortunate to keep his hair, some of us don't, you might lose yours early yourself boy, you don't know."

"And he's still got his own teeth Grandad," said that lad defiantly.

"Yes, yes, alright boy, don't rub it in. Who's side are you on? Different lifestyles. I met your grandma in my teens. I had to marry her, I won't go into that boy and then your dad came along, followed by his two sisters, your two aunts. I was stupid at times I admit. Them days was 'ard boy, we didn't have a telly in every room, Facebook or whatever you call it, smartphones and such like. You don't know you're born lad."

"And he's over six foot and built like a rugby player," the boy persisted.

"Yes, alright boy." An irate Rawlings flicked his cigarette end in the direction of the azalea bush. "I will accept he's got the looks and that. He likes his whiskey and has an eye for the women. Mind you, who wouldn't in his profession, lots of temptation. He's been married four times you know, don't bode well for the future do it, so let that be a learning lesson for you lad, don't get swayed by the rich and famous with their posh homes and that. I've tended for many of the privileged in my time boy, and in the privacy of their homes behind closed doors life is not what it always seems, trust me boy, so stick with horticulture lad, leave the entertainment business to others, even that karaoke nonsense in pubs, stay clear, don't chase fame, it's an illusion, contentment is in reach of us all, particularly those of us that are in the horticultural business boy, am I right?"

"You are indeed Grandad, you're the Willie Nelson of horticulture, you are Grandad, you really are."

"I am boy, I am. Hang on, who the hell is Willie Nelson?"

Swiftly upon the green, headed in the direction of the village pond intent upon following the path close to the water's edge, Bentley was confronted by an enraged swan intent on the protection of a female and a pair of signets nesting nearby. Chasing him with aggressive intent for some 100 yards or so, Bentley changed direction with haste, crossing the recently manicured cricket square at full throttle finally outrunning his feathered assailant at the boundary edge close to the pavilion. The noisy encounter between man and beast was witnessed by an incumbent Constable Willoughby seated in the comforting shade outside The Mariners, glass in hand. Recognising the approaching Bentley Browne from afar and mindful of the recent encounter, the constable took careful note of the mower's wild approach. Leaving the grass cutter alongside the cricket pavilion, Bentley approached Kathleen Judd, daughter of the landlord, collecting glasses from the outside tables. A recent unlucky contestant in the TV series, Cook for Four, she was in a sombre mood. Approaching quietly from behind Bentley caught her by surprise and whispered in her ear. "Does nobody work in this village apart from you m'dear?" She turned quickly nearly dropping the laden tray.

"Oh Bentley, it's you." Kathleen had nurtured a crush on Bentley Browne since her teenage years and his purchase of Barton Manor and usage of The Mariners delighted her somewhat.

"Hello sweetheart, Mr Rudd at large?"

"No, not at this moment, apparently he's on business in Southampton recovering a vehicle," she said having regained her composure. Kathleen gave him a broad smile. "That coach of his, it's in a police compound somewhere. I had to laugh when I saw it on the TV late last night, the traffic reached all the way to Winchester. Did you see it, it was a disaster."

Bentley shook his head. "No, unfortunately I had an early night and missed it. I have just heard about it. I shall be in deep trouble, my wife was involved."

"Yes, so I believe Bentley, I am sorry. The old fart Rudd was in last night raving about police attitude and such like. Back again this morning first thing, had a large one, on the slate, and then he shot off with his boys in the pickup. Once again, I am sorry about your wife Bentley, believe me." She picked up the tray and headed for the door. "Phew, I shall be glad when the weather changes, this heat is getting too much for me." She turned at the door. "You coming in?"

"No, I better not, a bit early for me Kathleen, things to do."

"Ah, such as apologise to Mrs Browne you mean?"

Bentley nodded in agreement. "Yes, perhaps. Oh, before I forget, I am sorry your cooking endeavour failed, maybe next time eh."

She shrugged. "I'm over it now, I got full marks for my duck a l'orange, it was my puddings that let me down. Still, I won't let it beat me, it was good publicity for The Mariners, and we've never been so busy."

"That's the spirit, catch you later."

"I hope so Bentley, bye."

Returning to the mower, Bentley was confronted by Constable Willoughby. "Have you a moment please sir?"

Bentley turned. "Oh, hello constable, nice to see you on your feet again."

"Beg your pardon?"

"Last time I saw you, you were a little bit under the weather."

"When was that, sir?"

"Yesterday constable."

"Ah yes, you are alluding to my dodgy stomach. Ah, I think it was a touch of summer flu."

"Well yes, you did appear to be a little unwell I must say, but I am sure that is what it was, flu undoubtedly." Bentley struggled to keep a straight face. "You feeling better now?"

"Oh yes, yes I am over the worst of it sir, thank you."

"Good good, now how can I help you?"

"Er, I noticed your dash across the green sir. In my opinion you were driving very, very wildly."

"Oh, how so?"

"Well, you nearly flattened a pair of swans for a start. The Queen, Her Majesty, is a patron you know, you are aware of that I trust?"

"I did alert it with a touch of the klaxon," Bentley retorted.

"Klaxon?"

"Yes, the horn."

"In my opinion sir, you displayed complete disregard towards a pair of Her Majesty's swans close to the pond's edge. From where I was situated you appeared to drive straight at them," the constable insisted.

"Are you suggesting that it was a callous attempt for some swan slaughter officer? Are we filming some episode of Midsummer Murders here constable?"

"I am aware of the difference between fact and fiction sir, I am Hendon trained, however, it has to be said that your driving was uncoordinated and wild. You drove straight over Silly Mid On. Cardinal sin. We have a match on Sunday, the game is pivotal to our progress this season.

"Look, I am sorry, perhaps I was a bit wild." Bentley extended a hand in friendship. "I will get my head gardener to look at Silly Mid On first thing tomorrow and if there's ground damage he will put it right I assure you, no expense spared."

"Mmm, well," the constable wavered.

"Come on, you're off duty, can't we forget this, er, little encounter?"

An indignant constable stiffened. "Off duty, I'm never off duty sir."

"Well I did notice your panda outside Patel's corner shop as I came across, and I saw you outside the public house with glass in hand when I was chatting with Kathleen so I assumed you were off duty."

"Ah yes well, I am off duty," Willoughby conceded, "that's officially true, but it doesn't change the fact that you were driving too fast and not for the first time I believe." He addressed Bentley with a knowing look. "Am I correct sir?"

"Well yes. It is being contested and I am awaiting the verdict," Bentley agreed.

Willoughby nodded. "It is not what you know, it is who you know isn't it sir? I shall speak with Sergeant Russell at Petersfield Station and clarify the position on my off duty regulations and if I get the nod, you're in trouble my lad."

"My lad, officer? Good grief, most kind of you to speak in such a fashion."

"Just copper speak, Mr Browne, police rhetoric, helps

to defuse tense situations."

"Tense situations, what are you on about?"

"Ah well, I've been taught to recognise aggressive body language Mr Browne. You did raise an arm to me."

"Just a conciliatory gesture. Good God man, please go finish your pint, I've had enough." Bentley turned and climbed aboard the mower.

"Hang on sir, I haven't finished yet."

"I have constable." Without a backwards glance, Bentley sped across the green returning to The Gables.

The remainder of the afternoon was spent trying to contact Mrs Browne aboard the ocean liner. With no response forthcoming, Bentley once again phoned the home of Chuffer Rudd. "Hello, me again, Bentley Browne, is he at home dear girl?"

"Ah Bentley, Mr Browne, yes he's just come in, I'll get him for you."

After a delay of several minutes, Chuffer Rudd picked up the phone. "What ho Bentley, you old thespian, what's the drift?"

"I'll get to the point Chuffer, my wife."

"Oh, you've heard have you."

"Yes, it's all over the papers, can't fail to hear, you almost brought southern England to a standstill yesterday. What happened? Why didn't you phone me and put me in the picture? I only heard the news this morning and from my damn gardener of all people."

"Ah, well it was my bloody fool of a nephew, Bentley. He replaced the oil filter, drained it and replaced it with the wrong oil and engine seized up, end of story, silly sod."

"And my wife?"

"Ah yes, Mrs Browne."

"Yes, Mrs Browne."

"Well, the police packed her and her luggage into a transit, got her there just in time to sail. Didn't she phone you?"

"Yes she phoned, but I was otherwise engaged."

"So I hear. You were with the delightful vicar's wife, lucky chap. Nothing goes unnoticed in this village old boy. Anyway Bentley, it's been a hell of a long day and I need a brandy, I'll catch you later. Give my love to Mrs Browne when you speak with her, bye bye."

In no mood for company that evening, Bentley retired once again to bed early.

CHAPTER 6
A Trip Outside

The following day brought welcome news for Bentley. After prolonged legal wrangling his driving ban had been reduced by half and his driving licence was restored. Once again, he was a free man. Seeking out the elusive Rawlings, Bentley eventually found him poised high on a pair of steps pruning the grapevine in the orangery.

"Morning Rawlings, it's another beautiful day for it."

"Depends what you're doing I'd say," came the dour reply from up high.

"Can I have a word?" Bentley continued good-naturedly.

"What about?"

"If you come down I shall tell you," Bentley said patiently.

"I can hear quite well enough from up here Mr Browne," came the curt reply.

"You can? Good. I would like you to know first-hand that my driving licence has been returned and I am able to drive once again."

"Not for long if Willoughby gets his way," came the dark murmur from above.

"What do you know of it Rawlings?"

"You had a run-in with him yesterday, he was in the pub last night. He was telling all about it, how you almost slaughtered a couple of swans crossing the green."

"Well if you believe that, you believe anything, Rawlings. It was just a blip I can assure you. That policeman is mentally unsound. Now Rawlings, let's move on. I want you and the boy to prepare the soft-top Rolls for a trip out. It has been static in the barn for weeks on end, unattended and in need a little love and attention."

The steps wobbled in indignation. "Hang on! I'm a landscape gardener, not a bloody chauffeur."

"Fair enough, fair enough Rawlings, I shall advertise for a landscape gardener able to do many tasks in this Friday's Portsmouth Echo, OK with you?" Without further ado, Bentley walked away.

"Hold on, hold on Mr Browne," came the anxious call from above, "I was just pointing out that my expertise lies in horticulture, not machines as such."

Bentley stopped and turned. "You're an expert on mowers though I recall, similar principle, forward movement, backward movement."

Rawlings coughed nervously searching for his tobacco pouch. "Ah well yes, you have a point Mr Browne, I will get the boy to do it." Rawlings hurried to ground level.

"No, you will both attend to the vehicle if you please and when it is done, shall we say in an hour's time, bring it around to the front of the house. Oh, but first cover the seats, you look a bloody mess, and if there is any damage it will come out of your tax free wages that you receive every Friday." Bentley headed for the door. "Are we at one on this Mr Rawlings?"

After a lengthy pause came a reflective reply. "Yes sir, I think we are."

"Good, good, hurry up then please." At the door, Bentley paused. "Did you say something Rawlings?"

"Me? No governor."

Within the hour, the convertible was ready for use parked up upon the courtyard. Leaving the village behind him for the first time in many weeks, Bentley re-joined the rarefied and intoxicating world of luxury motoring, admitting to himself many times what a fine job Rawlings had done getting the Rolls ready for the open road. The midnight blue coachwork was a joy to behold, the chrome work dazzling and the leather interior of the vehicle spotless. Although at heart an unassuming man, in truth preferring the use of a more modest vehicle, he had over the years had come to accept and enjoy the rewards of public acclaim with less embarrassment and soul searching. Spending much of the afternoon en route to nowhere in particular, enjoying the leafy delights of the Hampshire countryside, Bentley stopped just outside Petersfield at Greenfingers the garden centre. After a leisurely browse throughout, he was seduced by the heady aroma of coffee beans emitting from the re-vamped, newly decorated cafeteria. An oasis of art deco, painting and furniture. The emporium was almost empty save for a solitary figure sat down with beans on toast whilst across the way an elderly couple with a pot of tea between them and a chocolate éclair apiece sat in total silence. Ignoring the chef's special lasagne and chips with fresh salad at £8.75, Bentley sat down with a cappuccino and a chocolate flake. On his return from a visit to the counter for a second cappuccino, he had unexpected company.

"I thought it was you old boy, pleased to meet you, name is Smethurst, Nigel, farmer, entrepreneur, you name it, I do it. You may have heard of me, I also run a chain of butcher's shops from here to Havant. Here, take these, my speciality." Out of the deep recess of a

Barbour coat slung nonchalantly over his shoulder, he produced a packet of Smethurst superior pork sausages. "My top seller old chap, I always carry one or two with me, it's a habit and anyway it's good for business. Here, take them, take them. I recognised your car outside, she's a beauty, mind you, I haven't seen her about the village for some time and I thought perhaps you'd sold her. Glad to see you, been meaning to have a chinwag for some time." Pausing to remove his flat cap, Smethurst sat down dominating the table. Bentley thought him to be in his late 30's, large in stature, florid in face, handsome to some maybe, but a supercilious privately educated prat was Bentley's opinion. "Let me get straight to the point."

"Yes, if you would Mr Smethurst, please. My cappuccino is getting cold."

"Call me Nigel please. Let me get you another."

"No, no I'm fine Nigel. Now how can I help you?"

"Ok. You may be aware we are neighbours, our boundaries meet. Truth is I want to purchase some of your land."

"You do?"

"Yes."

"Why so?"

"Well, let's say I need to rotate my crops."

"You do?"

"I do. I'll pay you a very good price."

"You would have to Nigel, but the answer is no," Bentley said firmly.

"Ah hold on, chill out old boy. Think it through. You don't keep horses, grow strawberries, runner beans, sprouts, encourage wild flowers, it's all such a waste."

"It's a buffer zone, my security blanket, my castle moat if you like, Mr Smethurst. It provides privacy. Without it, your incessant ploughing would prove to be a distraction were you any nearer."

"Sound of the countryside old son, part of its charm, you will be helping future food supplies. We need more land under the plough."

"You and Tesco?"

"Well, not necessarily Tesco, I also supply local businesses."

"Such as Patel's?" Bentley hinted.

"Oh that sly old devil. Mystery to me where his produce comes from, always fresh though. Now and again he calls in for a few carrots and such." Smethurst shrugged. "To be frank Bentley, he's far too small, I need larger outlets."

"As I said, Sainsburys and Tesco."

"I was thinking Waitrose actually," Smethurst laughed.

"What's the difference? The answer is still no," Bentley replied firmly.

"Give it some thought, I will give you a fair deal," the businessman laughed. "Look, let's be truthful. Your greenhouses, they could be a very interesting project for me."

"Oh, why so?"

"Various reasons, you are keeping them I hope?"

"Yes of course, I have no choice, they are grade A listed, part of the manor and I wouldn't wish to part with them."

"Well, yes of course, I realise that but I know what you chaps are like," Smethurst teased.

"You do?"

"Yes, a few bob in your pocket, bend the rules, do the same myself given the chance."

"Such as?" Bentley was intrigued at the possible misdemeanours being hinted at.

"Forget local planning. Behind The Gables, no one knows what's gone on. No offence old chap, but that's life." He thrust his hands deep in his pockets. "But I do need those greenhouses for my future plans to succeed."

Bentley sighed heavily rising slowly to his feet. "Listen old boy, anything I do I try to do right and proper and receive permission for all alterations past and present. Check it out by all means."

"Oops, don't forget your sausages." Smethurst planted the sausages under Bentley's arms.

"Oh by the way, you involved in the summer fete?" Smethurst enquired as they headed for the door.

"In what manner?"

"Sponsorship possibly. A man of your wealth and popularity, I'd be rather surprised if you hadn't been approached by Mr Patel doing his public duty as usual of course."

"What has Mr Patel got to do with the fete?"

"Ah. Mr Patel is council chairman and into most things, naturally it would include the fete."

"Really, nice to know, thank you Smethurst."

"Yes, I know what you're thinking, he is a bit highly strung, but if I'm honest he gets things done. Wise move to keep in with him if you understand my meaning Mr Browne."

"Yes," Bentley nodded. "I have some idea, you mean local planning regulations and such like?"

Smethurst laughed. "Yes and such like, you've got it in one old boy."

They reached their respective vehicles. Smethurst's, a huge tractor with a trailer full of straw bales parked up close behind Bentley's convertible. Climbing high into his cab, Smethurst opened the side window to lean down to address Bentley.

"Oh by the way, you lucky old chap getting a visit from the vicar's wife I believe."

Bentley smiled tolerantly. "You're the second person

that's mentioned that today."

"Have you met her husband, the vicar?" Smethurst raised an eyebrow.

Bentley shook his head wearily. "No I haven't."

"Well, he's the most unlikely vicar I have ever come across, built like a brick outhouse, typical Aussie, swears like a trooper, middle aged I would say, but one of the boys, great guy, he's been coaching the village cricket team for the last month or two since his arrival, great improvement all round in just a few weeks. I'll be off then, I'll be in touch Bentley, bye bye."

CHAPTER 7

Global Warming

Late afternoon, returning to The Gables approaching St Michael's Church, all progress was brought to a halt by a continuous line of traffic cones set down upon the centre of the road restricting movement. Close by, parked up in the shade close to the village phone box a police car. Approaching the parked vehicle Bentley was greeted by PC Willoughby, stretched out upon the back seat, doors wide open and a pair of boots neatly placed alongside the back wheel. The uniformed figure was fast asleep.

"Ahh, greetings Willoughby, another dodgy stomach young man?"

A startled Willoughby struggled to his feet adjusting his cap. "Ah, it's you Mr Browne." Recovering his composure the PC reached for his boots. "Before you say, I'm on my afternoon tea break."

"I shan't say a word constable," Bentley promised.

"Good, good, I have no wish for a confrontation Mr Browne. Now, how can I help you?"

Bentley pointed towards the cones. "I can't get through constable."

"Touch of global warming, sir, I'm afraid."

"Global warming, here, today. You sure constable?"

"Your tone of voice suggests you're questioning my theory, Mr Browne. Follow me sir." Moving to the centre of the road, Willoughby pressed his thumb into the soft tar. "The tarmac has melted sir, I'm sorry to say, uneven surface, driving hazard, so I've closed the road. I am monitoring the situation closely...." Willoughby trailed off. "Just a minute." Straightening up he looked closely at the Rolls Royce and then back again at Bentley. "Have you got your keys handy Mr Browne?"

"Yes of course constable, they're here, hanging on my little finger."

"Would you mind handing them over to me." Willoughby held out his hand.

"And why would that be, may I ask?"

"I don't want you doing a runner sir, that's why."

"Runner?"

"Yes, a runner Mr Browne. Can you clarify something for me please, sir?"

"Such as?"

"Willoughby reached for his pocket book. "First and

foremost, I am puzzled Mr Browne. I would like you to help me out."

"I'll try constable."

"Right. I seem to recall an occasion some months ago when again, if my memory serves me correctly, you were convicted for speeding on the Guildford bypass. Am I correct, sir?"

"You are constable, spot on." Bentley agreed.

"Now sir, I recall that you received a three month ban. Once again, am I correct?"

"Once again constable, you are spot on, well done."

"As I recall correctly, the ban was in force at the beginning of June. Am I right sir?"

"Somewhere in that region constable."

"And yet Mr Browne," a gleeful Willoughby reached for his pocket book and pencil, "and yet here we are in the middle of July, some scarcely six weeks later and it appears that you, sir, are back behind the wheel. How do you explain the discrepancy in time sir?"

"Well constable, sorry to disappoint you, but my ban has been reduced on appeal, I can assure you."

A visibly dismayed Willoughby tapped on his pocket book. "I shall check, sir."

"Understandably constable, you are Hendon trained after all."

"Your insurance sir, I trust that is in order."

Bentley nodded. "I can produce evidence if you wish."

"No need." An unhappy Willoughby returned his pocket book to its place of rest.

"Can we move on constable? Are we finished?"

"Yes, yes, I suppose so. However, I must advise you to take an alternative route through the village, sir."

"Be realistic constable, this is the only way to Barton Manor. I need to reach the B2017. I live on the outskirts of Barton, constable. You do recall visiting the manor recently don't you?"

Fair enough Mr Browne, I can only advise. If you wish to ignore my analysis of the situation, that is your right. However, I do recall previous encounters with you sir when on both occasions you ignored my advice. I would like to remind you Mr Browne, I was a top trainee copper in my time at Hendon. My observation skills were recognised by all so believe me Mr Browne when I say, and I don't say this lightly sir, I recognise in you a malcontent. You're trouble and I keep a clean village here, zero tolerance is my motto, so mark my words sir, I shall be watching you closely.

You undermine my authority sir. In war times you would be put against a wall and shot."

"Really constable, a bit extreme don't you think?"

"Just my opinion sir, but I am sure I am correct."

"Er, tell me constable, have you ever considered psychiatry."

"No sir, I'm happy enough in police work, thank you, I find it very fulfilling. I have no wish to practice psychiatry." Willoughby handed over Bentley's keys. "Now run along laddy, you're holding up the traffic."

Originally of a mind to return to the manor, approaching the familiar picket fence surrounding The Three Mariners, Bentley entered the car park.

CHAPTER 8

The Three Mariners

The Three Mariners had been at the centre of village life since 1807 when, three sailors paid off after the Battle of Trafalgar with a handsome sum of prize money between them, bought the three farm workers cottages set down on the edge of the village green, converting the dwellings into The Three Mariners public house. It quickly became a popular and well-known watering hole on the route between Farnham and Portsmouth. Although a little rough around the edges, its popularity increased over the coming years. In the year 1826, the then incumbent landlord Jacob Hockridge, incensed by a loose remark criticising the quality of his finest ale, raised a fist to a man in military uniform standing among many others in the snug. Not a man to be challenged, he, a serving officer of the first Life Guards and a veteran of Waterloo, demanded his honour be restored by way of a duel with pistols out upon the green. The Mariners was well attended that lunchtime by many locals and dignitaries. Aware that a show of public reluctance to accept the challenge could affect future business left Jacob Hockridge with little choice but to follow the man of military bearing out of the door. Upon the green, he was no match for the serving officer. Mortally wounded, he lies buried in St

Michael's churchyard today opposite his beloved Three Mariners.

As the years passed, its reputation as an establishment worthy of a visit was cemented in place. At the end of World War I, it was purchased by a lino salesman from Portsmouth who brought about significant changes. Aware of the rise in the popularity of the motor car, he took a gamble enhancing The Mariners. He bought the further two adjacent cottages therein enlarging the bar and dining area and the purchase of a further acre of land increased the outside leisure area. As he rightly perceived, business multiplied and remained constant throughout the following years. Changing ownership several times, it always remained in the hands of private landlords, never tied to a specific brewery. Purchased in 2012 by the appropriately surnamed Albert Jugg, wife Jenny and young daughter Kathleen, it flourished, winning the Real Ale Pub of the Year for 2014 and also the following year. A purveyor of top quality real ale, the public house became a second home to real ale officialdoms for miles around. With the addition of an even larger kitchen area run by daughter Kathleen, it was to become the largest employer in the Barton area with some eight full-time and twelve part-time of the local personnel. Since his purchase of The Mariners, Albert Jugg had insisted on continuing its association with the Royal Navy, keeping many naval prints and artefacts tied to the surroundings, most notably numerous naval cups hung from the open beams above the counter, bearing many familiar names of past naval history. Doing little to dispel the belief among many that he was a retired naval commander, in truth however, during the consumption of many pints with Bentley one evening, assured of the musician's silence over the matter, he confessed he was in fact a retired conservatory salesman from Guildford who had done very well on the National Lottery. That said, the two became firm friends and never discussed the matter again.

Entering the surprisingly near empty pub, Bentley was greeted by Albert with daughter Kathleen, leaning on the bar discussing the proposed evening menu.

"Usual Bentley?" Kathleen asked.

"Please Kathleen, yes. Rather quiet tonight," Bentley commented.

"Yes, it's strange," he replied, "been rushed off our feet until dinner time and all of a sudden it's gone dead, never mind. Oh damn, sorry Bentley, must change the barrel, won't be a minute."

Kathleen Jugg disappeared to the cellar leaving the two men alone. Adding the final adjustment to the evening's menu Albert looked up. "I haven't seen you for a couple of nights Bentley, you ok? What's the matter, had a card from the wife?" he laughed.

"Steady Albert, not so simple, just ran across Willoughby. He's a strange chap. He is stopping people and turning them away from the village saying that the end of the world is nigh."

"End of the world? Good grief, has he gone off his head? How do you mean, end of the world?"

"Well, he is blaming global warming, says the tarmac is melting and causing the surface layers to soften, which in turn may result in motoring accidents. Stopping everybody and suggesting they take a different route and bypass parts of the village, including The Mariners."

"What! With quiz night tonight. Good God." Without a pause, Albert headed for the door. "Where is he Bentley?"

"Well if he's still there, he is up by the T-junction near the phone box."

"I'll soon sort this out." Without more ado, Albert was out of the door.

Emerging from the cellar Kathleen returned to the pumps. "Right, one pint coming up. Where's Dad?"

"Er, gone out for a minute."

"Go and sit down Bentley, I'll bring it over."

Finding a quiet corner by the bay window Bentley

looked out upon the green. Long recognised as one of the prettiest in England the area was in full use it being early evening with temperatures in the high 80's. Beside the pavilion, a well-attended cricket practice was in the progress. At the centre of everything, a tall muscular man wearing a baseball cap with an emblem of a kangaroo upon its peak was conducting all efforts with much finger wagging eagerness. On the fringe of the group, several of the younger players, stripped to the waist, were flexing their muscles to the obvious merriment and delight of several young women exercising some horses. Across at St Michael's Church a group of women gathering for the evening's WI meeting were trying to suppress many cheeky comments.

"Your drink sir." Placing the drink upon the table Kathleen Jugg leaned across Bentley to look out of the window. "What's caught your attention?" With her closeness came an intoxicating mixture of spices, rum, new bread and mint, mixed with a touch of Lenor fabric softener. "Push up Bentley I'm knackered." Pushing Bentley further into the deeper recess of the bay window she sat up close resting her head upon his shoulder. "Ooh that's nice, first time I've sat down today." Kathleen Jugg was an attractive young woman in her mid-twenties, enterprising, good humoured and hard working, with natural blond, shoulder length hair pulled back tightly to the back of her head when working, sparkling eyes, pretty full-face features, she was the epitome of womanly self-confidence. "May I?" She took a long lingering sip of Bentley's drink finally passing it back to him. "Thank you."

"You're welcome young lady."

"Bentley," she cooed. "If we were a couple of teenagers would you whisk me off to a corner of the green and captivate me with your charm?"

Bentley chuckled. "To me, you are a teenager young lady and anyway, I was under the impression it is the other way round these days."

"Is it? I wouldn't know, I've been locked up in this place for so long I've forgotten what day it is."

Bentley tweaked her nose. "What's up young lady, no love life?"

"No, not a sniff for months," she grumbled. Getting up closer to Bentley she whispered, "Can't you whisk me off somewhere romantic Bentley? You know I fancy you like mad."

"Very flattering and somewhat tempting suggestion young lady, but I am far too old and tired for such a prize as yourself. Anyway, I would have thought your recent TV exposure would have drawn the lads in for miles around lining up for your cooking. On the other hand, perhaps they feel intimidated by your fame,"

Bentley suggested.

"Yeah right." Kathleen laughed aloud. "As if."

"Anyway, if I were a young man I would be knocking on your door every day," Bentley said.

She cuddled up closer. "Would you?"

"Almost certainly," Bentley assured her genuinely "not only are you a cracker to look at but your cooking I am told is a triumph."

"Now you're teasing me Bentley."

"No, I can assure you I'm not. Is there no young bloke on the horizon, some young chap that is worthy of your affections?"

"Well there have been a few hanging about I must admit. A young policeman in particular is showing a bit of interest."

"Not PC Willoughby!" Bentley groaned.

"Yes, a bit wet but a nice line in dry humour."

"Well that rather depends on what you call dry humour I would have thought."

She reached for his glass to take another sip. "He was in last night and your name came up funnily enough, he said you were a motoring maniac and hated nature. What was that about?"

"Small matter of a mower I would imagine," Bentley answered.

"No matter, I told him in no uncertain terms Bentley that if he were to bad mouth you in my company ever again he can find another pub." Bentley laughed.

"What did he say to that?"

"He went off in a sulk to play darts." She looked up at Bentley full of admiration. "You look really good today Bentley, all smart and shiny, been out for the day?"

"Yes, I have actually. I received good news this morning. I got my licence back on appeal so took the soft top out, great fun, enjoyed it all."

"Oh yes, where is it now?" Kathleen asked.

"The car? In the car park, where else. Why do you ask?"

"Bentley, may I suggest you have just the one drink this evening before driving your car home because if he is around tonight or early evening which he will be it being quiz night, his eyes will light up seeing it in the car park."

"Ah yes, you have a point." Bentley conceded.

"And just to make sure you do," Kathleen reached over finishing his drink. "There." She stood up. "The sooner you are home the better. On a more serious note Bentley, how is the wife, has she been in touch?"

"No, not yet, she hasn't replied to my calls. I shall ring again later tonight perhaps."

"Are you worried?"

"Good God no. If the ship had sunk or was involved in piracy, I think it would have been reported on the world news by now, don't you? She is giving me the cold shoulder, as she would have found her spell on the motorway quite harrowing. I do miss her of course, but it's only been a few days as yet. The weather keeps me cheerful, I read a bit, sleep a bit, drink a bit, a bit too much possibly, but as soon as the weather returns to normal I shall crack on with the greenhouse, keep me out of trouble."

"What's with these greenhouses, Bentley?" she asked.

"Oh many things. Ornate Victorian metal work, I would like to see them back to their best."

Kathleen squeezed his knee. "You must invite me over one day, show me around." Bentley coughed.

"Yes, perhaps sometime. Talking of greenhouses, a link with food somewhat."

"Bentley, your stamina, are you eating well? At your age, you must eat wisely. Plenty of fruit and veg. Now take your gas-guzzler home, put it away, return on foot and dine with us tonight, I insist." She returned to the bar. "Since you've been here in Barton I don't recall you ever entering the restaurant, you just use the bar. Well tonight, I promise you will use the restaurant." Bentley moved out of the corner.

"What's on the menu?"

"You'll have to wait and see," came the reply.

"Well, make mine a double portion."

"You'll get what you're given, now buzz off and leave the door open Bentley, it's baking in here, excuse the pun."

"Yes miss, from lover to mother in two minutes flat, eh?" Bentley laughed.

"Was it ever, with you men," the answer came from the kitchen.

CHAPTER 9

Chilli Con Carne

Returning to The Mariners within the hour, the evening quiz about to begin, a full crowd in noisy expectation, landlord Albert Jugg, dressed in a dinner jacket with a gold top hat festooned in flashing lights, was about to address the evening's crowd. Moving through the crowd towards the restaurant doors Bentley was overtaken by an eager Penny Jugg. "Saved you a table Bentley hurry up."

Entering the dining table for the first time ever, Bentley was taken aback by the contrast. Although continuing the seafaring theme to some extent, it displayed a far lighter touch, predominantly Wedgewood blue on walls, tablecloths and light shades. No prints of man of war on the rocks but optimistic sightings of sailing ships upon calm seas. A pair of French doors opened up upon the rear garden, which displayed a large marquee set upon the lawn. Penny showed Bentley to a corner table. "Will this be OK Bentley?" Penny handed Bentley the evening menu.

"Oh I should think so; it will do fine, thanks."

"Kathleen suggested you would appreciate her chilli con carne."

"She did, did she?"

"She did indeed," Penny assured him. "Be patient Bentley it won't be long, it's just that in the past half hour everything has gone manic." She lowered her voice. "Did you hear what happened to Willoughby?"

"No, what's happened? Not involved in an accident I hope," he laughed

"He shut the road."

"Oh yes, I have some recollection of that."

"Well," she continued, "it was quite funny. Albert confronted him by the crossroads, told him in no uncertain terms that the roadblock was silly, affecting a day's business and if it continued he can forget his team's entry in tonight's quiz and all future events for months to come. Willoughby huffed and puffed of course, but you see him now at the top table with his team of police mates, Willoughby's Winners he calls them, loves his quizzes does Willoughby, wouldn't miss them for the world. Winning is everything to him, he's such a pillock."

"He wouldn't do for a future son-in-law then?" Penny turned in horror.

"There's not much chance of that Bentley. My Kathleen's far too sensible, thank God."

A big man some 6 foot 3 inches in height with build

to match and a long period of success in the public eye behind him, Bentley was often recognised wherever he went. Although approachable at most times entering good-naturedly into conversation with all and sundry, he had become some would say quite averse to being stared at, a figure of curiosity. When this happened, which was quite often he would, as his first wife put it succinctly, engage reverse gear, rise to his feet and leave without a word. Many fans considered such a prima donna act as childish, to be discouraged. To Bentley however, this was his only way out, such close attention from complete strangers no longer tolerable. Finding his visit to Kathleen Jugg's restaurant just such an occasion, Bentley hurried his meal, anxious to escape the close attention of four excitable women on a girls' night out seated at a table close by. Passing a sizable tip into the hands of an appreciative waitress, he slipped away through the French windows into the dubious comfort of the crowded garden, there to be immediately confronted by an exuberant Chuffer Rudd enjoying the evening sunshine.

"Bentley Browne, good to see you, how the devil are you? Take my hand sir."

"Always pleased to see you Chuffer whatever the occasion." Bentley shook his hand warmly.

"Good to be back Chuffer?" "Indeed sir, indeed. I returned with my coach this very afternoon. Slight hiccup in the police release of my coach, but it's back in my yard now, thank God. Running a bit lumpy but it can be returned to running order. Now tell me dear boy, that wife of yours, has she been in touch?"

"No, she has not."

Chuffer stood on tiptoes and placed a comforting hand on Bentley's shoulder. "Bentley, Bentley, face the facts of life. If the current position were reversed, would you be ringing home every five minutes?"

"Possibly not," Bentley agreed.

"Course not. Anyway, if you are that concerned, ring the cruise line's head office."

"I have so, several times."

"Oh good, and?"

"Well she is fine, in the pink, but incommunicado."

"Oh, well that is excellent news. She will ring when she is ready. C'mon let's have a drink together."

"Not today Chuffer, another time. But if you are stopping for dinner I would recommend the chilli."

Chuffer patted his stomach. "Good God no, I am fat as a pig as it is. Since my wife passed on, God bless her, my daughter-in-law looks after me like no other. You're very fortunate Bentley. I doubt your weight has changed much over the years."

Bentley nodded in agreement. "Mmm, few pounds here and there, not much, I've been lucky."

"My boys reckon I'm a dead ringer for Orson Wells."

"More like Humpty Dumpty," Bentley offered.

Chuffer roared with laughter. "You think so? Good. C'mon Bentley, come in and have a word with my boys, enjoy a drink."

"No, I'm going home. But while I've got your attention I think I am entitled to a refund after that debacle with the coach."

Chuffer paused for a moment. "She got there," he insisted weakly.

"Oh yes, escorted by the police," said Bentley.

"You have a point Bentley. 5% reduction."

"No, 15%, cash in hand."

"Done. Must go Bentley, quiz time, see you at the end of the week, I'll pop round. I have a business proposition to put to you."

On his return to The Gables, two phone messages awaited his attention. One from the vicar's wife confirming her appearance on Friday at 9.00am sharp ready for domestic duties and hoping to find him sober and in good humour. Second, a message from his agent, Maurice Gibbins, urging him to reconsider his decision to retire. Time for him to return to showbiz and make them both a few bob. Delighted by the first message and disregarding the second, Bentley watched a little television without a drink before retiring to bed.

CHAPTER 10

Team Work

The following day witnessed an unexpected return to grey skies and drizzle. Early morning news reports stressed a period of cloudy conditions would be short lived with a return to fine weather by the weekend. With this very much in mind, Bentley ate a hearty breakfast determined to begin work on the greenhouses. So, suitably attired, Bentley approached the barn all still and enveloped in silence. No sight nor sound of Rawlings and his boy. Across the way, silent protest against overlong neglect sat the glasshouses, conjuring up scenes from a Victorian melodrama. An addition to the garden area built in the summer of 1876 designed by Edward Binlow, a prodigy of Joseph Paxton, the structure was considered a masterpiece of the time, formed as a quadrangle some 120 yards in total, with a magnificent entrance complete with two huge boilers and over 500 yards of piping. It was considered one of the most innovative glasshouses of its time featuring in garden publications for many years. It was broadly accepted by experts that firing up the boilers could generate enough pressure to propel a battleship. However, sadly neglected over the years it was a poor reflection of its former grandeur. The walled garden by contrast had been cleared and returned to much of its former originality within eighteen months of the Browne's purchase and was now abundant with fruit and veg.

Up for the task ahead, Bentley Brown, within one hour, had deposited many years of unwanted rubbish inside a conveniently placed skip outside the entrance. Pleased with his progress and pausing in his labour for a moment of self-congratulation, Bentley's attention was taken by a movement in the south facing garden wall. A heavy wooden door set in the brickwork slowly opened to welcome Rawlings and his boy pushing their bicycles before them. Engaged in conversation, the pair were unaware of Bentley's presence.

"Good morning gentlemen. On time as usual. Good to see you at last." Momentarily surprised, Rawlings dropped the large door key into a bed of nettles. "Leave it to me Rawlings." Bentley dived forward retrieving the key and placing it into his back pocket. Leaning his bicycle against the wall buttress Rawlings reached down to remove his bicycle clips, momentarily speechless.

"In the interests of home protection Mr Browne, I urge you to return the key. Your good wife has been most insistent that I should have it."

"Ah well, I have been after this key for months, Rawlings. We don't want it falling into the wrong hands do we?"

Rawlings shook his head. "That's why your wife gave it to me governor, for safe keeping. If you think back Mr Browne to the last year, about this time, me and the boy reported for duty and found this door flung wide open with my fruit and veg in disarray. My runner beans and soft fruit pillaged." Rawlings slipped his bicycle clips onto his handlebars. "Everything I had worked for gone overnight, eh boy?"

"That's right Grandad."

"Look, can we establish something here Mr Rawlings. It is my home, my garden. How was it your loss?"

"My effort, gone," came the tense reply.

"From which you were well paid and rewarded, Mr Rawlings."

"Yes, yes, we were compensated but emotional loss is far greater than monetary consideration, Mr Browne."

"But it's my land Rawlings, my land."

"Ah, but my efforts though. Paid the price I did with emotional stress," Rawlings insisted.

Bentley reached for the key. "Here, have it back, I can't be doing with this nonsense."

"It's for the best Mr Browne, your good wife would

want it this way."

"Would she?" Bentley turned away in exasperation.

"What's up Mr Browne, something we said?"

"Good Lord, no, what gave you that idea."

"Oh, alright then. C'mon boy, leave the master to it." Rawlings reached within his pocket for his tobacco tin winking at the boy as he did so.

"See your wife's having a good time then eh sir.

Bentley paused in his work. "Oh, sent you a card has she?"

"No. But there's a bit in the paper, you can't miss it, good spread."

"Ah, can you show me."

"I haven't brought it with me, papers at home isn't it boy?"

The boy nodded. "Grandma's reading it."

Bentley paused. "I see. Payday tomorrow Rawlings I believe."

"Yes governor, payment in cash, that's how I like it, sir."

"Well yes, I am sure you do. Now Rawlings tell me,

what did you read in the paper this morning?"

Rawlings edged towards the skip, poking about in the bottom with a bamboo cane.

"Well," he said slowly. "Let me think. There is talk of a drought if this heatwave continues." He looked up at the sky. "Little chance of that, summer's been and gone in my view, you mark my words. What else you ask? Well, fares are up in London by 10%, that won't bother us, will it boy. I don't go to London, full of ponses innit boy." The boy nodded his agreement. "That's right Grandad, ponses." Rawlings rummaged deeper into the skip finally to reappear brandishing two empty wine bottles. "What's this, there's hundreds of them down here in my skip."

"Your skip, Rawlings, I think not, my skip."

"Well, our skip then," Rawlings conceded reluctantly.

"No, Rawlings, not our skip, my skip."

Rawlings blew out his cheeks. "Well I have always thought of the three of us as a team Mr Browne. You'll be upsetting the lad if you talk like this won't he boy?" The boy nodded mischievously in agreement. "Teamwork is paramount in horticulture Mr Browne." Rawlings winked at the boy.

"Yes, yes Rawlings I am sure, but this skip is for my own private use and I intend to work on the greenhouses, clear them out." Bentley said.

"Cor, some job governor. Me and the boy are up to our eyes in work at the moment, vegetable garden, flower beds, lawns, can't really give you any more gov, our energy is spent."

"That's fine by me Rawlings, find yourself a little part of the garden and stay there. Meantime, empty my skip of your cuttings if you will and dispose of them somewhere. I suggest a bonfire."

"Can't do that Mr Browne, health and safe, carbon emissions."

"Rawlings, this is my final word on the subject. Take your cuttings and burn them, far away from me. We are surrounded by twenty acres of private land, my land do you hear and if I want a bonfire, I shall have a bonfire. Now find a corner of the garden out of my sight, start a fire, a small bonfire. This is to dispose of your waste. And when I say small bonfire Rawlings, that is what I mean. I do not want to see a huge blaze that starts a panic in the village, comprende?"

Rawlings nodded his head. "You're the governor. I'll get the tractor. C'mon boy."

"Oh Rawlings, one more thing."

"What will that be governor?"

"What was in the papers this morning?"

"I told you, increasing train fares and the pound up against the Euro."

"Rawlings! Do you want payment in cash tomorrow?"

"Oh, Hong Kong you mean. Lots of celebrations and fireworks as your Mrs's ship entered the harbour. Quite good it was. I'll bring the paper in tomorrow and hand it over when we get paid in cash gov."

"Thank you Rawlings, much appreciated."

"Mr Browne, before we goes about our business, what is going to happen to these greenhouses when it's all said and done?"

"None of your business Rawlings," came the sharp reply.

A persistent Rawlings continued. "What I mean is them boilers for a start, don't try starting them up, you'll never get them going and they could blow us all to kingdom come. I say scrap them, I know plenty of people that will take them off your hands."

"Rawlings, they are rare and Grade 2 listed as you are well aware."

"Uh, they're sell for scrap if you ask me."

"Well I'm not Rawlings. I may spend some money and restore them to working order or sell the whole caboodle to my neighbour Smethurst." Rawlings stepped back in horror. Bentley smiled within himself having hit a nerve. "Is that a problem," he asked.

"Course it's a problem, don't want him here trampling all over my garden produce."

"Your produce?"

"Alright, our produce, your produce, whatever it is." Rawlings was plainly agitated, reaching again for his tobacco pouch.

"It won't really matter will it? If the garden goes with the greenhouses he can have the lot, there's plenty left."

"But the man's a philistine. He wouldn't know a carrot from a parsnip and have you tried his sausages," Rawlings protested bitterly.

"Yes, well that's enough now Rawlings, let's leave it for the moment shall we, I've got work to do. When you've emptied the skip of your cuttings, take that old armchair and burn it, I need every inch of space. One more thing, we had a visit from the deer overnight, the rear lawn needs a clear up. My apologies old chap but best get the boy cracking with a bucket and spade. Fond as I am of mushrooms, we don't want them all over the lawn do we?"

For the remainder of the day the two antagonists managed to avoid each other with some success.

Rawlings, incensed by the thought of Smethurst getting his hands on the greenhouses eyed the smouldering leather armchair with ill-disguised contempt. "My bloody pension gone if he has his way. I'm lost boy, lost. All my plans gone out the window. I was going to take your grandma on a trip to the Isle of Wight. That's gone. Thought of buying a new bike as well. We'll have to keep our eyes and ears open when we're around Mr Browne, spike any plans of an arrangement between him and Smethurst before it's too late."

"How will we do that Grandad?" the boy asked.

"Easy boy, easy. Your grandad is a master of trickery. Trust me boy, trust me."

CHAPTER 11

A Surprise Call

Early morning the following day, a slightly hungover Bentley answered a bedside phone call.

"Mr Browne?"

"Yes, I think so."

"Is this Barton Manor House, sir?"

"As far as I am aware, yes."

"Are you Mr Browne sir?"

"It's possible."

"Mmm, shall we start again sir? If you are Mr Browne and my information is correct, this is Barton Manor, hardly a two up two down is it sir? Now, I have a busy schedule. Could you perhaps send a servant to open the door or perhaps come to the door yourself personally?" Within four minutes, Bentley answered the door to a man dressed in green overalls carrying a clipboard. "Are you Mr Browne, sir?"

"Yes I am. And who are you young fella?"

"I work for JJ Plant Hire, sir, Basingstone and you are my first call but I am running rather late at the moment and I hope we can get this over and done with rather quickly." The driver turned and looked toward the forklift truck parked high on the back of a 15-ton pickup with obvious pride.

Bentley followed his gaze. "Yes, very impressive."

"The phone call was received at head office requesting the hiring, for one day only, of a fork lift truck sir and here it is. Top of the range sir. We were informed a large object was prohibiting easy movement in the driveway and surrounding area, this would be it sir would it?" He stepped forward and lifted a corner of the bubble wrap. "My word, a bit cheeky sir, even in these so called enlightened times."

"It is considered a work of art in many quarters," Bentley contested rather weakly.

"I don't think it would go down too well in Guildford sir."
"Do you live in Guildford?" Bentley asked, somewhat irritated.

"No sir, but I have visited Guildford many times, a very conservative area Guildford." At this very irrelevant observation of a Surrey town Bentley stepped back inside the door.

"Look, I've had a very unusual weekend and I'm feeling, to be honest, a little under the weather. Could you give me an hour or so to get myself together? Perhaps you could take yourself off to a café somewhere. Look, have it on me." Bentley reached for his wallet.

"No sir, none of that rubbish for me, I am self sufficient thank you, you have to be these days, you never know what the day will bring." the driver said pointedly "A flask, plenty of fruit, nuts, mint tea, key to a healthy lifestyle, sir."

"Fair enough, fair enough I will leave you to it," said Bentley.

"Very well Mr Browne, I shall unload. I have a very busy schedule ahead of me."

Bentley stiffened. "You can't leave that thing here, it is nothing to do with me," Bentley insisted.

"It's on my docket here sir." The driver tapped his clipboard. "Mr Browne, Barton Manor, clear as day."

"I have no recollection of ordering a forklift truck."

"Well it's a puzzle Mr Browne but there you are," said the driver.

"Well why don't you ring your head office and request some clarification," Bentley suggested.

"I have sir and I am at the right address."

"Well, I disagree. I am sorry, I shall say goodbye."

"Just a minute sir, Mr Browne, before you disappear, I must ask you something."

"Go on."

"Have you ever been on TV? You remind me so much of a chap who played a bent copper on television some years ago, very convincing it was, was it you, sir?"

"No, it was not me."

"Truly?"

Bentley nodded. "Sadly so." The driver's disappointment was plain to see.

"Shame. The wife will be disappointed, I don't meet many celebrities."

"Well, I am sorry young man, you've got two issues wrong here. I am not the bent copper and I did not order a forklift truck, so I shall say goodbye." Closing the door, Bentley allowed himself a small smile. "Price of fame, eh, a bent copper." After two pieces of toast, a shower and a shave, a slightly repentant Bentley opened the door to be greeted by an empty drive save for two spent tea bags discarded on the porch floor.

CHAPTER 12

A Turn on the Piano

Late afternoon, Bentley received a phone call. "Bentley? Albert. Sorry to disturb you at home but I wonder, will you be visiting The Mariners tonight?"

"I don't think I will Albert, I've had rather a busy day, thought I'd put my feet up and relax. May I ask why you require my company this evening my friend?"

"Ah well, never mind, I'm a bit disappointed but not to worry."

"Come on Albert, speak your mind, what is it?"

Well, I'd rather value your opinion on something."

"On something? On what may I ask?"

"A piano."

"A piano?"

"Yes, a piano Bentley, second hand of course."

"And how did you acquire this piano my friend?"

"Your pal, Chuffer Rudd, he's downsizing. Could turn out to be a bargain, you never know."

"Albert, Chuffer Rudd does not do bargains." Albert

laughed in agreement. "I know, but I may take a chance with it. It was dropped off earlier this afternoon by his two lads. It's in the lounge bar. Depends really what you think of it, otherwise it's heading for the auction rooms on Monday. I am in a mind to increase live music in The Mariners. Can't stand still in this business, perhaps also a stage somewhere, I'm undecided and that's why I would value your opinion before I make a decision." Albert paused for a moment. Receiving no response from Bentley, he continued hopefully. "I'll pick you up, drop you off, large whiskey in it for you. What do you say? Are you there Bentley?"

Finally, after much consideration Albert received an answer. "Yes, I am here Albert, listening, just. Now tell me this my friend. Why should I leave the delights of a comfortable armchair with glass in hand containing malt whiskey of such rarity and age that a small teaspoonful costs a fortune to thrash the keys of a worn out piece of furniture previously owned by a village bandit such as Chuffer Rudd?"

"For the same reason as always, Bentley. Despite your moans and protests you enjoy a little company!"

"Do I? How very astute you are Mr Jugg. Alright, you win. As it's you," Bentley replied generously.

"Thanks Bentley, pick you up in ten minutes?"

"Twenty, I need a shave."

"Twenty it is then," came the delighted reply.

"Well, what do you think?" Albert rubbed his jacket sleeve across the piano top. "Looks good to me Bentley."

Taking his time, Bentley stood back a little, casting a professional eye over it. "Yes, it's a good one Albert, I have to admit it. It's a Morrison, iron framework, a natural for a pub. They produce a sharp tone as a rule, good for jazz and blues. Not a Steinway of course, unsuitable for the concert platform obviously, but for here it's perfect."

Albert was delighted. "I thought so Bentley, thanks. It's a bargain then?"

"Oh, hang on, I haven't heard a note yet," Bentley cautioned.

Albert lifted the lid. "Have a go Bentley, bring it to life!"

"Steady on Albert, I haven't played in front of a crowd for years," Bentley teased.

Albert spread his arms wide. "Look around you Bentley, early evening, miserable night out, no-one's in yet. Couple on the fruit machine, Cyril with a newspaper over in the corner and oh yes, a couple in the bar just come in. It hardly constitutes a crowd surely! I'm not asking for a concert. Poke around a bit, tell me if it's in tune."

"Poke around a bit!" Bentley chuckled. "What a philistine you are Albert. Where's that drink you promised?" Bentley turned and headed for the bar followed closely by Albert. At the bar, perched precariously on stools an elderly couple waited patiently for attention.

"Shan't keep you a moment folks, just serve this gentleman. Now Bentley what's it to be?"

"Bitter, Albert."

"Bitter?"

"Yes, bitter."

"Bentley, you are well aware that I have over fifteen real ales to choose from. Which one would you prefer?" Albert looked at the waiting couple raising his eyebrows in exasperated apology.

"Anyone will do."

"Anyone? Anyone coming up then."

With a drink in hand and without a further word, Bentley returned to the piano watched with some interest by the couple at the bar.

"Is that who I think it is?" the lady whispered to her

companion.

"I don't know dear. Who do you think it is?" came the reply.

"Can't think of this name, looks familiar though. Excuse me," the lady expressed to the landlord "who's that man?"

Albert moved closer, putting his finger to his lips. "Sshh, don't let him hear you madam, he's wearing his temperamental head tonight. That madam is Bentley Browne."

"Oh." The woman clapped her hand in joy. "Of course it is, of course it is!" She grabbed her partner's arm. "Dave, it's Bentley Browne," she said excitedly "He hasn't changed a bit. Is he going to play? Oh Dave, imagine, Bentley Browne in here with us?"

An apprehensive Albert glanced over at Bentley who, unaware of the gathering excitement, removed the piano top and was peering within the framework with much interest.

"Does he come in a lot?" the woman whispered under cover of her hand.

"Yes, most evenings about this time. Very much a creature of habit," Albert replied.

The woman nudged her companion. "Hear that Dave?" We must come again. Is the restaurant open every night?"

"Oh yes, most evenings. My daughter runs the restaurant. She was on television recently actually. You may have seen her," Albert replied proudly, "she reached the final."

The woman beamed with pleasure. "Oh how wonderful, we shall come again won't we Dave?"

The man nodded with half-hearted enthusiasm. "If you say so dear."

"Tell your friends," Albert urged.

"Oh, we will, won't we Dave?" The man slid off his stool with a heavy sigh heading for the toilets. The woman reached out towards Albert. "Take no notice of my husband, been a bit low recently. Retired you know. He doesn't like gardening, he gets bored. I do my best but he has to help himself. But fancy, Bentley Browne in the flesh. I shall tell all my friends. I am so thrilled. I adored him when I was younger, still do!" she giggled.

"Yes, well he's in most evenings so a good excuse to come again. Now please excuse me, nice to have met you."

Beckoning a passing waitress over to cover the bar for a moment, Albert returned to the side of Bentley who was pressing down upon the keys in a thoughtful manner.

"Well?"

"Well what?"

"What's the problem, out of tune is it Bentley?"

"No, it's fine Albert."

"Well come on them man, play a melody."

"Albert, it may have slipped your attention but there is no stool to sit on."

"Oh God, sorry Bentley, it's in the office, hold on."

Awaiting Albert's return Bentley pulled upon each finger with a little nervous exaggeration increasingly aware of an ever-growing clientele in for the night. Within the minute, Albert returned with the stool, holding it aloft.

"Here you are Bentley, comfort at hand."

"Thank you Albert. Now bearing in mind I am a little out of practice what would you like to hear?"

"Ah, my choice eh? Well, not too much rock and roll. I've always been moved by that tune from the film Picnic starring Kim Novak and William Holden. Great atmosphere. Or the Casablanca one, the film with Humphrey Bogart."

"Right, right, good choice Albert. Moonglow it is then, followed by You Must Remember This. Hang on a minute, where's my drink Albert?"

"On top of the piano where you put it, Bentley."

"Oh yes, yes. Well I think we can forget best bitter from now on. If this instrument plays as well as I think it will, bring me a large scotch with ice every half hour on the dot. Ok Albert?"

"Whatever you say, Bentley. On the other hand, why don't I just leave the bottle?"

"Good thinking Albert. I'll take care of myself. Don't forget the ice, please. Put some in a mug close by."

"Very well sir."

Finally settling upon the stool, hunched over the keys like some predatory bird of prey about to strike, Bentley was quickly into his stride. Confidence in the piano itself growing by the minute, the evening progressed at a gallop, from Gershwin to Dorsey, jazz to blues, the music was almost continuous for over a period of two hours, finally coming to a close with several blues classics including his 70's hit Moonrock Rumble, a composition part written and arranged by his erstwhile musical ex-partner, acclaimed blues guitarist, Syd 'Nifty' Mitchell.

At the end of the evening, departing the bar to a

standing ovation, Bentley was escorted to the relative quiet of the kitchen area by an exuberant Albert Jugg, there to be greeted with further applause from kitchen staff and a warm embrace from daughter, Kathleen.

"Wonderful Bentley, wonderful! A lot before my time but nevertheless, now let's get you home while you're still standing."

Present in the crowd that evening, independent reporter Amy Nuxford, out for a night's revelry with current boyfriend, Neville Chaucer, was seated in a position well suited to observe the excitement generated by Bentley's impromptu display of musical accomplishment. Aware of his past history and suitably streetwise to its news value locally if not nationwide, her observations that evening were on the editor's desk of the Portsmouth Echo by 11.45pm that evening.

"This evening in a public house in the wonderful village of Barton-on-the-Green in wildest Hampshire, I witnessed first-hand the return of a musical God, Bentley Browne. A supremely gifted performer be it music, film or concert hall. Retiring in the late nineties, his reappearance draped over a small piano in the dark corner of a village pub was surreal."

Although now of an age more suited to thick socks and warm vest, he still strikes a commanding presence with his thick head of hair, easy manner and good looks. Although personally I am too young to remember his heyday during the eighties and nineties, his legacy lives on, in particular his portrayal of a hard-nosed Detective Inspector Dawkins, a TV favourite often repeated to this day on Talking Pictures television. Pausing only briefly to replenish his glass several times with Johnny Walker Red Label whiskey, he was seated at the piano for a period of two and a half hours. His range of musical numbers was immense, played in a manner of consummate ease bringing gasps of delight all evening from a rapidly growing audience. However, I wonder why such a return now? Is this old dog pulling on the lead just as his fourth wife disappears over the horizon on board a luxury cruise ship for a 5-week Caribbean cruise, or was his appearance as landlord Albert Jugg insisted, pure coincidence? A mere call to arms, responding to a request from his friend, said landlord Albert, to test a recently acquired piano. Did he indeed pop across the green initially to test this piano, one thing leading to another? Is the event likely to be repeated? This I cannot confirm. Bentley Browne being whisked away hurriedly out through the kitchen doors to be driven away by the daughter of landlord Jugg.

To sum up, I found the evening an unexpected delight ending unfortunately on a sour note. Off duty policeman PC Willoughby, attempting to control the excited crowd's movements after the pub's closure, some say with exaggerated enthusiasm for the rule of law, was pushed from behind into a flowerbed by a person or persons unknown. A second man, apparently the current vicar of Barton-on-the-Green, attempting to assist the hapless constable was soon to follow him face down into the flowerbed. Landlord Jugg put it down to a few high spirits bemoaning the fact that the particular flowerbed in question contained rare hybrids and were difficult to replace. This reporter however notes, with some caution to the many unaware, that The Three Mariners has a history of high spirits dating back to 1830 as a body in the local church yard will confirm."

CHAPTER 13

A Day of Reckoning

The following morning, somewhat approaching lunchtime, Bentley was finally prised from a deep slumber by frantic tapping upon the bedroom window. Rising somewhat reluctantly to his feet and approaching the French doors with some concern, he opened them out upon the veranda. Perched upon the upper reaches of a long ladder leaning somewhat precariously against a drainpipe was the somewhat agitated Rawlings boy.

"What the hell are you doing boy?"

"Grandad says get your arse downstairs as quick as you can, the vicar's wife is sitting in the porch outside the main entrance wanting a word with you and she's been waiting for ages."

"Waiting? Oh God, what time is it boy?"

The boy sniggered to himself. "Well, let's say it's a little late for a breakfast of egg on toast governor."

A concerned Bentley re-entered the bedroom, followed closely by the lad.

"Where do you think you're going boy?"

The lad shrugged. "I dunno, back outside I suppose, downstairs perhaps?" the lad answered somewhat vaguely.

"What's wrong with you young fella, go back the way you came, down the ladder."

"Well the ladder is a bit wonky skipper, it's dangerous. Grandad said he can't afford insurance, we don't get paid enough, that's what he said. Can't be too careful can we, health and safety and all that," the boy responded mischievously.

"Yes alright lad, point taken." The irate musician reached for his dressing gown. "Now go downstairs, make your way to the front doorway and let the lady in. Tell her I shall be down in a minute, I'm freshening up first, alright?"

"Well, where shall she wait governor?"

"Er, my study or, no, perhaps in the grand reception hall, anywhere as long as she's happy," came the irritable reply as Bentley headed for the ensuite.

"Hang on gov, I don't know where your study is or the grand hall or what you call it, I've never been in before, I don't know where it is, this house is huge governor."

"Yes alright boy," Bentley conceded, "I haven't got time for all this. Look," Bentley pointed at the bedroom door, "go out the bedroom, turn right, go to the end of the passageway, you'll find yourself confronted by a large stairway, follow it all the way to the bottom and you will find yourself in the grand hallway. You'll know it's a grand hallway because it's large enough to house two double decker buses or even have a game of football there, you can't miss it and hopefully you will find the outside door and let the lady in and there hopefully she will remain in place and I shall be down in 5 minutes. And be polite when you speak with her, she's a lady. Then I suggest you go back outside, remove the ladder and then go about your business workwise. Ok lad? Now I must get on."

"Right on governor, job done." Without further ado, the lad left the bedroom.

Showered and shaved within ten minutes, Bentley headed downstairs reaching the reception hall. Bentley was rather surprisingly greeted by Rawlings comfortably seated, feet up upon a bay window bench, tobacco pouch in hand.

"Who let you in Rawlings and also, no smoking inside thank you."

"Just relaxing skipper, just relaxing."

"Well, relax outside please." Bentley insisted.

"Oh steady on, skipper."

"Who let you in anyway?"

"The boy did."

"Well, what are you doing here, where is the lady."

"Lady, lady who?"

"Don't play games Rawlings, the vicar's wife."

"Ah the lovely Melody you mean, delight to the eye that woman. D'you know she's a local girl born in Barton-on-the-Green. I remember her in her youth, from way back. Win my horticultural award for spring blossom any time of year eh."

"Yes, alright Rawlings, where is she?"

"Not sure, she got tired of waiting for you, last I saw of her she was heading down the hallway, could be anywhere now, she's a real cracker thought aint she skipper? Bet she stirs your pot don't she?"

"Alright Rawlings, that's enough, keep the remarks for the pub and your mates. Good God man, act your age."

"What! I'm the same age as you are," came the indignant reply, as Rawlings sprang to his feet.

"Life spent in horticulture keeps a man fit, I'm not past it, I can still admire a good looking woman you know and provide a service when required. Mrs

Rawlings has never complained about my stamina."

"Alright Rawlings, I've no wish to know about your private life."

"Ah in my time I could have gone ten rounds with Sonny Liston," Rawlings continued in protest. "I'm as fit as a fiddle, I've got Irish blood in me, I'm the Michael Flatly of horticulture I am, look..."

Rising to his feet, much to Bentley's consternation, the gardener embraced a three-minute wild performance of an aggressive soft shoe shuffle before returning to his window seat, arms open wide displaying a show of triumph.

"There you are gov, what did I tell you."

"Yes, very good Rawlings I must admit, but you are acting a little excitable this morning, not quite like you at all, are you ok?"

"I'm in fine fettle thank you, never felt better, quite jolly I am."

"Yes, that's what I mean, not yourself, are you on pills or something, a pick me up perhaps?"

"No, course I'm not." came the retort. "Medically I'm as fit as a grasshopper, I've Irish blood in me you know, I'm the Michael Flatly of horticulture, I keeps telling you that."

"Yes, OK Rawlings, I'll take your word for it but I've no time for any further wild Fred Astaire if that's ok, I must greet the lady. Time you returned to work also Rawlings. What are you doing in the manor anyway? I know your boy let you in but why are you here?"

"I was concerned about you Mr Browne when you wasn't about this morning, so I got the boy to let me in. It's all over the village this morning, your return to the limelight last night. I was there, I saw it all. Debauchery, heavy drinking, a scrap in the car park, a good young copper Willoughby injured, where's it all going to end? When the boy and I couldn't raise you this morning we thought, well, I thought perhaps you had snuffed it, the excitement and all that, that's why I sent the boy up the ladder. I mean, since your Mrs has been away the place is falling apart. I mean the way this job is going, on top of everything else what are we, we're in horticulture; we're not multi-taskers. What have we become, the boy and I, firemen, lifesavers, window cleaners, it's all getting out of hand Mr Browne, more than we can cope with."

Suppressing a smile, Bentley addressed his gardener, offering a solution to his handyman's woes.

"If you find your work at Barton Manor untenable Rawlings, I suggest that you and the boy leave my employment this very day, I'm sure Mrs Browne would understand given the facts that you'd had enough. I shall get in touch with her this very afternoon. Until then, perhaps you can find your way to the door."

Reaching out, a concerned Rawlings grabbed Bentley's arm. "Hold on skipper, that hurts, there's no need for that kind of talk, I was just putting my view forward, no need for discord between us governor."

In haste to calm the rising discord between the two, Rawlings turned his attention to a line of photos running the length of the grand hallway, pointing to one in particular. "That's him then is it?" he asked.

"Who Rawlings, who are you referring to?"

"Your ex-musical mate, that's who."

"My ex-musical partner you mean, yes, that's him, why do you ask?"

"He went a bit divvy didn't he in the end, always in the paper for one thing or another."

With a heavy sigh, Bentley turned to defend his erstwhile ex-partner. "Well he could lack a little self-control at times, not unlike yourself Rawlings eh, but we are talking a long while ago, we've both moved on since then, done different things, our paths haven't crossed for years. Now come on Rawlings out the door, about your business, you've work to do I trust."

"Is he still about?"

"Yes, he's still about Rawlings, in deepest Devon, retired like myself. Now I must get on, I must get on, away you go."

"Ah, he was a class act though wasn't he?"

"Well, matter of opinion Rawlings."

"Aw, do I detect a smidgen of jealously there, governor?"

"No, you do not Rawlings."

"Well, I've got to say, it's not my choice of music really, bloody hippy stuff, but he was damn good in what he did." Rawlings headed for the outside door. "Your wife know about your return to showbiz last night, Mr Browne?"

"No. And there is no need for her to know either Rawlings, it was strictly a one-off." Bentley replied pointedly. "Understand? No need for her to know."

"Oh, I quite understand gov, trust me. Don't worry, you're secret's safe with me, I can assure you. I mean, I am your head gardener aren't I; a very important position for continuity within the manor house isn't it, eh? Right, I'll get on, see you later Mr Browne. Oh by the way, you will find the lovely Melody waiting for you in the conservatory gov, I meant to tell you, goodbye then."

Entering the conservatory, Bentley was greeted by the

vicar's wife gazing out upon the garden and beyond through open doors.

"Hope you don't mind Bentley, I opened the doors. With temperatures rising it's so damn hot again."

"Yes, it is. My apologies Melody, sorry to keep you waiting, got sidetracked, had to do a little pest control. Can I get you anything, coffee perhaps?"

"No, no please, don't go to a lot of fuss, I'm not stopping, I've been here far too long as it is, but I'm glad to see you finally made it out of your bed. I've come to tell you I shall not be at your beck and call for a few days owing to a slight accident involving my silly husband. You are aware of it I am sure, yourself being centre stage at The Mariners last night."

"No, first I've heard of it truth be told. What's the problem, Melody?"

"My husband has gone and damaged his knee in an incident at The Mariners last night, a little altercation between the village constable and a rather boisterous village youth leaving the pub. Didn't your right hand man Rawlings inform you?"

"No, he didn't actually."

"Ah, don't you chastise your handyman for not keeping you in the picture, if it wasn't for him I'd still be waiting at the door and you would still be in a deep sleep I imagine, looking at the state of you."

"Well thank you Melody, most kind, I do admire your honesty my dear."

With her hair piled high upon her head and devoid of makeup, she appeared much younger and prettier than he remembered and Bentley had to agree with his horticultural expert that she did indeed ring all the bells.

"Please tell me more. Your husband, is he ok?"

"Well without going into detail, let's summarise by saying he won't be bowling leg-breaks this Sunday that's for sure, even a trip to the top of the pulpit may be a problem, he will be a right old misery to live with believe me," she laughed ruthlessly and glanced at her watch. "God, I must go and pick him up, he'll be waiting."

"Where exactly is he?" asked Bentley with sudden concern.

"Petersfield, Accident & Emergency, they kept him in overnight."

"Oh God, can I help, let me get the car out and I'll take you."

"No, Bentley, that's quite alright, I have transport arranged. One of the girls in the WI is going to take me, must go now," she headed down the hallway followed closely by Bentley.

Out upon the courtyard she pointed at the statue still enveloped in bubble wrap. "It's still here then?"

"Yes, yes I'm still here," came the reply from the porch.

"No, not you silly, the statue, you asked for its removal I recall."

"Did I?"

"You did. Well, actually not you as such, I did it for you, don't you remember?"

"Er no actually I don't, remind me."

"What, you've forgotten our day of introduction so soon, Bentley, I'm bitterly disappointed in you," she teased. "You don't recall last Sunday afternoon? We shared a bottle of wine together, well two actually."

"Yes, I recall that," Bentley nodded "of course."

"Well, as I was about to leave you dashed into the house and returned with the Yellow Pages under your arm and as you are a non-believer in such things as email and mobile phones which you dislike intensely, you requested I ring a company in Basingstoke and hire a form of conveyance capable of moving a heavy object from A to B, correct?" Bentley nodded vaguely, "If you say so, I don't recall doing so."

Melody laughed. "I'm not surprised, the amount of wine you put away."

Bentley joined her in amusement. "Well you didn't do too badly yourself young lady, did you?"

"Too true, Bentley, too true, a bit of an addict. Perhaps we could do it again someday?"

"Yes, yes Melody, nice idea."

"Well I must be off Bentley, I must go and rescue my poor husband. Perhaps I'll see your lordship on Monday, perhaps not, bye bye."

As she disappeared towards the green up the drive, Bentley was loathed to admit even to himself that he had no recollection of a phone call to Basingstoke that day.

CHAPTER 14

A Day to Forget

After the vicar's wife's departure, Bentley took to the landline to contact the cruise offices in London's Pall Mall. After a delay of some five minutes, he was put through to a young lady from marketing.

"Good afternoon, how can I help you?"

"Well quite a lot I hope. My wife is on board the cruise ship S.S. Splendide."

"Your name sir?"

"Browne."

"Oh, would that be Browne with an 'e' sir?"

"Yes that's correct."

"Haven't we heard from you several times Mr Browne?"

"Yes you have. I am very sorry to bother you again but I wish to speak to my wife and I cannot get through to her and I am rather concerned."

"Well Mr Browne with an 'e', it certainly rings a bell, hold on a moment and I'll see what I can do."

After the passing of several minutes, she returned to the phone.

"Mr Browne, the answer is the same as before. We have contacted the ship itself and even spoken with the captain and requested that he contact Mrs Browne with a view to her answering your calls personally. He has met your wife on several occasions along with her sisters. They are all in excellent spirits and I understand she has stated forcefully several times she will return your calls when and if she has the time."

"Oh alright then, I understand. Thanks for your help Miss..."

"Brenda, Brenda Rokins."

"Thank you Brenda. Oh, as a matter of interest before we go, where is the ship at the moment?"

"Hold on sir, I'll check, bear with me Mr Browne with an 'e'."

Within seconds, she was back on the line. "Panama Canal sir. You could fly out there and surprise her," she added encouragingly.

"I could, yes, what a cracking idea."

"Shall I arrange the flight for you Mr Browne?"

"No thank you."

"Ah shame, you don't fancy a cruise, we have many options at present, discounted at 10%, 20%, some even 25%."

"No thank you, I have an exciting time ahead, I plan to explore Hayling Island by bicycle."

"Oh, sounds delightful Mr Browne with an 'e', I am quite envious."

"Well it's a simple life for me you understand, good for the soul."

"Too true Mr Browne, too true. I'll say goodbye then, I'm sure we'll talk again at some point in the near future unfortunately, bye bye."

At 2.22pm that afternoon precisely, Bentley sought out the irascible Rawlings and his boy, the search finally coming to a close in the barn finding the pair knee deep in spanners servicing several grass mowers.

"I have your wages here Rawlings, rest assured it's all there."

Taking the envelope, Rawlings immediately checked the contents. Once assured, he slipped the money in a money belt hidden under his waistcoat.

"Mmm, your trust is most reassuring Rawlings, I thank you."

Rawlings rose to his feet slowly and the gardener

tapped the boy upon the shoulder.

"C'mon boy, this week's hard graft is behind us now but before we leave you Mr Browne I should say to you, man to man, face to face, that this mower here has just been serviced by the boy and me saving you a small fortune by way of service charges from that bloke in Petersfield you call upon from time to time. I can assure you that this machine will transport you across the green at a fair old rate of knots should you ever feel an urge to repeat your trip across the green on the back of a mower, but should you do that, I would advise you, Mr Browne, to wear a hat and pull it well down over your face because should you do so, and I have it on good authority, PC Willoughby blames you for encouraging the riot outside the pub the other night, jeopardising his opening bat for the village cricket team on Sunday. What with him being pushed into a flowerbed, he says he will get you for something even if it takes him a lifetime. He says you're the source of all that's wrong in this corner of England governor, so I suggest you keep a low profile until Mrs Browne comes home. I wouldn't want to see you hanging from a gibbet at the crossroads leading down to Lower Barton, would we boy." Unable to suppress their mirth any longer the pair reached for their cycles and headed towards the greenhouses and the door in the wall. "I'll leave you to shut up then Mr Browne, what with you not wishing to pay us overtime now, we'll leave you to secure the barn, alright sir?"

Bentley nodded, "Leave it to me."

"Have a good weekend, Mr Browne; we'll be seeing you at the cricket match on Sunday I hope."

Bentley pulled upon the barn doors. "Not if I can help it," he muttered.

Later in the day, returning to the manor house after his customary stroll upon the green with the dog, Bentley was confronted by Mr Patel seated within the porch out of the unremitting afternoon sunshine. Visibly relieved at Bentley's appearance, he rose from the shadows and extended a hand in warm greeting.

"Ah, Mr Browne, at last my dear friend, your appearance is most welcome sir. I fear I have agitated your alarm system, most unfortunate my dear sir, so sorry. I feel I may have knocked upon the door rather harshly, so sorry once again."

"Indeed you may have Mr Patel, let's get inside the house and turn the damn thing off."

Crossing the threshold, Bentley hurried to his study and within a minute returned to the porch way.

"Step inside Mr Patel, bear with me for a moment, I must ring the police, reassure all is well here."

Within a minute, his call was answered. "Hello, this is

Sergeant Murray, Petersfield Police Station, how can I help?"

"Afternoon sergeant, my name is Bentley Browne, I have just returned home to find my alarm activated, you may be aware of it at your end?"

"Ah could be, let me check, whose residence is it?"

"Mine."

"Yes of course it's yours sir, where is it exactly?"

"Barton Manor, Barton-on-the-Green."

"One minute sir." After some delay, the sergeant returned to the phone. "Yes sir I can confirm it has been noted," adding rather wearily, "now bear with me, I must confirm you are who you say you are sir."

"Must we sergeant?"

"Yes sir we must," came the firm reply. "I am duty bound to confirm that you are who you say you are, not some villain testing our response time, or worse a damn nosey reporter out for mischief."

"Sergeant, I am who I say I am, believe me. I could question you sergeant. Are you who you say you are? You could in fact be a spotty nosed constable having a laugh, or worse still an office cleaner, who am I to know?"

"Point taken sir, but please do not test my patience further, I am on a short fuse today. Now let's establish your credentials shall we sir?" His words, measured and firm in tone, forbade further questioning.

"Name and nationality, followed by date of birth sir, if you please."

"Bentley Browne."

"Correct. Nationality?"

"English."

"Aye, I thought so, can't say I'm surprised. Another question sir and I should warn you, this is a tricky one. How do you spell your surname?"

"B R O W N E Browne."

"Aye, that's it. I think we can safely say...." the sergeant's voice trailed off.... "One minute sir." After a short pause, the sergeant was back on the phone. "My apologies sir. Browne with an 'e', unusual, rings an alarm bell, a little disquiet somewhere, I don't know why, I can't quite make the connection but I will in time, police instinct, but let's put it to one side for the moment, let's see, ah yes, I can have a bobby at your place heading your way within ten minutes, how would that suit, to investigate the break in? But I must impress upon you that having taken you into police confidence regarding our response time you would keep it to yourself sir, got to keep the villains on their toes at all times, you understand, don't you agree sir?"

"I do sergeant, most informative, but may I say that…"

"One minute Mr Browne, please let me finish, I'm here to offer advice and to reassure the public of our commitment to law enforcement. Of course, our response would have been swifter if Barton's local bobby PC Willoughby was on call but unfortunately the poor lad was injured in the line of duty, pub brawl, out of action for a few days but he'll be back fitter than ever, rest assured. PC Willoughby is one of the best young coppers about, as vibrant and energetic as a Bosch sparkplug that lad. I help him all I can of course, my duty to do so, the future of the force that lad." The sergeant sighed heavily. "Now sir, back to business. Can you identify the culprit sir?"

"Identify?"

"Yes, the culprits, what exactly have they taken?"

"Nothing."

"Scuse me, nothing did you say? You interrupted them then in their misdemeanours did you sir, well done."

"No, there has been no break in sergeant, that is what I was trying to tell you but I rang to report the alarm had gone off by accident."

"Accident?"

"Yes, unfortunately" Bentley murmured.

"So this is all a waste of police time Mr Browne."

"Well yes, but not intentionally sergeant I can assure you. With respect, you didn't give me much of a chance to get a word in."

"Just doing my duty sir, keep the public informed."

"And you did sergeant."

"Oh well, under the circumstances I'll say goodnight Mr Browne with an 'e'. That rings a bell you know."

Returning to the hall, Bentley beckoned Mr Patel to join him in the study. Entering the room, Mr Patel looked around him in admiration.

"Ah this sir is your retreat, a man's room sir. I can identify with such a room, magnificent and upon the wall sir I can observe your finest moments captured forever, a lifetime's triumphs, such memories Mr Browne, how I envy you."

"Sit down Mr Patel, can I offer you a drink?

"Oh no sir, I can assure you, I must not delay my

return to Patel's Emporium. Early evening is a busy time sir. Mrs Patel is a fine woman, I am grateful for her support, but sadly she is just a woman." Bentley nodded in silent commiseration. Mr Patel reached out for a photo claiming pride of place upon the Steinway. "Her Majesty with consort and your good self Mr Browne, ooh such wonder." He placed a pair of glasses on the end of his nose viewing closely. "Royal Albert Hall. You performed this day Mr Browne?"

"Yes, yes I did. I performed at the hall many times but I have not embraced serious music for quite some years but wonderful memories Mr Patel, I do miss days like that."

"But Mr Browne, surely your days of retirement are not at an end, I've heard much to the contrary sir."

"You are referring to last night Mr Patel?" Bentley reached for a glass.

"I am sir, I am, at the public house. The maestro returns, an outstanding display of virtuoso brilliance I am informed, Mr Browne. I only wish I could have witnessed such universal approval for your sleight of hand sir."

"Hush Mr Patel, it's all very much exaggerated I can assure you. It was a privilege to play in public once more and be appreciated I do confess but it was a one off sir, no more." Bentley gestured towards an armchair. "Now Mr Patel, please take a seat, you have left your place of business in the care of your very good wife at a busy time, there would be a reason, what is it you wish from me?"

Mr Patel rolled his head from side to side in delight. "Mr Browne, your shrewdness is legendary sir, legendary."

"Let me guess Mr Patel, you wish me to settle my account, say no more." Bentley searched in his back pocket for his wallet. "One moment, it must be in my jacket."

"Mr Browne, Mr Browne, man of your stance sir, such an insult, the sum of £9.88, such a paltry sum to even consider. I have no doubt it will be settled in the near future, you're a man of honour sir. Now, the purpose of my visit Mr Browne is very simple, to request a huge favour from you."

"Speak your mind Mr Patel and whilst I wait for your deliverance, I shall pour myself a small one. Won't you change your mind and join me?"

"No, no sir, I do not drink. Mrs Patel would return to India if I were ever to succumb to such temptation."

"As you wish Mr Patel, now what is it you require of me?"

Mr Patel shifted uncomfortably in his chair leaning forward earnestly. "I am here Mr Browne on behalf of Barton Village Community Association to approach you sir, a man of immense public recognition to consider a request to open Barton Village fete in August as the guest of honour Mr Browne, it would generate immense joy throughout the county sir I am sure, what do you say?"

"Well, if I'm honest Mr Patel, first of all I say you have left it a little late to ask me. The fete is in a few weeks time I believe? Something tells me somebody has dropped out."

"Dropped out Mr Browne."

"Yes, my instinct tells me that somebody has dropped out, that is why you're here sir."

"Ah Mr Browne, your shrewdness, indeed you are right sir, somebody has dropped out. If it were left to me you would always be my first choice but..." he shook his head sadly, "you cannot win every point in a game of chance Mr Browne."

"True enough, Mr Patel, true enough, but as a matter of interest, who was first choice?"

Mr Patel coughed nervously, "Angela Rainsborough I believe."

"What, the newscaster?"

"Yes it was."

"Good choice. So what happened then, is she ill?"

"No sir, I believe she is to be married on this day."

"Good God, again, how many husbands is that, five, six, seven?"

"Quite a few I believe Mr Browne."

Bentley rose to his feet. "I will give it some consideration Mr Patel. I am flattered you asked me. Of course I am retired from public life, but why not, I don't see why not at all, a few words on the mike and then to the beer tent, am I right Mr Patel?"

"Yes, yes something in that order Mr Browne."

"Well, yes, I'll do it, I'll do it."

A delighted Mr Patel clasped his hands in rapture. "Wonderful, Mr Browne, wonderful, you are a gem sir, just as I suspected you a man of immense civic pride, I must shake your hand sir and of course Mr Browne, you live within the village boundary, part of village life, few expenses I would imagine, a bonus for Barton, wonderful, wonderful." Mr Patel rose to his feet. "Now sir, before I go, how do you manage such a magnificent house. No sign of any footmen, butlers, maids, anywhere to be seen, you have given them all the day off surely?"

"Well Mr Patel, we have a housekeeper, that is sufficient, at the moment anyway. In truth, there are many parts of this house I have yet to visit, shut down and awaiting my attention, much to my poor wife's consternation I confess, but it gives me pleasure to own such a residence, so I shall continue to spend a small fortune on its maintenance and improvement and then perhaps we will embrace staff, we shall see. It would delight my wife, but as for me, I have no grand ideas of my station in life, I am a loner if truth be told, to be waited on hand and foot does little for me but cause embarrassment. I have stayed in all of the best hotels in the world and never yet rang for room service, and yet I can be a little awkward and demanding at times, so I am told. We all contradict ourselves from time to time do we not, Mr Patel?"

"Indeed we do sir, indeed we do, but you are a man with determined righteousness."

"Mr Patel, please, I have known many smooth talkers in my life, but you sir, you top the list. I am just a useful musician who has been fortunate in life."

"Well, you must forgive me Mr Browne, but I am still amazed. No army of footmen, butlers, maids, not possible in such a wonderful house without them, I cannot believe it."

Bentley rose to his feet. "Mr Patel, whilst you are here

let me show you around."

After a brief tour, the pair returned to the conservatory stepping out upon the veranda. "Such a house Mr Browne, such a house. I understand during its long history it was used as a hospital after the Great War?"

"Yes, so I believe Mr Patel, the impressive hall was once a ward in itself, housing many beds I believe."

The shopkeeper turned his attention to the outside world.

"What a wonderful evening it is Mr Browne, and all that lays around us is all yours sir, all your property?"

"Yes, yes, Mr Patel, as far as the eye can see and beyond, some fifteen acres of meadow land, woodland, open fields, you name it, it's there. In the distance that is my nearest neighbour, Mr Smethurst, you may have heard of him, entrepreneur butcher of sorts, our boundaries meet just beyond the wall garden," Mr Patel nodded gravely.

"Oh yes your neighbour. I believe he wishes to purchase some of your land Mr Browne."

"You're well informed Mr Patel, who told you so?"

Mr Patel smiled knowingly. "I am a local government officer, I hear much."

"I'm sure you do Mr Patel, I'm sure you do. He has particular interest in the greenhouses for some reason. What the attraction is I've no idea, they are listed so they must remain and they need an awful lot of money spent on them so to bring them up to scratch and make them serviceable would cost him so much, but at the moment I am undecided what to do, but we shall see, we shall see."

"Surely Mr Browne if you dispose of your greenhouses that would include the wall garden etc?"

"Well, yes certainly, they go together."

"But surely such a productive vegetable garden would be sorely missed by yourself and your good wife."

Bentley laughed. "Are you serious Mr Patel? We see very little of the end produce, Rawlings always insisting it is plagued by black fly or scurvy, God knows what, all is decimated by disease. At times he shows a little at the fete so I imagine he has something in mind for this year's extravagance but we see very little of it. I try not to interfere but if I were to dwell on the subject I would consider the view that a lot disappears somewhat undercover."

"Oh, never Mr Browne, never such underhand behaviour, I do not believe it, your man Rawlings is a gem sir, a gem. Every morning he arrives at Patel's for his paper and half an ounce of rolling cigarette tobacco, a bit rough and ready but a decent man essentially, I don't think such deceit is possible with him."

"Well, your defence of him is very commendable Mr Patel and rather fanciful of you to suggest that he is such a paragon of virtue but ok, I'll give him the benefit of the doubt."

"You must Mr Browne, you must. Now sir, I must be off and thank you for your hospitality. Your house I have admired from afar and now I have seen it I desire it even more. Stay where you are Mr Browne, I know the way out and I shall be seeing you soon I hope, good bye."

Following Mr Patel's departure Bentley wondered the house in morose contemplation unable to settle, his mind a mixture of contentious foreboding, the previous night's pleasure having loosened the cork from the bottle of temptation leaving him wanting more.

Returning to his study, he took a turn upon the Steinway repeating many numbers from the previous night's programme without a quarter of the satisfaction. Not for the first time in his life, he was reminded how an appreciative audience could ignite one's performance. Quickly tired of playing he paced the hallway returning time and time again to the photo of Sid Mitchell that so excited Rawlings, taken in the foyer of the Albert Hall during the first tour in 1982. As he studied the photo, the memories came flooding back, some good, some not so. Bentley felt a wave of nostalgia for the good old days and for the first time in many years wondered how Sid was doing. Anxious to avoid revisiting many negative memories regarding his ex-musical partner, Bentley turned to the television briefly hoping for a little entertainment. None forthcoming, turning to the local radio, there again nothing was of interest. His favourite presenter, Bill Reynolds, was not on until late evening. Tired of solitude within the manor house and in need of a little company, he decided for a further visit to The Mariners.

Out upon the green, all was quiet, many unwilling to embrace the current heat wave suffocating southern England that day. Reaching The Mariners Bentley was mindful of PC Willoughby's prediction of the world approaching a meltdown.

CHAPTER 15

A Slice of Oyster Pie

Behind the bar, a radiant Catherine Jugg was flirting outrageously with a group of builders in for the evening. Surprisingly alert of Bentley's arrival she deserted her young admirers to reach behind the optics, from there to produce a newspaper which she waved triumphantly above her head and tossing it on the counter before a bemused Bentley Brown.

"Hey there handsome, who's in the papers then?"

"I've no idea, who?"

"First things first, what are you going to have to drink Bentley, large whiskey?"

"No, not tonight thank you, I'll have a house red, that'll do me fine, going to be a good boy tonight, but I may stop for dinner, I'm rather peckish, I'll take a chance on your cooking again."

"Oh, glad to hear it, you overdid it last night Bentley, do you remember who took you home?"

"Yes, of course I do, even now the sweetness of your lips upon mine remain with me."

She raised an eyebrow. "Do you, that's not how I

remember it, a quick lunge, a peck on the cheek and then out of the door is how I remember it," she laughed.

"Well I thought I'd better go Catherine before I expressed my earnest desire for you."

"You were full of something Bentley that's for sure, but I wouldn't have said it was passion, more like Black Label Whiskey. Now go and claim your seat before we get busy, I'll bring your drink over, you must see this newspaper."

"Must I?"

"Yes, it's a hoot."

Within several minutes, she was by his side. "Here you are Bentley, look at this."

Placing his house wine safely out of the way, she spread the paper in front of him. There, a double page coverage central to all was a photo of Bentley from his halcyon days. "Good grief, where did all this come from?"

"Well, read it and see," Catherine urged.

"I can't, left my glasses at home, do the honour for me Catherine."

Sitting back, arms folded across his chest, Bentley closed his eyes listening with mixed emotions upon the article's disclosures. Finishing, Catherine flicked the newspaper with a flourish and reached for Bentley's glass. "Why the long face Bentley, I think it's brilliant, feasts the ego somewhat," she punched him on the shoulder and Bentley grimaced.

"Hey, that hurt."

"Oh, don't be such a misery Bentley; what's the matter with you?"

"Well as I said before Catherine, I've retired, full stop. If the Italian firebrand gets wind of this she'll divorce me and take half of all I've got, I'll lose the manor house that's for certain."

"Well Bentley, it's none of my business I know, but why would your wife view your night out with such hostility, just a bit of fun surely."

"To us may be," Bentley grimaced, "not to Christina. A few years ago she gave me one last chance, leave the business altogether and retire from all temptations."

"What temptations?"

"Catherine please."

"And it's worked, almost, we're closer than ever. I don't miss the limelight at all, truth is, my time was almost over anyway, so it is no big deal to pack it all in, but unlike Christina, travelling the world bores me.

I've seen most of it anyway, so a good few months ago I put it to her that we leave Hampstead and London behind us to buy a property in the countryside, find one rich in history that required attention and the manor house fitted the bill, so here we are, but and it's a big but, Christina was most reluctant to leave the big city and has found it most difficult to adapt to country life. She would love to return to, in truth, Italy, Milano, so the slightest suggestion that I broke my promises then she would take me to the cleaners and I'd lose everything, and I mean everything. Do you know how much divorce has cost me over the years, millions upon millions, a huge fortune I can assure you. This would be my first separation that I would be left with very little at the end of the day, a semi in Ruislip if I'm lucky."

"Is that where you come from Bentley?"

"No, of course not, I just hate the place."

"Oh." She nodded sympathetically. Bentley pointed towards the bar nudging her in the ribs. "You're wanted madam, the natives are getting restless."

"Yes, so I see, but Bentley, how is she to know, your wife has not been in touch for days and she is miles away enjoying herself."

Bentley brightened slightly. "Yes, that's a consideration. So, what I will do is I'll open the fete for Patel, a few words, retreat to the beer tent and sneak away after half an hour or so, job done. Keep a low profile at the manor house for several weeks and it will all be forgotten, yes, no trouble."

Catherine leaned closer. "Bentley, what did you say, opening the fete?"

"Yes, I've been approached by Patel, his first choice has dropped out, a newscaster of some renown, so he asked me, rather chuffed in a way, quite flattered I am, a few words, then into the beer tent and away, job done."

"Bentley, be practical. You are concerned about publicity, your performance last night caused a stir, justifiably too, it was brilliant, you're in the Portsmouth Echo the following day, today, tomorrow no doubt you will be in the tabloids and on television. You say no to the publicity but cast a thought; Patel is no fool, he has a vested interest in the fete, he'll use you and your profile for all its worth to bring in the crowds. Much of the catering is done by him and his family, he makes quite a packet and so do we here in truth, we are very, very busy, the fete weekend is good news for all Barton folk and for us and if this weather holds, well with you on board, posters everywhere, fliers, this paper," she flicked the Echo, "who knows what else. For someone who wishes to remain in the background I would say opening the fete is a mistake."

"Yes, you're right of course, I'll see him first thing in the morning. You're a bright young lady you know that?"

Catherine rose to her feet. "If I were you Bentley I would go and see him now, go and get it sorted, don't leave it a moment longer."

"No, no I will leave it until tomorrow. I can't put up with the sanctimonious garble twice in one day that's for sure. I think he thinks I am a servant of flattery that man."

"Alright, fair enough, you know best." Catherine looked at her watch. "Crikey, it's nearly 6 o'clock, the evening menu to prepare, the staff will be in soon, oh God. Hang on Bentley, watch it, I think you've got a visitor."

Leaving Bentley, Catherine headed directly to the kitchen, much to the disappointment of the group of young men at the end of the bar waiting for her expected return.

With a theatrical bow and a wave, Catherine disappeared into the kitchen with loud groans of good-natured dismay from the crowd at the bar.

CHAPTER 16

A Return Visit

"Ah, cool, here you are again Mr Browne, how are you babe. Mr Jugg implied you were a man of habit, and so it seems you are. Let me introduce myself, my name is Amy Knutsford."

The young lady produced a card with a flourish, handing it to Bentley.

"Freelance reporter, part-time beautician, I was in last night, I saw your show, may I sit with you for a moment?"

"Indeed you may, Amy, yes."

The reporter flicked at the paper left by Catherine.

"You've read my article then, what do you think, good eh?"

Bentley took a deep breath. "I have, yes, very complementary, I thank you for that but I have nothing further to add, so if you will forgive me Amy, I'll say goodbye."

The anxious girl grabbed fiercely at his sleeve. "Oh come on babes, just a few words, I'm on a pilgrimage."

Bentley recognised in Amy Knutsford the so familiar traits of ambitious young women in reporting, anxious to make their mark early in life, hopefully leading to a job in television or even better, film work. Bentley remained seated at the table. Perched on the end of the bench seat, shapely legs to the fore, pocket memo at the ready, Amy began to probe. "I am told you're wife is away on a luxurious cruise, how are you coping without her. May I ask, is your marriage in trouble?"

"You're a cheeky young lady. If my marriage was in trouble do you think I would tell you, I think not."

"It's true then," Amy Knutsford persisted.

"No it's not; the truth is much more mundane young lady. You may or may not be aware that my wife is Italian?"

"Yes, your third marriage I believe." Ignoring the interruption Bentley continued.

"May I? As you say my third wife is Italian by birth and as such adores sunshine and we've not had much of it in this country of late have we? Oh, I know what you're going to say, apart from this week, how odd is it that this is the week she sets sail. Well, such is life, however," Bentley paused for emphasis, "she also adores olive groves, pasta, siestas, extended family meals and gatherings, fine wine, opera, what else, oh yes fashion. All her delights are to be delivered on this voyage with many stops along the way, so to combat any unexpected boredom, after six weeks of bliss she will return to further enrich my life in mid-August. Now will you excuse me please?"

"What ship is she on?"

"That's for you to find out young lady."

"Final question babe, after such a long time in the shadows why have you returned to the sunlight, is it money, poor investments, Brexit uncertainty perhaps, what's the reason, will you be joining the old rockers endless summer tours in the near future?"

Plainly stung at such a horrifying suggestion, Bentley rose to his feet. "Amy, I am out of show business for good," he tapped the paper, "for good," he repeated firmly. Amy held his gaze.

"Is that so, then why are you opening Barton Green's fete, do you not consider this a branch of show business?"

"Hardly an Albert Hall booking is it," Bentley faltered in his reply sensing danger in her knowledge.

"You don't deny it then," she persisted.

"It's just a playful gesture on my part, just a harmless bit of fun."

"Not to Angela Rainsborough it's not."

"Who?"

"Come on Bentley, don't play games, you know who I mean."

"Of course I do, she declined the offer and she is getting married again."

"She's not."

"She is."

"She is not Bentley."Amy had a triumphant gleam in her eye. "I was told that she was informed emphatically, very, very recently that she was no longer required to open Barton-on-the-Green's extravaganza this year as a bigger beast had been approached and it's you babe and she's not too happy about it."

"Where do you get all this drivel from Amy?"

Amy smirked. "I'm a reporter darling, it's my job. Also I have been reliably informed that without a shadow of a doubt you are committed to playing the concert on the Sunday evening, full works, stage accompaniment, band of big names, full publicity, the lot."

"Whaaaat!' Bentley exclaimed. "Where did you get this from? You're making it up as you go along."

"Do you deny it?"

"'Course I do."

Amy rose to her feet. "So Bentley in short, you are not divorcing your wife, or she you, and a return to show business is out of the question?"

"Quite." Bentley spluttered.

"Quite. What does that mean?"

"Yes, it means yes," Bentley growled.

"Yes, yes, or yes no," Amy teased

"It is impossible to say. Look, I've had it with you Amy, that's my lot, I'm off."

Turning abruptly, Bentley pushed his way through the early evening regulars, who along with the ever-attended builders, had moved closer and closer with ill-conceived mischievous delight to listen to the exchange of words between the confident young reporter and the increasingly beleaguered Bentley.

Torn between a return to The Gables or a few hopefully reassuring words with Catherine, Bentley chose the latter eventually finding her laying tables in the empty restaurant in readiness for the evening meals. Grabbing a chair Bentley sat at a table.

"You knew who that was then?" he asked.

"Yes of course, she's a reporter, she was nosing around last night, spoke to Dad among many others," Catherine replied.

"Oh God." Bentley rested his head on the table. "That's it then, my marriage is over."

Catherine turned to him. "Why, what's up, what did she say? Look, where's your drink? Sit down and relax, I'll go and get it for you." Returning with said drink in hand, Catherine found an anxious Bentley pacing the floor. "Here's your drink Bentley, relax. Look, don't blame Dad Bentley, I'm sure he kept all your confidences. It was all pure coincidence her coming in on the night you chose to play, pure coincidence. What harm's done, I don't understand it. However, she is making herself too much at home here, getting far too familiar with my builder boys. Not in my pub, I'll soon put a stop to that. Cheryl, where are you?"

A young waitress seated in the far corner polishing cutlery raised her head. "Here."

Catherine prodded a brooding Bentley. "Listen to this Bentley," she whispered before addressing the unfortunate waitress. "Cheryl, I want you to go into the bar and tell that woman flirting with my..." she sniffed disdainfully, "boys and tell her that the car belonging to her is parked dangerously and would she move it now."

Cheryl grimaced. "Must I?"

"Yes, you must."

"How will I know her?"

"You will, she laughs like a donkey, skirt up to her arse surrounded by men."

Cheryl pulled a long face. "Why me?"

"Because it is good management skills, something for the future, it'll come in handy when you're older," Catherine laughed.

"But what about this lot?" the girl asked, rattling the cutlery tray forcibly sending several spoons spinning to the floor. Approaching the unfortunate waitress, Catherine took the tray prodding the young woman in the rear.

"Now get in there and sound convincing, otherwise you'll be off the roster for Sunday afternoon's cricket match."

"Catherine, that's not fair, you promised me weeks ago, all the boys will be in their lovely white gear."

"Well then, see how you get on out there, harass the tart, go on, earn your money." Prodding the unfortunate girl through the swing doors Catherine returned to Bentley's side rubbing her hands gleefully. "See Bentley, easy, fight fire with fire, you're too easy going, you should have told her to clear off, still," Catherine paused reflectively, "just doing her job I suppose. Now then, what did she want to know?"

"It wasn't so much what she asked, more what she knew. She was aware that my good wife is on a cruise suggesting some nonsense that we were about to separate and to cap that knew that I had agreed to open the fete. How for God's sake, I only agreed with Patel this very afternoon, and then to cap it all...." Bentley paused as the young waitress re-entered the restaurant. Approaching Catherine, she put her hand to her mouth suppressing a giggle.

"Well?" Catherine asked.

"I told such fibs, said her car would be clamped if she didn't move it straight away, it was parked badly and there was a horrible smell coming from the boot and people were complaining." The two women hugged each other giggling profusely. "Now do I get to work on Sunday?"

"Of course," Catherine giggled, "I had already pencilled you in."

"You conned me Catherine," Cheryl grinned ruefully.

"Just a little, but you enjoyed it though didn't you. We don't want flash birds corrupting our boys do we?"

Cheryl nodded in agreement. "Yes, she picked up her

bag and left without a backward glance."

"Good," Catherine nodded approvingly "Now, finish cleaning the cutlery and see what you can do to help in the kitchen, I'll be in there in a tick, must help this unfortunate man first. Now Bentley, what were you about to say, I've two minutes at the most. The restaurant is fully booked and I've things to do, come on, half a minute's gone already, what else did she say?"

"Well, I can't believe what she said. She suggested I was to play on Sunday evening at the end of the fete weekend. It was all cut and dried and I would be centre stage surrounded by top musicians to wrap up the weekend with a flourish. Can you believe it, where did this all come from Catherine?"

"Ah, Bentley, you're so naive, Patel has read you like a book and he is tempting you out of retirement."

"Why should he do that?"

"Bentley, as I told you earlier, your appearance at the fete would be a delight for him, put thousands on the gate and make him a lot of money. Well, I suppose we would all benefit, us included. As I said before, Patel has his fingers into everything and I would suggest that he heard of your success last night confirmed by the report in the paper today. Bingo! Two and two together make four. He's read you like a cheap novel.

He's a shrewd old devil, had you sussed in no time, despite your repeated denials, I bet he takes a gamble that you can't say no to him come the day." She leant upon the table, her elfin face a picture of amusement. "Admit it Bentley, you'd love to do it wouldn't you?"

Bentley began to pace the floor. "That I admit, but I'm not ready to call time on my marriage, there's much mileage left, I hope."

Ignoring Bentley Catherine climbed upon a chair lifting her apron high above her knees pirouetting in front of him. "What do you think? I've got good legs and not such a big bum as that cheap reporter. What do you think, Bentley?"

"Please Catherine not now, I'm trying to think, get down you'll hurt yourself."

Catherine let go of the hem quickly, disappointment evident. "You're no help to a girl Bentley, here help me down." Returning to the floor, she retrieved the tray of cutlery and headed for the kitchen. "If you are that concerned about unwelcome publicity, why not take yourself off for a few weeks, join your wife, why don't you," adding cuttingly, "that would please her no end, you appearing out of the blue, I'm sure."

"Catherine, that's it!" Bentley exclaimed excitedly. "Come and sit down, come back, great idea, holiday, get away from it all, not with the wife though," he added.

"Now you're talking Bentley, just say the word, I am due time off, I'd love to visit the Greek islands or Turkey, I've always wanted to go to Turkey, no-one would recognise you there either, I'd pretend to be your daughter Bentley, we'd be fine."

"Well, that's very kind of you Catherine, but if you don't mind I was rather thinking of Eastbourne."

"Eastbourne!" Catherine exclaimed, screwing up her nose. "That's for the elderly."

"Yes of course, Eastbourne," Bentley repeated to himself. "I've a place there, good old Eastbourne, why didn't I think of it myself. Catherine, you're a genius." Bentley nodded his head in satisfaction murmuring once again, "What a damn good idea."

Catherine joined him once again at the table drumming her fingers on the tray. "Well, it's not quite what I first thought of Bentley but a saucy weekend could cheer a girl up, yes, walks on the pier, fresh cockles and muscles, country pub, early night, yes, yes, I could be persuaded Bentley, ask me nicely and I'm all yours." With eager eyes, she looked at Bentley with excited expectation.

Bentley coughed nervously and pulled on his earlobe. "Ah yes it would be fun Catherine of course, but you forget I'm a married man and to go away now might be interpreted as a coward's action by Patel and such, a bit like running away from a fight, don't you think? I mean honestly, what's a bit of publicity when it's all said and done."

Catherine slammed the tray upon the table in exasperation. "Really Bentley, you're impossible, you'll be sorry one day." Heading for the kitchen she turned, "Are you stopping for dinner?"

"Well yes, it was my intention," Bentley replied, almost apologetically.

"Well, prepare yourself for a bloody long wait shipmate," came the angry reply as Catherine slammed the door behind her.

For the next half an hour as the restaurant grew busy, Bentley remained at the table unattended. Finally, an apologetic Cheryl approached the table to address him in a quiet manner. "I'm sorry Mr Browne, Catherine instructed me to keep you waiting, it's not my idea, I am so sorry and she pays my wages you know."

"Oh don't worry Cheryl," Bentley reassured her, "I'm clearly out of favour at the moment." Cheryl bent low to whisper in his ear. "Catherine told me to inform you there is a reporter from the News of the World out front asking as to your whereabouts and as you have reaffirmed your love affair with the press shall she direct him to you?"

Bentley groaned. "No, no, I would rather you didn't Cheryl if you don't mind, I think I better shoot off home."

"Catherine thought you'd say that and suggests that you leave the back way now, through the marquis, there's a wedding party due to arrive, you'll get lost in the crowd."

Bentley rose reluctantly to his feet. "I've not eaten yet, you are aware of that I trust?"

Cheryl produced a bag from behind her back. "I am, Catherine said to take this with you."

"What is it?"

"Slice of oyster and steak pie fresh out of the oven." She pressed it into his hands.

Bentley gratefully accepted the offer heading for the outside disappearing by way of the marquis.

Entering the sanctuary of Barton Manor, Bentley was welcomed by a flurry of noise and a recorded message left on the phone from his excited agent. "Bentley you old charmer, you're all over the news. Good man, welcome back, I expect you're out on the lash knowing you, catch you later I hope, well done boy, big bucks on the way." Steak pie consumed accompanied by a glass of red, Bentley took to the

TV with a troubled mind.

CHAPTER 17

Look to the Future

Despite retiring early, Bentley slept poorly, rising from his bed earlier than usual the following day in the vague hope of encountering Rawlings and his boy on their arrival for work that morning. Aware of Rawlings' favoured entrance, Bentley lay in wait close to the arched wooden doorway set within the high brickwork encasing the vegetable garden. At precisely 8.41am, the pair entered the garden. Leaving their respective bicycles leaning against the brickwork, they skirted the greenhouses approaching the potting shed engaged in idle chat. Unaware of Bentley's presence they entered the hut, there to be confronted by a mischievous Bentley seated upon a large upturned flowerpot.

"Morning chaps, a bit late this morning?"

Rawlings stooped down to remove his bicycle clips. "Ay, the boy had a slow puncture, had to use an emergency repair kit." Returning to full height, he eyed Bentley with suspicion, searching for his tobacco pouch. "Don't normally see you this early in the morning governor, what's up, another fire or summat?"

"Yes, very droll Rawlings, very droll. The reason I am

here so early as you've put it, is to enquire as to what you have in mind to accomplish today, bearing in mind the wonderful weather that is still with us."

"Why do you want to know?"

"Because I pay you Rawlings, that's why."

Rawlings considered his options for some time reaching for his tobacco pouch finally. "Well as you say, it's hot so I was going to get out the sprinklers before the sun reached its peak, that's what we planned, wannit boy?" The boy nodded "That's right Grandad, do the lawns, they're getting a bit worn out."

The pair eyed Bentley with some uncertainty.

"Yes, yes that's fine, sounds good," Bentley replied, "but before you start, as late as it is, I would like you to visit the lodge and shut the manor gates."

"What!"

"Shut the manor gates if you would please, up tight."

"Give over governor, them gates are as big as Buckingham Palace, they're huge, give me heart attack."

"Talk some sense Rawlings, those gates have been sandblasted, re-sprayed, returned to their former glory, re-hung perfectly, round rollers replaced, everything works in perfect working order, that is apart from the electrical connections to the lodge house but that shall be done in time, so please get up there and as I said, close the gates."

"Well I'm not moving into the lodge house if that's what you think, being on duty night and day opening and shutting, no way, Mrs Rawlings wouldn't want that, stuck in there away from her friends, no water, no light, ah no, place is a disgrace, mind you if we had it done up, I might consider it, I am sure Mrs Rawlings would."

An exasperated Bentley rose from his flowerpot. "The chance of you of all people becoming a resident of Barton Manor Rawlings is nil, rest assured, so don't worry yourself any further."

"Well I should think so too."

"Now, please get on with it the pair of you, I've things to do."

Leaving the pair to their task and returning to the house, coffee on the go, Bentley phoned The Mariners

"Hello?"

"Hello Catherine, it's me, Bentley."

"I am well aware who it is."

"Can I speak to your father?"

"He's having a few hours away, busy day tomorrow, cricket match remember?"

"Oh yes, yes. You sound a little brittle this morning Catherine."

"Do I, you've a short memory, Mr Browne."

"Catherine, may I ask, are there any reporters hanging about your establishment?"

"We're not open to the public yet Bentley," came the curt reply.

"Ah, what time is it?" Bentley glanced at his watch. "I thought it was later, mmm, what about the car park? Pop outside and have a look for me sweetheart would you, be discreet."

"Bentley, I am double busy."

"Please Catherine."

"You are a complete pain Bentley Browne, grrrrrrrrr."

"Thanks Catherine."

Within a minute, she returned to the phone. "You're ok, not a soul about, you're yesterday's news Bentley, there's been a passing of time, now if you don't mind I have work to attend to."

"Thanks Catherine"

"Grrrrr, men!"

After many years at the mercy of the press and acutely aware of how an inappropriate remark or action could, and often did, transform the lifestyle of many overnight, be it for good or bad, Bentley was wary of publicity and in mind to distance himself from public engagements for a while until his recent performance at The Mariners lost momentum in the world of social media. Thus in mind for the immediate closure of the main gates leading to Barton Manor, the most sensible option open to him to avoid press harassment further from the likes of Amy Knutsford. Well aware of further work to be completed on the gates and lodge house, a resolute Bentley vowed to engage suitable tradesmen, experienced and familiar with all aspects of high tech security systems as soon as possible.

Crossing the green and reaching the corner shop, Bentley encountered Mr Patel. Unaware of Bentley's approach the shopkeeper engaged in thoughtful consideration, standing before an impressive display of fresh fruit and vegetables piled high upon wooden racks outside the store.

"Another fine day, Mr Patel."

Lost in the world of commercial enterprise the

startled businessman stepped back in alarm spilling several apples to the floor.

"My dear Mr Browne, such a surprise sir, I can explain it all sir, I can assure you."

"Explain! Explain what, Mr Patel?"

"Oh forgive me Mr Browne, you must excuse the ramblings of a poor old entrepreneur, let me get the door for you."

Both men pushed hard upon the shop door, finally entering as one.

"Such a delight to see you Mr Browne, so soon after our recent meeting, how can I help you, such an honour."

"Well, you may not think so in a moment Mr Patel, I've come across the green to withdraw my services for the forthcoming fete."

"My dear sir, why so?" Mr Patel removed his glasses. "You have greatly shocked me, such a change in destiny's pathway Mr Browne." Removing a handkerchief from his trouser pocket, he patted his forehead furiously. Mrs Patel, behind the post office counter blinked wearily shaking her head and reaching for a box of tissues, sliding them under the grill towards her anxious husband.

"You have cut short all our celebrations Mr Browne, I

had such good news, let me explain."

Bentley raised a hand. "No, no, please Mr Patel, hear me out. I feel your previous choice of Angela Rainsborough was the correct one and in truth, I have no wish for the publicity, I am finished with all of that."

"But Mr Browne, it's an adventure for you, I have contacted several members of your past band. A joyous celebration is on offer Mr Browne. I have also contacted Mr Mitchell down in deepest Devon sir. Ah, you're in shock Mr Browne, with delight no doubt. Let me make you a strong cup of tea my good man."

"Not shock Mr Patel, dismay. This is not Alice in Wonderland and I have no wish to perform in public again, least of all with Sidney Mitchell and you have no right to involve me in this deception. I agreed to open the event with a few words and then away, and now you expect me to perform, certainly not sir."

Mr Patel lowered his head, spreading his arms wide in an act of contrition. "My dear Mr Browne, I had no idea you would view a business arrangement with such trepidation."

"Mr Patel, I agreed to open the fete with a few words and then away, now I feel something sinister is afoot."

"Mr Browne, what a suggestion, I am a man of my word sir; I just felt in my heart of hearts that you would view a reunion with your ex-partner as a moment of pure joy sir."

"Well you thought wrong Mr Patel, not for me. Had I wished a reunion with Mr Mitchell I would have arranged such a meeting myself."

Turning sharply, Bentley headed for the door, there to be confronted by a grinning Rawlings emerging from behind the ranks of cut-price toilet rolls.

"Trouble skipper?"

"Ah, it is you Rawlings; I thought I recognised your bike outside."

"You sound agitated Mr Browne."

"Well I'm not Rawlings. What are you doing here anyway, everywhere I go?"

"Ah, free country innit, come and go as I like. I don't work for your good self on Saturday afternoon Mr Browne, in case you forgot, although I could arrange for me and the boy to work all day on Saturday in the future if you wish, mind you, time and a half, may be double time."

"No, no leave it as it is Rawlings, thank you, five days a week is more than enough for both of us."

Rawlings shrugged. "As you wish governor, although I'm sure your beloved wife would be of a different mind." Rawlings smiled ruefully. "Talking of your good lady, has she been in touch governor?"

"None of your business Rawlings."

"That means no in my book."

"Take it as you wish, I've nothing more to say on the subject."

"She don't know about you opening the fete then?"

"I am not opening the fete."

"But I heard you and Mr Patel talking about the fete governor."

"Well, you heard wrong Rawlings, Mr Patel jumped the gun a little."

"Really!" Rawlings chortled. "Sounds like it's all done and dusted to me. Your poor Mrs will not be a happy bunny when she finds out that's for sure."

"There is nothing to find out Rawlings, I shall not be appearing, trust me."

"Well I believe it, some wouldn't. You know your trouble governor, you can't let go. Fame eh, it's a curse innit. I mean look at me, I'm happy, don't live in the past, content with what I've got, I got me baccy," he tapped his top pocket. "I got a woman at home looking after my every need, what more do I want?"

"What more do you want Rawlings, well, if you don't mind me saying so, you've never come across as one of the most contented I've ever met. You're one of the most disagreeable men I've ever come across if truth be told, not a good word for anyone."

"You talking about me? I find that most hurtful Mr Browne, your good wife would never speak to me in such a fashion."

"True enough Rawlings, true enough. My irritation gets the better of me sometimes, my apologies; however, if you will move to one side I shall get on. Goodbye Mr Patel, no need for extended farewells, sir."

"Mr Browne, Mr Browne, before you go, a small matter of remuneration sir, your account sir, it would seem to be a good moment to settle up, sir."

Bentley turned to Rawlings. "You got any money on you Rawlings?"

"Why?"

"Never mind why, have you?"

"Yes, well I've got a small amount, enough for me baccy and a few necessities, I'm not on the best of wages if you know what I mean, not like some I could speak of."

"I'll ask again Rawlings, can you help me out, have you any cash on you?"

"Well a little, as I say enough for some baccy and a daily paper, why should I help you out?"

"Because it would be in your best interest. Settle up with Mr Patel for me and I'll square up with you later."

"Eh, I can't give my hard earned money away like that."

"Ah, but is it your hard earned money Rawlings? After your late arrival this morning, that could be owed to me, so what we do is call it quits, fair enough?"

"Whaaatt?"

"Oh yes, and while you're at it, add the cost of this paper to the bill."

Grabbing the newspaper from the counter Bentley left the shop amid cries of indignation from an angry Rawlings. "Bloody cheek, tight git, he's pushed me too far this time, I've had enough, bloody bourgeois ponce."

Quickly approached by a shocked Mr Patel, Rawlings

was ushered out the door. "No foul language in my store Mr Rawlings, such unfortunate behaviour in the presence of Mrs Patel, such vulgarity. Please Mr Rawlings, leave now sir, and take your bicycle with you."

CHAPTER 18

A Stroll Upon the Green

Out upon the green and keeping to the bridle path that meandered close by to the church, Bentley's attention was drawn to an elderly couple leaving the vicarage. The woman was talking with great difficulty, hanging on to her companion's arm with grim determination. With a courteous nod to the pair as their paths crossed Bentley hurried on his way, head down lost in thought.

"Coooeee Mr Browne, forgot me so soon. Bentley!" Blood running cold as a familiar voice cut through the air, Bentley slowed dramatically to a halt. Turning, he awaited the couple's laboured approach with an ill-concealed apprehension.

"My dear Mrs Clemspon, my apologies, didn't recognise you, how are you dear lady?"

"Dear lady," she choked reaching his side. "My my, I am honoured, not how you usually address me Mr Browne, things are improving." Mrs Clemspon leant upon her cane breathing heavily

"Steady on Alice, don't exaggerate, your perception of me is a little harsh. How are things with you brain wise that is, all sorted? Sparkplugs back in working order I hope?"

"You can laugh Bentley, it's been a nightmare. I don't think I could have survived this past week if it weren't for my dear Bunny here." Close to tears, she grabbed her companion's shoulder to steady herself almost dragging the unfortunate man almost to the ground. Stepping forward smartly Bentley steadied the pair.

"Good girl, well done, well done. So this gentleman would be your husband, would he? Bunny, did you call him? Pleased to meet you Bunny, in fine fettle I trust?"

Her companion, a short rounded man clearly her junior in years was wearing a red tracksuit with white piping on the sleeves. Upon his feet were matching trainers, a baseball cap upon his head shielded his eyes and an earring was prominent upon one ear. He puffed contentedly upon a small cigar,

"Not quite no," came the singular reply from behind a pall of dense smoke.

Alice beckoned Bentley closer whispering in his ear.

"My Bunny don't say much, a man of caution in his dealings with folk," she giggled. "He's a chap of raw passion, you mark my words, but a husband he's not, don't want another one of them buggers, thank you very much." She returned to her companion's side, searching for his hand. "He's my toy boy, we have an agreement, don't we Bunny."

The man nodded gleefully in agreement. "That's right Alice, a game of cards on a Friday night, egg and bacon for breakfast on Saturday morning, couldn't be better, she's my saviour." Grabbing her waist, he pulled her to him. Feigning indignation, a blushing Alice struggled free from his sudden embrace striking upon his leg with her cane.

"Naughty man, Mr Browne's my employer, he doesn't want to hear such talk, do you Mr Browne?" she said coyly.

"No problem Alice, no problem." Slightly embarrassed by the prospect of further such disclosures, Bentley turned to leave. "Well, lots to do, must get off, lots to do, I'll say goodbye now."

"Before you go Bentley, how are things at the manor, are you managing OK without me?"

"Yes, yes fine, spot on, no problems Alice." Bentley assured her. Mrs Alice frowned heavily sniffing the air dismissively.

"Not what we've heard is it Bunny?" Alice pulled on Bunny's arm for confirmation. At length he nodded in agreement.

"That's right my dear."

Sensing forthcoming criticism about to enter the

conversation Bentley applauded the cloudless sky. "Another wonderful day in store, we must make the most of it, so, must be off, things to do."

Alice tapped his foot with her cane. "Did you hear me Bentley?"

"Difficult not to Alice, what is it?"

"Well?"

"Well what?"

"Are you behaving yourself?"

"What are you driving at Alice? Come on, say your piece please."

Alice swung her cane at the molehill situated between her feet sending clods of dried earth high into the air. "Not for me to comment Bentley, I'm just a humble housekeeper, but I will say this, no sooner is your poor wife out of the country then you're out on the town. A night in the public house gets out of hand, I'm aware of that much and you can't get up in the morning to greet your visitor, a woman who went to see you, a vicar's wife, as a result of an over indulgence the night before," reducing the molehill to a ruin, she turned her attention to a larger mole hill close by.

Prudently retiring out of the line of fire Bentley sought to reassure his housekeeper. "Now steady on

Alice, that's a complete exaggeration I assure you. I was testing a musical instrument for a friend and it turned into an evening's entertainment for the many. It was all good fun, quite innocent."

Alice swung determinedly at the pile of earth with continuing success. "That's as maybe if you consider a parish vicar face down in the flowerbed entertainment. What would your dear wife have to say about all these unsavoury goings on in Barton, instigated by her erstwhile husband as soon as her back is turned?"

Curtailing a vicious attack upon the pile of earth Alice rested upon her cane breathing heavily. Taking advantage of her breathlessness Bentley moved to defend himself.

"Alice, if truth be told, since the day she left, my wife has declined to answer my calls. No phone call to the manor house to enquire as to my well-being, which all rather suggests a lack of interest in my good self, doesn't it?"

Alice returned gamely to the reduced pile of earth between her feet. "Hardly surprising, sending the poor angel off on holiday in a motorised wreck supplied by Chuffer Rudd of all people, a man whose family have terrorised this village for generations, she's a delicate woman is Mrs Browne, a woman of breeding, well accustomed to all the good things in life. My Bunny wouldn't send me off on holiday in a clapped out old wreck, would you my love?"

Bunny hesitated for a moment. "No my dear, horse and cart more like."

An indignant Alice struck out fiercely with her cane striking the man's knee with a resounding blow. "Wash your mouth out Buddy Ford or there'll be no cocoa for you tonight."

Returning to the molehill, a final skirmish levelled all remaining earth. She turned with satisfaction, waving her stick threateningly at Bentley. "Don't you miss her, just a little?" she demanded to know.

Bentley brushed a clod of earth from his shoulders. "Yes, of course I do very much, the house is empty without her, and of course your dear self Alice, without question, I miss you both."

Alice allowed herself a satisfied smile. "I should think so too. If I were you Bentley I would try a little harder to get in touch with her before things go too far."

Bentley growled with exasperation. "If you would listen for one moment dear lady, in my defence, I was unaware of Mr Rudd's intention to send a bus to collect my wife, and subsequently breaking down on the motorway was unfortunate but," Bentley shrugged dismissively, "things happen. Quite frankly she refuses to answer my damn calls, so how can I get in touch with her?"

Alice fixed him with a glare of icy distain. "If you are going to be abusive about your dear wife Bentley, I will take my leave of you. Come on Bunny, let's be off."

"When are you coming back to work Alice?"

"When I'm ready Mr Browne, when I'm ready."

Approaching the store the pair were accosted by Rawlings pushing his bicycle laden with shop purchases. Clearly irate, he engaged the couple with an angry rhetoric bemoaning his earlier treatment at the hands of Bentley Browne.

"What am I, first a valet, then a chauffeur, and now I'm settling his debts, me, trained, a master of horticulture. Where's it all going to end? I'll have him, just you see."

Over at the cricket pavilion there were increasing signs of activity. Two young men emerged from the tractor shed dragging a roller between them heading towards the cricket square. A group of female joggers out upon the green slowed down to exchange many ribald comments with the pair as they passed close by. After several moments of good-natured banter with the lads, the girls continued on their way headed towards the pond passing close by to Bentley. Several of the girls, recognising Bentley immediately as they passed by, whooped with delight, young faces, eyes sparkling with mischievous intent, surrounded the aging musician. The group leader, a tall girl with bright red lipstick and hair in a tight bun, jumped from her bicycle and curtsied in front of him saying, "Well well, it's our local celebrity. Mr Browne, how are you sir?"

"Very well thank you girls, kind of you to ask."

The young woman giggled. "Most of us were in the other night, in the pub and it was a great night from such an old codger, you're almost as old as Mick Jagger, surely." She turned to her friends, "eh girls?" the group burst into laughter.

Bentley nodded, gravely suppressing a smile. "Well not quite, but almost," he answered good-naturedly. A short plump girl moved towards him. Reaching up she planted a kiss upon his cheek. "Well, I thought you were fantastic and my mum adores you, my dad doesn't though, a bit of jealously I think. I am told you will be performing at the forthcoming fete, Mr Browne, is that true?"

Bentley shook his head. "No, I shall not be performing at the fete girls. Now tell me, during your excursions upon Barton's highways this morning, have you noted anything unusual?" The question induced much shaking of heads.

"Such as?"

"Well, parked cars, strangers, reporters, TV, newspapers?"

The girls shook their heads again as one. "No Bentley."

"Oh, alright then, thanks for your help, I must get off."

The tall girl turned to her companions. "Come on girls, let's go. Bye Bentley darling, we'll see you around. Come on girls, last one to the pavilion buys the drinks."

Amid much shouting and cheering the girls soon passed the church and out of sight, leaving a thoughtful Bentley mindful of Catherine's comments earlier in the day that his recent return to the limelight was already a damp squid.

Reaching the gates of Barton Manor, Bentley was confronted by a post office van with a damaged door flung wide open, drawn up outside the entrance. The driver clearly agitated speaking on his mobile phone.

"I can't secure the van, I have to dump the mail, send somebody out, yes, yes, Barton-on-the-Green, yes, yes, the manor house, the pianist place, the rock star bloke, no he's not around, oh hang on a minute." Acknowledging Bentley's appearance, the postman returned to his mobile. "He's here now, catch you later, don't forget, send somebody out." Returning to the cab with weary acceptance, the driver reached for his flask. "Coffee, Mr Browne? It is Mr Browne isn't it?"

"Yes, yes I'm Browne, but not at the moment, no coffee thank you." Bentley surveyed the scene. "What exactly is going on?"

"You might well ask sir. I thought you were away or something. I can't get in, gate's all bolted."

"Oh yes, I see your point, but there is a tradesmen's entrance. Look see, there."

"I'm not going through there all the way down to your manor carrying a bloody great sack like this, you are joking."

"Don't you carry a bike with you in the back or something for emergencies?"

"A bike. I'm not going back on a bloody bike, I'm in the union you know and I'm an official. Riding about on a bike, those days are gone, no sir. And then to add to my troubles I'm just about to go and I reverses up to go back to the yard and I hits a bloody tree stump, here look, look, it's damaged the door."

"Well, I'm sorry for your predicament, surely they can find you another van somewhere to help you out but before I go, didn't I see you earlier having a bit of a run in with Mr Patel down at the corner shop, something about shorts in hot weather?"

"Yes, that's another bugger too, comes to my country and tells me I can't wear shorts in this sort of weather, bloody cheek."

"Well yes, it's all very unfortunate. I do understand but I've things to do, I'm off now. Have you got any mail for me?"

"Mail. Mail. Why the bloody hell do you think I'm here?"

"Well, are you going to let me have it?"

"I'll let you have it alright matey." Reaching inside the damaged door, he dropped a sack at Bentley's feet. "Bloody hundreds there are. Next time you'll have to come to the depot, I'm not having this. Can you believe in this day and age of email, internet and such, people still communicate in this fashion? Baking hot day and I am forced to deliver hundreds of sheets of paper down a driveway a mile long. That's something out of the dark ages I tell you, I've had it, I've had enough."

After a brief fumble beneath the driver's seat, he returned with a crowbar securing the back door. "That's it, that'll have to do. Right, if you don't mind matey, pick up your mail, I'm off."

"What shall I do with the sack when I've finished."

"That's up to you matey, I could tell you but I'm too much of a gentleman. Right, I've got to go."

CHAPTER 19

Moving On

Returning to Barton Manor, once seated upon the terrace, coffee in hand, Bentley spent much of the afternoon sifting through the mail with a mixture of dread and delight. The majority welcomed his return to national consciousness expressing huge interest in any future appearances. A few, less complementary, suggested playing in a country pub should be the limit to any future aspirations concerning a return to the limelight. One letter signed *Cathy from Broadstairs* recalled travelling to London with several friends at the height of his success to see him play at the Apollo. After the show, invited backstage by Bentley's then manager Billy Boyle, she found Bentley amusing company, not at all the predatory figure she had expected, unlike his partner Syd Mitchell, who in her opinion was a complete self-centred berk. A surprisingly large proportion of the mail was full of praise for his portrayal of Detective Inspector Jack Dawkins, a hard nose copper of the old school, a series running for eight years during the 1990s, much acclaimed at the time. The programme was unexpectedly dropped by the BBC citing production problems. However, press coverage at the time hinted that the relationship between Bentley and his long running co-star Beverley Dalton had "lost its magic" and that increasing salary demands were no longer tenable. Moved by the warm display of many of the letters a resolute Bentley Bowne vowed to reply to each letter in kind, given the time of course, save one however. Among the cavalcade of mail, a less exuberant example, a letter in plain light brown format from JJ Plant Hire, Basingstoke, requesting immediate payment of £380 including VAT. The sum total being payment, now overdue, for delivery of a forklift truck Monday, July 14th as requested for removal of large statue and plinth from a prominent spot upon the driveway to one of a less intrusive position. The request for forklift truck being received Sunday evening, July 13th by phone made in the name of a Mr B. Browne and was dutifully recorded. The address given, The Manor House, Barton-on-the-Green, was double-checked, verified and dutifully acted upon with all good faith. This being so a request for payment should be answered with equal good intention, signed *JJ Skinner, Managing Director, JJ Plant Hire, Basingstoke.*

As the afternoon temperature reached its peak, Bentley sought refuge in his study. There, despatching all unsavoury correspondence to the shredder, JJ Plant Hire's invoice to the forefront. In need of change, Bentley took a turn upon the Steinway, finally calling it a day around 5.30pm to phone The Mariners.

"Hello, Three Mariners."

"Hello, Catherine, it's me."

"And who is me exactly?"

"The aging musician who lives up on the green in a posh house, you must have seen him about?"
"Oh him, yes I've seen him. What do you want then?"

"I'd like to book a table Catherine if I may? I am going crackers here on my own and I need some company."

"You would?"

"Yes, I would. Why is it a problem?"

"No, not to me Bentley but I would advise against it tonight, your friend is in, the reporter from the Portsmouth Echo, Amy Knutsford, she booked a table for 8.00pm. She asked about you."

"Did she? Ah, that's no problem, I will come across at 6.30pm or near enough and I will be gone before she arrives."

"Entirely up to you Bentley," her voice softened. "Er Bentley, I am sorry about this morning, I was a bit grumpy, do you forgive me?"

"What's on the menu?"

"T-bone steak courtesy of Smithurst Farm Shop with garlic mushrooms on a bed of watercress and hot chestnut garnish with homemade horseradish sauce," came the reply.

"I forgive you."

"Good, we're friends again then are we?"

"Certainly young lady. I shall not be late. 6.30 to 7.00pm."

"You better not, we are fully booked tonight."

"Oh, I'll be there. Catherine, before you go."

"What?"

"A quiet corner table for one out of the way."

"Bentley?"

"Yes?"

"Have you ever considered meals on wheels?"

"Often Catherine, often. See you later. Bye"
Replacing the phone and leaving the kitchen in the

care of others, a weary Catherine entered the bar. Despite the early evening The Mariners was filling up rapidly. Several dozen booked in for the evening meal having arrived by coach were standing knee deep at the bar. Many, displaying irritation at the long wait for attention. Ignoring the beleaguered bar staff in desperate need for assistance Catherine made her way outside in urgent need of a quiet corner of retreat from the maddening crowd. Finding such a refuge out of the sun behind the wedding marquee, she lit a cigarette, an occasional weakness she herself deplored. The week had taken its toll since Bentley's impromptu concert. Due to the evening's subsequent publicity in the Portsmouth Echo, trade had increased significantly at an almost unmanageable level, not to mention Sunday's cricket match in the offing and forthcoming weekend fete to consider. Catherine felt her world was spinning out of control.

A moment of relaxation short lived she was brought back to earth by the ominous sound of three pulls on the ship's bell hanging within the kitchen indicating ten minutes remaining to complete preparation of that evening's menu. A call to arms to ensure all kitchen and restaurant staff were at their post promptly for a 6.45pm opening. Cursing the day she instigated such a practice, Catherine re-entered the restaurant with the weary acceptance of a convicted felon.

Despite the many changes of ownership and

alterations over the years, the five cottages that constituted the core of The Mariners still retained much of its original identity. Although never a coaching inn in the accepted sense, being somewhat off the main highway to Portsmouth and beyond and having no provision set aside for the overnight stabling of horse or carriage, The Mariners was nevertheless well considered by all and remains so to this day. Inside, away from the main bar and restaurant area, much of the original decor survives, nooks, crannies, small areas of cosy seclusion, oak panel passageways and welcoming bay windows overlooking the green. Albert Jugg, a keen historian and cricket fanatic had left much as it was, indeed turning one such alcove into a testament to many years of test cricket between England and Australia over the years. Prints and memorabilia of past encounters festooned the walls. This area was set aside for the comfort and use only by bona fide members of Barton-on-the-Green cricket team and card carrying registered supporters, rules strictly adhered to at all times save when moments of severe overcrowding, where good business sense dictated, a relaxation of the rules.

No such relaxation of the rules was in evidence this particular evening however, the area being full of Barton's cricketing warriors, the prevailing mood most sombre. Constable Willoughby, right leg encased in plaster from ankle to knee, addressed his captive audience in an increasingly aggressive fashion. Several of the players, plainly unimpressed, made their excuses and returned to the bar leaving the remainder sitting in abject silence, unwilling to question his tactical nuance. In the meantime, the vicar, arm in a sling, sitting close to an open window, looked out upon the cricket square occasionally turning and nodding in vague agreement to the constable's excitable rhetoric concerning Sunday's local derby, before returning his gaze upon the green and an approaching Bentley Browne.

Meantime, over at the scoring shed, close companion to the pavilion, a second pair of eyes bore witness to Bentley's passage across the green. Securing the shed door behind him, Chuffer Rudd, paragon of virtue and eminent life president of Barton's esteemed cricket club sped across the green in urgent pursuit of his quarry, finally catching up with Bentley at the rear of The Mariners.

"Hold up Bentley old chap." Pausing at the doorway Bentley turned to greet his old drinking companion with foreboding.

"Chuffer, where have you sprung from?"

"Spotted you from across the way old chap, setting up for the game tomorrow."

"Oh yes, the big game, heard of little else this past

week. Are you the opening bat Chuffer?"

"You can take the mickey Bentley as much as you wish but not so long ago I was the Kevin Peterson of Barton, top man, a village legend."

Bentley chuckled. "I believe you Chuffer."

"You're new to this village Bentley, the Rudds go back a long way. Anyway enough of that, how's the wife's holiday going?"

"No idea."

"Oh well, no news is good news eh? Tell me, are you in for a pie and a quick pint then away or are you stopping longer? Only I need a word or two, I have a business proposition."

"I've booked a table Chuffer."

"Have you? Good, I will join you."

"Table for one Chuffer."

"Ah that's no problem, I'll squeeze in somewhere, come on let's get out of this sun. If it's like this tomorrow there will be a lot of tired cricketers come tomorrow afternoon. Tell me Bentley, why do you always enter The Mariners from the rear entrance?"

"Hopefully to avoid people such as you Chuffer," Bentley replied with a chuckle.

"Oh I see, ok. Lead the way Bentley, lead the way."

Entering the restaurant, the pair were escorted to the least desirable corner of the room imaginable by a contrite Cheryl, whose apologetic mutterings disclaimed all responsibility for their unfortunate position seated close to the kitchen doors pressed up hard against a large welsh dresser housing many condiments, a constant path of pilgrimage for many customers that evening.

Once seated, an uneasy Bentley, finding little room for manoeuvre or path of escape, listened with ever-increasing reluctance to his dinner companions bullish business overtures.

"Trust me Bentley, it is a most generous offer, could run into millions. What have you got to lose except a few old greenhouses, a few acres of surrounding area and a couple of fallow fields? What is that to a chap of your eminence? Plenty of remaining acres with privacy intact. It's worth considering old boy, makes good business sense to me."

"Tell me old boy, who is this interested party and what's in it for you?" came the immediate reply.

"Nothing, nothing I assure you Bentley, I am acting

on behalf of a client in a purely advisory capacity of course. The gentleman wishes to remain anonymous at the moment."

Bentley poured himself a glass of house wine before proclaiming solemnly, "no name, no further discussion, end of story."

Chuffer Rudd drummed nervously upon the tabletop in solemn contemplation before answering. "Smethurst sausage producer."

"Can't say I'm surprised it's him. I ran into him a couple of days ago, said no to his offer then, so why should he think that your involvement as a go-between would change things?" Bentley retorted.

"Well think on Bentley, we have done business in the past," an impassioned Chuffer protested.

"Mmm don't remind me." Bentley snorted. "Our last business dealing was farcical. Bloody broken down old coach with my wife abandoned on the motorway who is no longer speaking to me, abroad somewhere, I know not where. So tell me, does the thought of any future business dealings with you my old friend fill me with dread or delight, what do you think?"

"Ah come, come Bentley that was very unfortunate."

"Yes, it was indeed for me so why now would I consider another arrangement such as an offer to sell part of my estate to that man. If he gets any closer I shall hear his kettle boil of a morning. This past week his infernal tractor has created a din from morning to nightfall. I accept that the weather has been exceptional and a boom for farmers but imagine his hive of activity moving even closer and closer. It would be a nightmare. I have no need of the money, I am in good health and I am content. I have it in mind to restore the whole estate including lodge and greenhouses and it is my intent to do so in my own time, so why should I consider selling out to a pork butcher and lining the pockets of a go-between such as yourself. Come on Chuffer, what percentage is it, 10%?"

"Er, 15% actually old boy."

"Could cost him millions Chuffer old boy, has he got that kind of cash?"

"Oh without a doubt Bentley, the man is loaded. You will give it some thought Bentley, please old chap?"

"Perhaps Chuffer, perhaps. Now I see our evening meal is about to arrive. Perhaps we can change the subject?"

"Yes certainly. Good show on tonight Bentley I

believe. A chap called Art Nouveau, a comedian of some sort and two fine women with him. Have you heard of him Bentley, you being in showbiz and all that sort of stuff?"

"Yes I have actually Chuffer, run across him several times in his early days, born in Slough, unfortunately likes a drink, his real name is Maurice Biggins but I shan't be stopping on. Might catch a quick pint at the bar, but I have been informed a certain lady has booked a table here for the evening at 7.45pm and I wish to avoid her." Bentley glanced at his watch. "7.10pm. Good. Half an hour, that should do it, so stop this chatter Mr Rudd, our food awaits."

CHAPTER 20
Good Management

Meantime, outside the main entrance, Albert paced the crowded car park with ever-increasing unease, anxiously awaiting the long overdue arrival of that evening's entertainer. Very much aware of the generous publicity and excitement generated by Amy Knutsford's recent article in the Portsmouth Echo and subsequent TV coverage regarding Bentley Brown's impromptu master class at the piano, prompting much speculation that a return to the world stage was on the cards. Albert, anxious to exploit The Mariner's involvement wasted little time in exploring many avenues in a quest for a well-regarded artist of comparable stature post haste. Common sense naturally dictated that to secure talent of equal ability was out of the question both financially and artistically. Albert however was determined to avoid crass disco music, karaoke and such like, finding such entertainment past its time. As good fortune would have it, success was almost immediate with the booking of new wave comedian and musician Art Nouveau with female accompaniment. His availability at such short notice was due entirely to a last minute cancellation he insisted, not lack of demand for his craft, indeed, his popularity was at a higher level than ever. Confirmation that his time of arrival that Saturday would be no later than 5.30pm, a convinced Albert secured his services immediately.

A genial man by heart but somewhat fastidious by nature, Albert was at war on several fronts that day. The ongoing heatwave being instrumental in several bad tempered encounters between landlord and clientele over ever-increasing numbers of male customers of all ages entering The Mariners topless leaving Albert with little option but to escort the miscreants back outside from whence they came with ill-disguised annoyance displayed on both sides. Events having reached such a stage that to avoid escalating confrontation, Albert displayed a notice board in prominent position in the foyer proclaiming in large print:

"PUB MANAGEMENT WOULD LIKE TO POINT OUT THAT ANYBODY ENTERING THE MARINERS WITHOUT APPROPRIATE CLOTHING IN SITU WILL BE SHOWN THE DOOR WITH LITTLE CEREMONY – MAY I SUGGEST THAT IF ANY INDIVIDUAL, MAN WOMAN OR CHILD, OBESE OR OTHERWISE WISHING TO DISPLAY ACRES OF FLESH IN OUTLANDISH FASHION SHOULD PAY A VISIT TO THE PLOUGH & HARROW SITUATED ON THE B184. THANK YOU. ALBERT JUGG, LICENSEE, LANDLORD, OWNER."

Another cause of some irritation between mine host and the public occurred during moments of relative quiet. Albert would patrol The Mariners inside and out passing from table to table moving any offending glass, he felt placed too close to the table edge closer to the centre, a wave of the finger conveying all disapproval necessary. Dispensing justice with cold eye determination, leaving in his wake a bewildered mixture of customer, some quietly amused and others not so. If questioned he would be retort abruptly, "if you are not happy go to the Plough & Harrow B184." Further strange behaviour causing much dismay to wife and daughter was a propensity to follow customers entering the restaurant wearing dirty shoes with a brush and pan in hand. All in all, it must be said such behaviour was accepted with surprising good humour by the public at large. With the time fast approaching 7pm, having completed a further visit to all corners of the car park without success, Albert approached The Mariners entrance with a heavy heart when a VW camper van, entering the car park driven at speed, caught him a glancing blow on the shoulder blade sending him spinning backward to land somewhat forcefully among a flowerbed of colourful pansies. The vehicle, circa. 1970, bright blue in colour, restored to pristine condition, shuddered to a halt barely feet away from a prostrate licensee leaving two young women unconcerned and giggling in the back of the vehicle. The driver leapt from the camper van approaching Albert with extended hand.

"Mr Jugg, you are he of course, the crimson blazer a dead giveaway. You took me back in time sir, Pathé News, Billy Butlin and all that. Before my time of course but you can't fool me. Sorry for the late arrival sir and particularly knocking you to the ground but there's holiday traffic everywhere, everybody on the road it seems taking advantage of this wonderful weather and why not, why not." Helping Albert to his feet, he turned to address the girls yet to emerge from their place of comfort. "Come on girls, chop chop, unload the van, take the props inside and let's get moving." He winked at Albert Jugg in a salacious fashion. "My girls do everything I say, know what I mean governor?" Placing an arm on Albert's shoulder, he drew in closer to him. "Now Mr Jugg, to business. Me and the girls require little from you save a quiet corner of the car park for use overnight away from the pack, I am sure you get my drift sir. Also the humidity is affecting my voice somewhat so may I request a fan on stage," the artist laughed, "a proper fan you know what I mean?"

Albert nodded. "It can be arranged."

The musician gestured towards the pub. "A fine pub sir, fine, it does you proud, now shall we get inside Mr Jugg, it has been a long trip up from Cornwall and I am rather in need of sustenance if you get my drift. A pint of bitter perhaps, scotch to follow, to put me in the right frame of mind sir for the evening's entertainment, perhaps on the house?" He gestured towards the girls. "Leave the girls to set up Mr Jugg, they know the drill." Albert removed the entertainer's hand from his shoulder with icy distain.

"May I be brutally frank with you Mr Nouveau?"

"Yes sir, go ahead," came the reply.

"I must question if you are indeed who you say you are. No offence intended but save for the ponytail you bear scant resemblance to your publicity photos. Truth be told Mr Nouveau, you could pass for a much older man in the flesh. I suggest you update your publicity stills, this almost amounts to fraud sir." The entertainer dismissed Albert's comments with cold contempt flicking at his ponytail with agitated nervousness.

"We all age Mr Jugg. I cannot update all publicity at every appearance of a grey hair or a receding hairline, it would cost a small fortune and if I may say so, here we are. We stand in late afternoon sunshine during the hottest spell for years that has reduced the countryside in appearance to a dried prune and I must further add that you yourself have no room for complacency. On observation, I would suggest you yourself have seen better days. Now, come show me the bar for a quick one before I start the evening show. Let me assure you sir, once inside on stage with subtle lighting, all the years will fade away. Come sir, to the bar." Meantime, the girls, unaware of discord between the pair and having unloaded all relevant props within the foyer were away in search of a quiet corner of the car park to park overnight.

The following 40 minutes were to test Bentley's patience and good nature to the limit. Constant interruptions by many ladies, young and old alike, seeking his attention in hope of an autograph or a selfie, the current craze that Bentley disliked to the extreme finding such a request a little intrusive.

Meantime, within The Mariners restaurant, good food and wine consumed and bill paid, settled by Bentley as usual, the pair headed in the direction of the main bar, on their way advised by a passing waitress to avoid the lounge as entry was obstructed by a crowd gathered outside the doorway due to an altercation between that evening's entertainer and landlord, Albert Jugg. The point of issue being the portable stage erected that afternoon in the lounge bar leading to a vexed Art Nouveau voicing his disapproval objecting to the size to quote, "far too small to accommodate such an artiste as myself and all my musical equipment such as speakers, keyboard, mikes and most importantly, my two girls, bereft of enough room to display their version of modern day salsa." Having consumed several pints of best better and a whiskey chaser, adrenalin flowing and feeling badly let down and in no mood to begin that evening's entertainment, Art Nouveau sat upon the stage edge head in hands staring morosely at the flagstone floor. Albert Jugg however, in no mood for compromise, was adamant that all was well, the stage large enough and the show must begin at the time specified on the written agreement between the two. If not, the alternative being in the best showbiz tradition of no show, no dough. Albert Jugg's firm stance was greeted with approval from the many standing within the doorway anxious to find suitable seating within the lounge bar. As tensions eased and the crowd slowly dispersed, among them Bentley Brown, head and shoulders above many in the crowd that night, he was immediately recognised and greeted with warm applause. Several of the crowd even giving to cries of, "sort him out Jack, lock him up DI," which involved further applause much to Bentley's discomfort. After a further ten minutes delay Art Nouveau returned from a visit to the gents and approached Albert Jugg indicating a change of mind and a willingness to begin the evening's entertainment. Displaying surprising agility for a man of senior rank, a relieved landlord leapt upon the stage to welcome all to The Mariners that night encouraging a warm welcome for artiste Art Nouveau adding despite his appearance being half an hour adrift, wishing all present an enjoyable evening. With a nod to the entertainer, that evening's entertainment began.

Seated in an alcove, early arrival freelance journalist Amy Knutsford accompanied by current squeeze Rafael Winstone, a law student, was keen to follow up her much-read article concerning Bentley Browne with another of a similar nature. Watching all events unfolding that evening with a keen eye and notebook at the ready, her interpretation of events that evening appeared as follows in a two page spread in the Portsmouth Evening Echo the following Monday:

"Once again your ace reporter Amy Knutsford, reporting from one of my favourite watering holes on a Saturday night out in search of entertainment. However, firstly I must express my disappointment. Having reported previously upon a splendid evening's entertainment at the majestic Three Mariners public house, Barton-on-the Green, I returned this evening in expectation of a repeat performance, if not by the maestro Bentley Browne then perhaps one of comparable God given talent, however sadly, this was not to be. The evening's entertainment was in the hands of a chap by the name of Art Nouveau, a name to excite many an art historian I am sure, however, his act, if you can call it that, was a mixture of so called progressive humour, blue jokes and bad language. My poor mum and dad would have left the room within minutes, bless them. However, I shall continue. It was a tribute to west country punk, endless shouting in my mind, snatches of new age Vaudeville, whatever that is, all accompanied by several dance routines presented by two giggling young girls wearing little more than flimsy nylon tassels leaving little to the imagination bringing many young men to their feet in appreciation. Even for

me, never a prude, I found the performance a complete embarrassment, I was also not the only one. Within twenty minutes the lounge was half-empty, many having left the room voicing disapproval causing Albert Jugg to take action. Leaving the bar in haste, he climbed upon the stage grabbing the microphone from Art Nouveau and he called all to a close from that minute on. From where I was seated, I don't know who lost control first.

With the excitement that followed Albert Jugg's abandonment of the evening's entertainment, it was difficult to define who struck the first blow. I would suggest that it was a clearly upset Art Nouveau but who is to know from my position in the room. Difficult to deduce but what I will report however is that off duty Police Contestable Willoughby once again was in the thick of it. Having reported last week upon his injury to his leg whilst doing his duty once again he took a knock, also hard to pinpoint who did what to whom, however, my hero Bentley Browne made my day. Stepping in he separated the antagonists despite taking a severe blow to the forehead. His presence was fundamental in calling the discord to a halt. Finally taking to the piano, the big man produced 70 minutes of profound pleasure to calm and re-energise The Three Mariners. Finally calling it a day, at approximately 10.30pm he left The Mariners to much applause once again.

Let me finish my report with the admission that leaving The Mariners that evening I was in good spirits, one too many perhaps, however, I was driven home that night by my current squeeze, so no problem, however I digress. Once outside I happened upon Art Nouveau, a little inebriated to say the least, spouting off to all and sundry upon his feelings of unjust treatment that night deploring the fact that his act was abandoned for reasons unknown and that he was much appreciated by many and only last year had been top billing at the Guildford Folk and Frolic Festival, drawing much attention and appreciation from the vast crowd, unlike tonight's audience, all conservative prats or words to that effect, and voicing his opinion that a Corbyn government would reduce all saloon bars throughout the land to dust increasing the size of public bars overnight at last ridding the world of middle class Tory ponses, not his exact words but you get the gist. On that note, I end this report with one thing in mind, if that is Art Nouveau, give me art deco anytime. Bye for now, your babe, Amy Knutsford."

CHAPTER 21
A Fine Sunday

Sunday, July 18th 2018. With a forecast of yet more fine weather to cast its spell upon many parts of southern England that day, the much heralded cricket match between fierce rivals Barton-on-the Green versus Lower Barton due to be contested that afternoon was greeted with indifference by some, others with much eager anticipation. Although quite a devoted fan of the sport in whatever form, Bentley preferred the initial conception of the game, that being polite applause, good-natured rivalry, the game played with good intent in mind, not today's version with its sledging, foul language, win at all cost, the very concept of the game under attack. To Bentley's certain mind, had he ever played and been subjected to any such treatment he would have in all certainty put the antagonists in hospital no matter the consequences. Just before 2.00pm Bentley crossed the green with time to spare, carrying underarm a light folding camping chair and shabby golfing umbrella brought to light after a quick rummage within Rawling's potting shed that morning. Following the footpath alongside the village pond, he headed towards the cricket pavilion for the umpteenth time that week. He was delighted to encounter a past acquaintance pleasure evident in their chance meeting, the two greeting one another with great delight. Finally, bonding over, the pair parted, Bentley continuing upon his way, the dog returning to the water's edge. Crossing the village green approaching the pavilion aware of a large crowd gathered outside Bentley changed direction heading towards the cricket nets in hope of a little quiet relaxation.

Once settled, chair and umbrella in place, Bentley gazed upon many aspects of village life bringing to mind Alice Coate's enlightened record of Barton Village over many previous years. According to the well-respected historian, many changes came about upon the death of MP Sir William Wiggins in the year 1912. In his Will, he bequeathed 9½ acres of fine land to the village, on one condition however, this being the formation of a cricket club to be named after Barton-on-the-Green, his dying wish that one day Barton would become a major player in county cricket. The Will was challenged by elder son Charles, his concern that many of the villagers were of low stature and should not be handed his inheritance to wander aimlessly upon the land once his.

Whilst having much sympathy with his concerns, the High Court dismissed his plea but conceded that a village committee should be put in place consisting of local villagers of some stature on the understanding that the Vicar of St Michaels, Reverend Ernest Bellway should preside over and be accountable for all decisions taken and approved by a formed committee. A man of resolute standing, Ernest

Bellway accepted all responsibility without a word of descent and the by end of 1913 much had been achieved with a cricket square in place and nurtured to receive much admiration by many and the surrounding area cleared and levelled, a task of some undertaking accomplished by local folk confirming much village pride. In 1914 further village pride was confirmed by the village committee when, by a majority of 13:1, the village would from that moment in time be addressed as Barton-on-the-Green and favoured point of contact for the cricket team would be The Mariners public house. With the outbreak of World War I, all future development was put on hold as many young men joined the military. In 1915, the neglected green was given over to the army with the erection of many wooden huts, put upon the green to house conscripts. After the Armistice, normality was somewhat restored and the green cleared of all military presence save for a large hut retained in place, courtesy of the army for future use as a cricket pavilion. A large board set upon the south facing wall overlooking the cricket pitch honoured those that fell in action.

During the summer of 1919 the landlord of the Plough & Harrow public house, running close to the extreme eastern edge of Barton village situated on the B184 on route to Churt village and beyond, sought out the Reverend Bellway suggesting a cricket match be arranged between Barton-on-the Green now named as such and the outer reaches of Lower Barton village, where having little connection with the green as such, the village, with a population of seven thousand being rather widespread was divided, many feeling allegiance to an area of the village addressed by many as Lower Barton. The suggestion was greeted with great enthusiasm by many, the game taking place on August 10th with many villagers present. Intense rivalry plainly evident from the beginning of a much contentious match, play was brought to a close suddenly during the fortieth over with Lower Barton at the crease on a score of 147 for 8 when the landlord of the Plough & Harrow, going for a third run, out of breath and yards from the crease, was struck upon the head by a returning ball thrown in from the boundary with some venom. Pronounced dead by the outfield umpire Arnold Shippard, the game was abandoned immediately and pronounced a draw, a decision Barton-on-the-Green contested, their view being that Barton-on-the-Green was the superior side that day and would have outscored Lower Barton no doubt whatsoever. Such talk at the time was ill advised and is still a great source of provocation between the two pockets of village life. The following year both teams joined the local league and remain so to this day. Both teams when playing at home use the green on alternate Sundays.

Eyes closed immersed in deep thoughts upon many

aspects of Mrs Coate's history of Barton Village, Bentley was brought back to earth by a pat upon the shoulder.

"Afternoon Bentley, all ok? I didn't recognise you in your Panama hat, very swish."

"Oh it's you Chuffer, sorry, I was miles away in dreamland."

"As I thought Bentley, recovering from last night eh?"

"No, not at all, I'm fine. Yourself? If I may say so Chuffer, you look a little weary."

"Yes, perhaps I overdid it a little yesterday. I stayed on after you left and didn't leave 'till gone 11. Mind you, this heat doesn't help, very humid isn't it?" Reaching out, he removed the clip holding the umbrella in place upon the back of Bentley's seating. "Ah, that's better, bit of shade."

"Yes, thank you Mr Rudd."

"My pleasure Bentley, my pleasure. Tell me, that comedian come singer, whatever, Art Nouveau, well, I am at a loss what to say. What a disaster. All that terrible music, bloody awful and his jokes, good grief, then he lost his temper, threw punches at everybody.

I noticed you were involved in the thick of it Bentley somewhat."

"I was on my way to the toilet, Chuffer, pure bad luck."

"And that Constable Willoughby. Took a nasty smack on the nose poor chap. Always in the wars that lad."

"Goes with the job," Bentley murmured.

"Mind you," Chuffer continued, "the girls were good to look at if nothing else."

Bentley nodded his head in agreement. "Yes, a very nice pair indeed."

Chuffer reproached his pal playfully with a wave of the figure. "Less of that smutty talk Mr Browne, I'm a born again Christian you know."

"Indeed you are Chuffer, indeed you are."

"That'll be the day eh, Bentley. Still, no harm in appreciation of a nice figure, despite my age, eh Bentley," he prodded Bentley on the shoulder. "What do you think, eh Bentley?"

"Quite so, Chuffer, quite so. Tell me. Recently I read an article relating to a game of cricket held many years ago between Barton-on-the-Green and Barton Village that was called to a halt when a poor chap was struck on the head by a cricket ball and died on the spot. He was the landlord of the Plough & Harrow. What with you and your family being Barton bred for hundreds of years, what do you know?"

"Ooh everything."

"Tell me then Chuffer, it interests me for some reason."

"Well, what can I tell you Bentley is the ball was thrown in from the boundary by my grandad, Ernest Rudd."

"Your grandad, Chuffer?"

"Yes, good player was Grandad, taught me everything I know about cricket. Once upon a time, I could bowl at 90 miles an hour, hard to believe now looking at me but I was very quick Bentley. I know it's sad what happened and Grandad was a little upset naturally but..." Chuffer shrugged his shoulders. "In them days there was little protection, no health and safety nonsense and the Great War had just finished where men had spent four years in trenches fighting. Terrible times, King and Country and all that. Those that returned home weren't concerned about a flying cricket ball, men was men in them days, no bloody health and safety, not like today, ruling the roost." Glancing across at the clock sat upon the pavilion wall Chuffer rose painfully to his feet. "Crikey, I must be going, the game is due to start and I have to address my boys, words of wisdom and all that stuff, you'll have to forgive me Bentley or are you coming now?"

"No, no thanks Chuffer, I am content as I am, no offence."

"None taken my friend, enjoy the game. One thing though, any thoughts on the greenhouses, land sale, anything?"

"No."

"And the wife, heard from her?"

"Not as yet, no Chuffer."

"Oh well, must go, see you later."

"Chuffer?"

"Yes?"

"My umbrella."

"Oh sorry Bentley."

Within several minutes of Chuffer Rudd's return to the pavilion, players already in white appeared outside the pavilion eager to get going. Within minutes the toss was taken, Lower Barton to bat first, the match began on time. Despite much partisan fervour clearly evident, all good firm sportsmanship prevailed within both sides on the field of play.

CHAPTER 22
Old Pals Reunion

As the afternoon drifted on, time approached for the customary tea break. Bentley considered his options; a visit to the pavilions for tea and a chat as wished by Chuffer, a quick trip to The Three Mariners for a pint and a pie and a little relief from the unremitting sunshine or perhaps a choc-ice purchased from an ice cream van parked up close by. As the players left, the field for a well-earned rest and a pot of tea Bentley plumped for an ice cream cone topped with coconut flakes. Upon his feet, he headed for the ice cream van to join the ever-increasing numbers waiting patiently in line. Standing in the queue, somewhat half-asleep, he slowly became aware of familiar music bursting forth from the loudspeaker sat upon the vehicle's rooftop, played in short repetitive bursts of bass guitar rather than piano; the result was a compilation of Bentley Browne's first monster hit, Moonrock Rumble. Reaching the end of the line standing behind a group of noisy teenagers Bentley caught a glimpse of the figure in the hatchway. With disbelief, Bentley looked across the way once more. It was, as he feared, his old musical partner Syd Mitchell.

"Can I help you mate?"

Panama hat pulled low over his eyes Bentley faced his old friend. "Large vanilla with coconut topping please."

"Don't do coconut topping."

"Oh make it walnut topping then."

"Don't do walnut topping either."

"Oh, what have you got then?"

"Look mate, come on, make your mind up, I'm a busy man, people are waiting. What have I got, I ask you, good grief, it's written in colourful print all over the van, can't you read, come on mate, make your mind up."

Bentley raised his head removing his hat. "Afternoon Syd."

"Good God, I should have known, Bentley Browne." Reaching down from within the hatchway, a grinning Syd Mitchell offered his hand. "Good to see you Bentley."

Bentley took his hand with surprising warmth. "And you Syd, and you."

Growing impatience from within the gathering crowd behind him, Bentley went for a vanilla cornet. "Just a cornet Syd, no topping, that'll do fine." Bentley handed over the required £3.50. "I shan't ask you what you're doing here Syd, but good to see you, perhaps we'll have a chat one day."

"Oh Bentley, don't go," came the anxious cry from within the hatchway, "I've come a long way to see you, can we meet up later?"

"I'm rather busy Syd."

"Please Bentley, I need your help."

Bentley nodded somewhat reluctantly. "Ok. The Mariners across the green, an hour's time, provided you pay for the drinks Syd."

"You're on, Bentley; you're on, one hour."

Acknowledging several waves of recognition from the many seated outside The Three Mariners Bentley entered the building. Passing through a surprisingly deserted lobby, he entered the lounge bar. Behind the counter landlord Albert Jugg, extravagantly attired in fancy waistcoat and bow tie and engrossed in polishing several trays of pint mugs, put all aside to greet his much-esteemed customer with open arms.

"Bentley, you old thespian, good to see you, what are you having?"

"A pint of your best bitter please Albert. I am dying of thirst, the day's got hotter by the minute."

"Coming up Mr Browne."

"Very quiet in here Albert, what's going on?"

"Cricket Bentley, cricket. Where have you been? You wait, in a short while we will be rushed off our feet."

"Oh God, yes of course, what am I thinking, I've just come from the green, sorry Albert, my mind is elsewhere."

"Here you are Bentley, a pint of the best, on the house." The landlord leaned upon the bar top beckoning Bentley closer, his voice a whisper. "Bentley, last night, thank you for what you did, what was I thinking of, eh, Art Nouveau, the name alone should have warned me off booking him."

Bentley reached for his pint. "On the house you say Albert, oh thanks, cheers. Well, I must say I was surprised you booked him, as you say the name alone should have warned you, I should have put you in the picture I suppose, but well, it was not for me to comment. I met the chap some years ago, he was a bit off the wall then, but that's showbiz Mr Jugg, we all behave badly at times or in my case, did."

Albert took a cloth to the counter, polishing the top with some aggression, "Yes but what a prat, eh, couldn't sing, blue jokes, then starts a scrap, ruined The Mariner's reputation I shouldn't wonder, business will take a tumble I'm sure and then he took a swing at you didn't he? He missed though," the pair chuckled in unison.

"Yes, fortunately Albert, hit the young copper instead. By the way, how is he?"

Albert suppressed a laugh. "Ha, he got a black eye to go with his damaged knee, not the best week for the boy was it? Not for someone fresh out of Hendon Police College, hey?" The pair suppressed further laughs.

"You don't appear to have a lot of time for the officer, Albert?"

"Ah, he's a bit of a phony, but only doing his duty as he would put it, I have some sympathy." An elderly couple entered the bar. "Oh at last, some customers, duty calls Bentley as our constable would phrase it, excuse me."

"Erm, before you go Albert, anyone been in asking for me, I am due to meet someone."

The landlord paused for a moment. "Man or woman

Bentley?"

"Man."

"Well no, not as such, but a chap was in just before you arrived, no shirt on, so I sent him out to put a top on or stay out, not your type, a bit of a hippy," Albert laughed, "not been back since, could that have been him."

"Yes possibly Albert, thanks."

Choice of seating plentiful, Bentley made for his most favourite corner of the lounge overlooking the green. Feet under the table for no longer than four minutes, he was joined in the alcove by a contrite Syd Mitchell. Despite his status of showbiz royalty seated close to Bentley for the first time in many years dressed in t-shirt, knee length shorts and a flat cap, he put Bentley in mind of an aging window cleaner. "Sorry Bentley, been chatting to a young lady in the restaurant, making me a cheese sandwich to eat on the way home later, very attractive, I might be in with a chance there."

"You might, you think Syd."

"I might, you never know."

"Huh huh, nothing changes with you eh Syd."

"Nothing Bentley. Now tell me, how are you? We've not been in touch for a good few years, everything ok? You're looking well I must admit, kept your hair as well." He removed his flat cap rubbing his thinning patch somewhat ruefully. "More than I have. How's the wife Bentley?"

"Which one Syd?"

"Well, the current one I suppose Bentley."

"Away on a cruise at present. And you Syd, you and Cheryl still together?"

"We are Bentley yes, 25 years on believe it or not."

"And the lads?"

"Doing fine. Jack's at university and Roberts in America working for Disneyland, doing rather well."

"Good, everything is going OK then. So what's your problem Syd?"

"No problem Bentley. Well not quite, er, let me get you another drink."

"I'm fine as I am Syd, thank you, now spell it out, what are you after?"

Syd Mitchell looked back towards the bar. "That barman, miserable old sod, made be put a shirt on when I arrived, said he doesn't do nudists in here, particularly at my age, made me go out as he put it and smarten up. What a pillock. I'm in good shape me. A few years ago I would have given him a right hander, it's not as if I'm out of shape is it Bentley?"

"No Syd, no, still as thin as a Cumberland sausage, no doubt about it. Now Syd, once again, what are you after?"

Syd Mitchell addressed his old partner with some foreboding. "I need your help Bentley, are you sure you won't have another drink with me?"

"Spit it out Syd, what is it you're after?"

"Well, it's your assistance as a fellow artist, Bentley."

"Oh yes?"

"Yes Bentley, I need to make a sizable sum of money. I'm not after a loan, don't worry, you've done enough in the past for which I shall always be grateful but the truth is, I made a heavy investment that is running short of cash so I need to make a few shillings."

"What, selling ice cream cones at £3.50 and you're short of cash, little unlikely Syd."

"Take the mickey if you must Bentley, I would do the same if our positions were reversed but I'll be honest with you, when the price of diesel goes up so does my expenditure so I have no choice but to raise my prices. I have five ice-cream vans on the go, spring and summer, employing six drivers and a full time mechanic on board to keep things moving which is fine, it's an ongoing business and I'm doing fine, but in the winter I start to struggle a little to keep the lads on the payroll, can't lose them, never get them back, but recently I invested a large sum of money buying a hotel in Paignton, you know Devon?"

Bentley nodded, "Of course. Very well."

Syd continued. "Well I've spent more on renovations than I bargained for and I have now run out of cash. I don't want to tie myself up with a bank loan to finish the job or borrow money. I was a bit stuck as to which way to turn then; believe it or not, as good fortune would have it, I was in Portsmouth last Monday making my way home from selling my wares at a fete in Epsom. Taking the long way home, I stopped off in Gosport for a break. Picking up a local newspaper in a cafe there was an article all about you implying you had returned to the business and I thought well yes, that's it, get back together with my old pal Bentley, he'd have me back. The reporter, obviously a fan wrote a glowing report and I thought wow, you're back on song, you sly old devil, so I thought I'd look you up. Just think Bentley, your return to the bright lights for a well-paid gig or two would bail me out and I wonder if perhaps the two of us, with one or two of the old lads in tow, could capitalise on the newspaper's interest on your return to the limelight while you're still hot, you do read the papers Bentley? You're buzzing. I rang our old manager, Morris Gibbins and he said he'd get on to you and for me to polish up the guitar for a nationwide tour in the offing."

Bentley raised his arms in protest. "Syd, for God's sake, it's just silly talk, you know what a chancer Morris is, it goes with the job, he's a manager."

"Oh come on Bentley," Syd persisted, "we could all do with a few more shillings including you, I'm sure. A few months on tour, then pack it in."

"Syd, Syd, I have retired, I don't need the money or recognition, I am happy as I am. If you're so keen, announce your availability out there on social media or join one of the many tours of the legends of the 80's, pop stars unable to let go. I am sure they can all do with an accomplished guitarist."

Syd snorted disapprovingly. "No way man, I'm not performing with a bunch of B celebs, I was the top man, still am, no second rate Christmas tour for me Bentley, no it must be you and me and the boys, one more time Bentley, please, give it some thought eh?"

"Syd, Syd." An irate Bentley tapped the tabletop. "You've got it all wrong. That gig that the girl reported on was a one-off, I was helping your friend," Bentley pointed in the direct of Albert Jugg "to test the piano, that was it. The report was a little over the top, sorry and all that."

Disappointment evident, Syd Mitchell persisted. "But Bentley, the support for you in the newspapers is overwhelming."

"Syd please. My dear wife and I agreed that my decision to retire some years ago was the right one, away from temptation and all that was the way to go and to return to that would result in the end of my fourth marriage and a large pay out in divorce fees, plus I am 68 years old, an old age pensioner, almost creaking at the knees old son."

"Nonsense Bentley," Syd laughed. "You look fine, you could pass for half your age and so could I with a little make up in the right places." The pair laughed in unison restoring a little harmony between the two.

"You always were a poor liar Syd, nothing changes."

Syd looked at his watch. "Oh well, I've tried. I must be going home soon it's a long way back. By the way

Bentley, a wonderful home you've got."

"Very kind of you to say so Syd. How did you find me?"

"Bentley, you're a national treasure, everyone knows where you live good grief. I made my way to Barton then popped into the corner shop on the green and asked the chap behind the counter if he knew of you. He said yes and implied you were good friends and pointed in the direction of the manor. He said you were thinking of making an appearance at the local fete in a few weeks time and that it's a very big event, almost as big as Glastonbury and you were keen to appear at it."

Bentley looked at his old partner with disbelief. "Syd, you're off the wall. First, I said no in person to the man, second, the event is no bigger than a village garden show with a few children and a couple of slides, perhaps a Punch and Judy if you're lucky."

"Ah, I see Bentley. I did try and come to see you personally but the main house was all locked up, couldn't get in. I came back to the green and saw the preparations on hand for the cricket match so I thought I would mix business with pleasure, make a few bob and then you arrived at the van, couldn't believe it, I thought my luck was in. Oh well, never mind." Somewhat reluctantly, Syd made to leave. "So long Bentley, must go, good to see you again. I know you can be a stubborn old bugger but you're also a softy. Have my business card in case you change your mind. Give it some serious consideration Bentley for old time's sake; help your old pal out."

Bentley rose to his feet reaching out to his old friend. "I will Syd, I will take your number and I will phone in a day or two. I will give it some thought I promise you. Come here Syd, give me a hug." A little awkwardly, the two shared a quick embrace.

"Steady on Bentley, I've got my reputation to consider." Bentley laughed.

"What reputation Syd, anyway I thought you were in need of publicity."

"Depends what sort Bentley. Before I go, I must say once again that you've got yourself a wonderful home, very desirable with gates and surrounding brickwork of such magnitude. I wouldn't mind living in Lower Barton myself, given the chance."

"Lower Barton? I beg your pardon Syd, Barton-on-the-Green."

"Ha, sorry Bentley, you're at the posh end then."

"I certainly am Syd."

The two laughed together, genuine warmth between the pair, past differences put to one side. "Well Bentley, once you get your knighthood you really will be lord of the manor and if you should ever need a gatekeeper give me a ring and if my business collapses I'll move in."

"I'll bear it in mind Syd, but you'll have to tidy yourself up a little for that position in life."

"Bloody cheek, time for me to go I think." A brief warm handshake between the two and Syd headed for the restaurant emerging within minutes with a cheese and pickle sandwich in hand. A nod of the head and a quick wave. "Hear from you soon Bentley I hope." Then he was gone. Standing at the bay window Bentley watched the familiar ice-cream van leave the car park. From within the cab a quick wave accompanied in sound by a loud rendition of Moonrock Rumble and a blast upon the horn. With that, he was gone.

Re-seated, finishing his drink, he reflected on their time together. Some good memories, some not so, times with great expectation and plentiful reward. Bentley felt a surge of regret for leaving that life behind him. Finally came the reconnection with the present day by a tap upon the shoulder by a concerned Albert Jugg.

"Everything OK Bentley?"

"Yes, why?"

"Well you looked a little thoughtful, not like you."

"Thank you Albert."

"Was that the chap?"

"Yes Albert, it was."

"Scruffy Herbert, I had to tell him to dress properly or push off."

"Yes, so he told me Albert."

"Who was he Bentley?"

"Oh, just an old acquaintance Albert."

"You sure you're OK Bentley? You look a little strained if I may say so."

"I'm fine Albert thanks, just re-awakening of long forgotten memories. I think I shall head for home, it's been a long day."

"Oh well, alright, as long as you're OK I'll leave you." Albert reached for the empty glass. "Have another

Bentley?"

"No thanks Albert, I'm heading for home."

"Not stopping for a meal? With chicken masala on the go, Catherine will be disappointed.

"Well, tell her another time, I shan't stop tonight, thanks. I have it in mind to try and contact my good wife."

"Oh right, well I wish you luck Bentley." Albert looked out upon the green. "Oh! D-Day approaches; sound the alarm, games over, the crowd is headed this way." Bentley followed his gaze. There out upon the cricket square all was at an end, bales off, stumps withdrawn, handshakes over, a surge of supporters headed towards The Mariners and with them the victorious cricket team, in line joining a steady flow already entering the building in urgent need of sustenance. Within minutes of Bentley's decision to head home, all was bedlam within both bars and restaurant alike. Raising a hand in farewell to an already beleaguered Albert, Bentley headed for the main exit.

Once outside, imprisoned upon the uppermost step of the many leading to The Mariners main point of entry, Bentley was confronted by the Barton-on-the-Green's victorious cricket team. Drawn together in a tight unit standing upon the lower steps, hemmed in by many supporters with little chance of easy exit from the dense crowd Bentley had little choice but to remain in place, witness to the noisy celebrations below. Instrumental in the large gathering and offering further encouragement for others to join the carnival atmosphere was part-time reporter and amateur photographer Quentin Wetherby, a keen contributor to local paper The Barton Gazette. Hopeful of a worthwhile photograph suitable for publication the following Friday, he cajoled many to join the throng. Among the many enticed to stand upon the lower steps were local dignitaries including entrepreneur and sausage magnate Nigel Smethurst, Barton Village Committee Chairman, Mr E E Patel, the local vicar, Australian Sean Reagan, skipper and Barton-on-the-Green cricket team president, Chuffer Rudd. All was put on hold shortly however as village bobby, PC Willoughby interrupted the celebrations. Standing at the forefront calling for a halt in proceedings, he addressed the crowd.

"In the pursuit of my moral duty I am duty bound to follow all procedures to ensure sensible decisions should be taken in the interests of health and safety, therefore I would advise the many upon the steps to move forward a foot or so away from the possible, however remote, of a loose or perhaps damaged basket hanging from the eaves above the entrance falling and causing havoc upon the gathering below."

The constable's instructions were greeted with much good-natured derision and laughter from the many upon the steps. Ignoring his command, all remained stubbornly in place, much to the constable's disapproval.

Finally, photos completed, the crowd quickly dispersed, a noisy majority entering The Mariners in wild abandonment following some distance behind an unhappy PC Willoughby. Hat well pulled over his eyes and head down, Bentley slipped through the oncoming throng without hesitation.

Upon the green a sizable crowd remained, still in party mode, many accompanied by children. Relieved to have distanced himself from the frenzy about to engulf The Mariners, Bentley headed for home, avoiding many youths on bicycles chasing one another across the green. Deep in thought, his reunion with old partner Syd Mitchell upmost in his thoughts. Avoiding close contact with the many gathered at the water's edge, Bentley was spotted by his erstwhile housekeeper Alice Clemspon accompanied by toy boy Bunny Ford in close company with the vicar's wife Melody Regan. Crossing their path without recognition a swift swipe on the leg with a cane brought Bentley to a sudden halt.

"My my, Bentley Browne. My word, surprised to see you here, why aren't you in The Mariners celebrating our winning team, I thought any excuse for raising a glass to your lips was your idea of heaven Bentley."

Despite the sharp pain inflicted upon his kneecap, Bentley greeted his housekeeper with warmth. "Good to see you Alice, how are you my dear, coping alright?"

"Of course I'm coping Bentley my dear sir, I am a woman, that's what we do, it's men that fall apart at the slightest excuse, isn't that so Bunny?" She prodded her companion with her cane.

"Yes, quite so Alice, quite so. To suggest otherwise is an unreasonable suggestion my dear."

"Thank you Bunny for your support. Now Bentley." She turned to a radiant vicar's wife. "You have met the young lady in question here I believe, the delightful Melody?"

"I have indeed Alice. How are you Melody?"

"Fine, thank you Bentley, nice to see you again."

"Did you enjoy the game ladies?"

"We did Bentley, yes. We were rather hoping to run in to you seated somewhere in the crowd, no chance however, so we paid a visit to the manor house in the hope of finding you perhaps at home. I couldn't get through the entrance, all padlocked and secure, very unwelcome. We wondered if perhaps you had sold up and left the country in a hurry, perhaps without paying the milkman. What's going on Bentley?"

"All in hand Alice, don't worry yourself, we don't want unwelcome visitors do we, able to come and go as they please."

"Like us you mean?"

"Alice, please!"

"Perhaps you have a point Bentley but we could have saved ourselves an unnecessary journey if I could have contacted you by phone at home or heaven forbid you carried a mobile phone with you like, well, most of the modern world."

"Sorry Alice, but my view of modern technology is unprintable. The world depends on Facebook and Google whatever. It's unbelievable, where is the world headed? I will stick to pen and paper and an occasional phone call to express my thoughts and opinions, thank you my dear lady."

"Well Bentley, how you have achieved a long career in show business without the use of technology is beyond belief."

"I left all such things to my managers Alice, that's what they get paid for."

"You are old fashioned and out of date Bentley. What of your poor wife Bentley, unable to get in touch, always out somewhere enjoying yourself."

"Nonsense Alice, I am at home every evening."

"Well I would dispute that Bentley. From what I hear you were involved in a fisticuffs in The Mariners only last night, not for the first time either so I'm informed."

"Not my doing Alice, it was the artiste Art Nouveau."

"Yes, but he was a friend of yours," Alice insisted.

"Nonsense, I had met him once, years ago that's all, hardly a friend."

"Well an association then, that's good enough."

"Alice please, where is this going?"

"I'm just trying to get you to curb your wild streak Bentley before it gets out of hand."

Bentley turned to Melody in exasperation. "Excuse me young lady, I've had enough of this. I've had a long day. See you tomorrow I hope, 9.00am. I believe?"

"Bentley Bentley, if you would only listen, that's why we're here, tell him Melody."

"Tell me what?"

"Change of plan I'm afraid Bentley, I shall not be

paying a visit to the manor house as planned. I do apologise but my poor husband has many engagements next week, all for the church of course, but with the poor man still in plaster due to his involvement in that set to in the flowerbed at the beginning of the week, he needs me to accompany him most of the time. I am so sorry Bentley but you will have to continue with the housework for a further week at least. Life can be very hard at times, can it not," she laughed, her eyes dancing with mischievous delight.

"Ah well, perhaps I should have advertised in the Barton Weekly for a young lady of suitable temperament to look after me for a short spell until your husband recovers. I shall look into it further."

"You will not Bentley Browne," Alice intervened forcefully. "You must put up with the inconvenience a little longer, perhaps use a duster occasionally Bentley, does wonders for your well-being, you'll be surprised," the women laughed in unison.

"Yes, well you've had your fun ladies, I must be off, things to do, same as you, anxious to get home eh?"

"Good Lord, no," Alice explained, "we're off to The Mariners, Bunny is going to treat us to a drink, aren't you Bunny?"

"I am?"

"Yes, you are Bunny."

"Ah yes, well of course."

"So see you Bentley. Oh by the way, I almost forgot, your good wife may phone you tonight."

"How do you know that Alice?"

Tapping the side of her nose she said knowingly, "Bentley, women know everything my dear, we are all in touch you know. Come Bunny, you're going to buy me a gin and tonic. Are you coming with us Melody?"

"I am indeed please, yes. I promised to meet my dear husband, let's hope he's still standing. Bye Bentley, see you sometime."

"Um, Melody?"

"Yes Bentley?"

"May I suggest you cover up a little before you enter the bar."

"Why so, Mr Browne?"

"To avoid words with Mr Jugg Melody."

"Concerning?"

"Your mode of dress madam."

She acknowledged Bentley's concern with a smile.

"We have spoken of this concern previously Bentley but he implied that as I was from Australia, all nature lovers and part of the commonwealth, he would put aside his concerns and I was very welcome within The Mariners."

"What a hypocrite."

"Yes Bentley, but aren't all you men. See you when I see you, bye bye Bentley."

"Bye bye Melody."

CHAPTER 23

A Change of Direction

At home, seated upon the terrace, large whiskey close to hand, the evening sunshine still dominant upon the landscape, Bentley reflected upon the past week's turn of events since his wife's departure. A week spent with countless trips across the green with little point or purpose many ending in an almost pantomime fashion, hours wasted that could have been better spent in pursuit of his dream, the restoration of Barton Manor House. Rising to his feet, he looked around him. Surrounding him were acres of land supporting a residence so large and overpowering that for the first time since his purchase over two years since, the musician felt some sympathy with his wife's misgivings concerning the purchase of the building and moving so far away from family and friends and a rich social life in Hampstead. Despite his success in renovating 90% of the surrounding garden, returning much of the ground and first floor to former grandeur, much remained to accomplish with more money to be spent on the servant's quarters, the lodge house and returning the greenhouses to Victorian splendour. For the first time the enormity of the task ahead promoted a feeling of isolation and uncertainty concerning his decision to move to Barton Green.

As the sun dipped behind the red cedar, Bentley turned to the comforts of television and a further large scotch. Time approaching 9.30pm, he received a phone call.

"Hello, how can I help you?"

"Ah Bentley, at last you old soak, need to see you pronto."

"Hello Maurice, what are you after?"

"Bentley, don't sound so glum, I'm your agent, I am duty bound to remind you of the many piles of dosh awaiting your return to the big time. You are hot news pal. Not a day goes by without mention of your name on social media. If you don't take advantage of your re-emergence into the world of entertainment, you're a mug Bentley. I must see you, tomorrow, Monday, any time. Look, we must get together as soon as possible. I'll drive down to your place early tomorrow and discuss all the possibilities. Syd and the boys are up for it, what do you say…? Bentley, are you there? Do you hear me?"

With a heavy sigh, a reluctant Bentley spoke to his former manager. "I heard you Maurice. May I remind you I do not have a manager as I am no longer in the music business. What is it you want? I am awaiting a call from Christina, my good wife so make this short will you?"

"Bentley, Syd your old pal has been in touch in need of a little financial help. He reckons a few months back on the road with you and the lads would solve his problems. He hopes I can persuade you to give it some thought. What do you say? I can pop down tomorrow if you wish. All options are open. I have been approached by many big venues Bentley believe me, a return to Glastonbury included, what do you say?"

"No, I'm sorry Maurice, far too busy at the moment, I wish you well. Goodbye."

Once again settled before the television came a further phone call. Crossing the great hall entering the library once again that night in hopeful anticipation of a few pleasant exchange of words with his current wife was surprisingly fulfilled.

"Hello, Barton Manor, current occupant speaking, how can I help you?"

"Silly as ever eh Bentley, nothing changes." came the warm response "How are you Bentley?"

"Missing you Chris, believe it or not."

"I'm missing you too Bentley very much. Drop everything and come out and see me. Join me and the girls. Forget the house. We are due to dock at Barbados tomorrow. Come out please Bentley; join us, like the good old days." Her voice dropped a little, clear emotion evident.

"My darling, I'd love to but I've so much to accomplish. I promise you when I'm done we'll return to the old days, I promise you Chris."

"Have it your way Bentley but I am aware what you've been up to this past week. A night of over indulgence in your favourite watering hole, a night on the piano I believe, well received I heard resulting in a poor police constable stepping in to calm things down and ending up with a black eye. It sounds really charming Bentley."

"Excuse me Christina, if I may interrupt, that is far from the truth. Where did this nonsense come from?"

"You will be surprised Bentley, from many sources of information. I have also been reliably informed that the exterior gates to the grounds are shut and bolted excluding entry and leaving deliverymen, including the poor postman, no alternative other than to drop everything outside. I thought your intention was to have the gates in full working order upon my return, plus the lodge renovated and occupied. From what I've heard, Barton Manor is going to pot, so here is my final word on the subject. If you will not come out to be with your wife as I request, I expect to find, when I return to England, if I ever do, Barton Manor restored to its splendour, gates in working order and the lodge house occupied by security, do I make myself clear Bentley?"

"Yes, you do my love. What you wish is my intention to produce, that is why I have not joined you abroad as much as I would wish to."

"Enough Bentley, I shall leave you to your glass of whiskey, the captain's table awaits me, cocktail hour. Once again, I am guest of honour, must not delay, I shall speak to you again Bentley. In time, hopefully I shall be informed a little less readily of your somewhat dodgy involvement in Barton Green and all its comings and goings. Goodnight Bentley, sleep well."

Spot on 10.00am the following day, Bentley was seated at his desk in the library, phone directory close by, determined in his quest to find experienced builders to complete the restoration work at the manor house as soon as possible. Phone in hand and reaching for the directory, Bentley was reluctantly forced upon his feet to answer frequent irritating tappings upon the French window. Once opened he was confronted by his junior horticultural operative.

"What's up boy, I'm busy?"

"Sorry governor, it's Grandad, he won't be on duty today, Grandma says he's suffering from a summer virus, it's the heat she says."

"Oh, does he boy, sure it's not too many pints consumed at a cricket match on Sunday afternoon?"

"No, no governor, nothing to do with the best bitter, anyway, Grandad enjoys a brandy, he wouldn't touch bitter," came the solemn response, "makes him go to the lav too often."

"Oh well, thanks for telling me lad, nice to know, still, that's saved me a few shillings in wages eh, your grandad being absent for the day."

"Huh, Grandad said you would say that skipper. He told me to tell you he is entitled to three days sick pay, it's on our contract, signed by Mrs Browne."

"Oh is that so? News to me, still I'm sure I'll find the money from somewhere, perhaps sell an acre or more of pastureland, what do you think boy?"

"Up to you governor," came the bemused reply.

"It is boy, up to me. Now on your way, plenty to do have you, that's if you're stopping lad, after all it has gone 10.00am."

"I'm here for the day gov, yes."

"The day, don't you mean the afternoon, the morning has almost gone."

The boy pulled a face. "I got caught up with Grandma, sorry gov."

"Yes, well OK lad, carry on then." Plenty to do have you?"

"Well Grandad said I should concentrate on watering. The way things are going heat wise he said sooner or later there would be hose ban, so I'll get the sprinklers out and set them up by the front, is that OK governor?"

"Well, you've had your instructions from your grandad boy, so I should carry on with it. I'll catch up with you later, I've got a lot to do, busy, busy."

"OK gov."

"Look hang on lad, can you stop calling me gov?"

"OK skipper."

Returning to his desk, seated for a further two hours contacting many local firms, a waste of time and energy all proving to be too small in personnel or ambition to consider such a challenge as Barton Manor. Finally calling it a day and locking all doors securely behind him, Bentley took to the outside world, encountering the young lad out among the front landscape, hose in hand.

"Ah there you are lad. I need a favour from you. Stop what you are doing if you would please and nip along to the barn and return here with one of the sit on mowers, I'm going for a trip across the green, enjoy a spell of the weather for a change, pop into The Mariners perhaps, it doesn't matter which one you bring back providing that the tyres are full of air. I will meet you at the gates, that ok?"

The lad looked at Bentley with some misgivings. "I can't do that guvnor."

"Oh, why? Don't tell me there's no petrol in the tank, bit like me eh?" Bentley laughed. "What's the problem?"

"Oh it's not that governor, there's no keys."

"What do you mean, no keys?"

"Well, Grandad takes the keys home with him after work in case we have a break in. Mrs Browne told him to do it ages ago, said it was too inviting, them being left on the machines."

Bentley looked at the lad in disbelief. "You're telling me that your grandad takes home the keys of the mowers on the orders of my good dear wife due to fear of a break in at the manor house?"

"Yes governor. Don't forget the gates aren't fixed yet, they are always open to the world and your Mrs was worried."

"But I lock them now boy, with a padlock and chain."

"Yes you do now governor, but not before."

"Well yes, you may have a point, I stand reprimanded, but here we are or should I say here I am, living in the grand manor house, a reward for many years of toil and trouble, a home of magnificence, within a courtyard for protection, wired to the local police force, brick walls some sixteen foot high, three miles in length, embedded at the top with sharp metal spikes preventing any climber, embellished by two iron gates almost as large as Buckingham Palace, locked and bolted to restrict entry and your grandad and my wife implied Barton Manor is in danger of a break-in with the theft of a mower or two, a motivation, good grief lad." Bentley turned away in exasperation. "When you next see your grandad lad tell him I want all ignition keys back and to remain in place from now on, comprende?"

"What? I don't understand?"

"It's Spanish for do you understand lad or perhaps Greek or something else, what does it matter, do you get the point?"

"I think so, skipper, yes."

"Good, right then, now let's move on. What is your name, I can't keep calling you lad or boy, it's disrespectful, similar to you calling me governor or skipper, my name is Mr Browne or Bentley, now tell me your name. I'm sure it's a long time since you've heard it I imagine, always being called lad and boy by your grandad, can you remember your name?" Bentley teased.

The boy adopted a sour expression biting upon his protruding bottom lip. Avoiding the jet of water heading his way Bentley raised an arm in warning. "Steady on lad, just a bit of fun."

"My name is Nigel, Nigel Rawlings."

"Ah, thank you. Alright then Nigel, how old are you just for the record?"

"Seventeen and a half, just over."

"Right, we got that sorted, good to meet you Nigel. And Nigel, if I may be so familiar, if at some point today you should see a chap arrive outside the gates, middle aged, short in stature, moustache, possible red bow tie, full of himself, stands out like a boil on the nose, driving a yellow Rolls Royce, you can't mistake him, he's my agent but I don't want to see him at present, so please tell him I'm not at home, OK Nigel?"

The boy nodded thoughtfully. "Where shall I tell him you are then governor?"

Bentley looked at the boy in exasperation. "Nigel, please call me Bentley or Mr Browne. Listen, you don't know where I am Nigel, that's the point, I don't want him to know or you actually where I am. If he persists hoping to get in by whatever the method by ramming the gates or climbing the wall, shoot him with a shotgun, OK Nigel?"

The boy pursed his lips. "Well in the first case Mr Browne I haven't got a shotgun, second, I'm without a licence and to own a shotgun without a licence is against the law and to shoot a chap would be a crime, right? I am not into that governor, sorry."

Bentley sighed wearily. "Ah OK lad, just another bad joke. Tell him I've gone on holiday for a few days."

"Where to governor?"

"Oh God help me, best you don't know lad, I'm off out. As you can see, I'm taking the keys to the gates with me." Bentley spun the key fob around his index finger. "Ok Nigel?"

"Yes skipper."

"And don't dream of letting him in through your private point of entry in the walled garden OK, now or at any point, otherwise your three day sickness agreement with my wife is at a risk, understand?"

"Yes, governor."

"Right I'm off, see you later."

"What time skipper?"

"Oh, Lord above."

As the clock struck 12.00 midday, Bentley reached the entrance to The Mariners entering the familiar comforts of the lounge. He was greeted, as often the case, with good-natured banter from the familiar crowd of regulars standing at the bar. Making his way through the midday gathering Bentley headed towards the only available bar stool standing somewhat isolated at the far end of the bar close to the entrance to the restaurant. Hoping to catch the barmaid's eye, he was subject to a deep-throated roar from the far corner of the room calling for his company.

"Bentley, Bentley my friend, over here, join me."

Across the way seated in the most favoured spot within the room overlooking the green, Albert, discarded newspaper to one side, coffee cup in hand, was a picture of relaxed contentment. Seated with him were three female employees. Having dutifully received final instructions relating to their afternoon shift they rose to their feet, ushered away with a good-natured clap of the hands. "Away you go ladies, bye bye."

Crossing the floor, the three young women, encountering an approaching Bentley Browne, came to an abrupt halt. Standing politely to one side, in unison, the trio acknowledged the passing musician with a deep sweeping curtsey followed by an exaggerated bow, much to the amusement of many onlookers and indeed Bentley himself.

Finally overcome with a prolonged fit of the giggles,

the trio left the lounge to much noisy appreciation from the many men standing at the bar.

Joining Albert in the alcove, he was greeted with a warm handshake. "Good to see you Bentley, you are a popular fella old chap, no doubt about that."

"Reward of show business Albert."

"Quite so Bentley and why not. Come on, join me for a drink, I am in relaxed mode, well at least for an hour or so I hope." He turned to Bentley displaying a boyish optimism. "Bentley, business is booming my friend, however, there is a downside, I'm washed out, ready for the knackers yard, so is the wife, daughter and loyal staff, what with the cricket match yesterday, accompanied by high temperatures and endless sunshine. We didn't shut shop until way after midnight so today we are all hoping for a little light relief hence my determination to remain seated for the next 60 minutes at least. Now, enough about me, what about you, what brings you in so early, escape from the chateau?" he laughed.

"Yes, very good Albert, strangely enough there are similarities in lifestyle. Today I am here because I need a break from a worthless quest to secure decent building contractors to continue work at the manor so I thought I'd visit my spiritual home, The Mariners, well according to my wife it is anyway."

"Ah Mrs Browne eh Bentley, have you managed to speak to her yet?"

"I have, yes Albert, last night, she phoned me believe it or not."

"How is she?"

"Fine, in talking mode, just off to have dinner at the captain's table. She would like me to fly out and join her in the Canary Isles as soon as poss."

"Really, are you going to?"

"No, I have to push on with the construction work, if I can find anyone to do it that is."

"If I may say so Bentley I just can't understand why it is such a problem, why don't you get the previous contractors that did so much when you moved in to return, you were full of praise for them, what's the problem?"

"Please Albert don't go there, it's not something I want to talk about, it's a long story."

"That's OK Bentley, I've got the time, it's my hour off remember," Albert laughed, "I like a little relaxation and gossip. So tell me all Bentley. It will remain between us, trust me."

Bentley sighed. "Well, unknown to me at the time the workforce tired of the wife's criticism."

"Was she not happy with their work?"

"Yes, something like that. I never realised at the time, mind you, my interest in golf was at a high. Do you remember Albert, you introduced me to it."

"Of course I do Bentley, although we haven't played together for a while have we, every time I suggest a game these days you say you are much too tied up with the manor, I thought you'd gone cold on the game if truth be told."

"No, not that Albert, it's just that as soon as Musgrove & Co walked out I've been in limbo land, I need another company as soon as possible to carry on the work and then perhaps I'll return to the putting green, who knows."

"Well, I'm all for that Bentley but tell me old boy, why did Musgrove Limited walk out on you in the first place, it wasn't money problems I hope?" Albert teased. "You did pay the bills I trust, it couldn't have been just because of criticism surely."

"It was Albert and yes, money is no problem. The cause of dissent according to their managing director Norman Giddings was that the lads tired of endless interference by my wife. They packed up and left almost overnight without apology or explanation, unbeknown to me. The following day I received a phone call from head office telling me they would not be returning, the reason being I was told in no uncertain manner was that whilst I was away most days playing golf my good wife would patrol the manor house forever fault finding be it excessive dust filling the house from floor to ceiling, general noise, music played at an excessive level but most hard to take and most infuriating to them all was her endless questioning of the quality of their workmanship, endlessly citing her Italian heritage and the wonders of Italian craftsmanship, belittling English workmen producing poor standards of workmanship. So that was that. After over a year of never-ending fault-finding, they'd had enough. Giddings even suggested that one of the chippies suffered a mental breakdown, can you believe it? Mind you," Bentley reflected, "I often returned home from the course mid-afternoon to catch sight of the workmen packing up for the day looking as miserable as sin. They didn't say a word to me about their problems, most of them ignoring me. I thought it was because they had little time for my dated music. Life in show business can make you very sensitive you know Albert," Bentley laughed, "but thankfully it was nothing to do with me, it's a critical wife, not unusual though is it Albert, we've all been there."

Albert nodded in agreement. "We have indeed Bentley, such is life. What did she have to say in her defence when you told her the reason for their departure?"

"Nothing. I didn't tell her the truth, I told her they had other commitments to attend to."

"Well, how did she take to that?"

"Fine, she was glad they had gone. Thankfully she said the manor house had returned to peace and quiet, suggesting we move out for some length of time, perhaps have a holiday and during our absence find another firm to continue with the renovation and then return home with everything completed but I said no, insisted she would have to take a break on her own and I'd stay home, that was my wish. I have seen much of the world, I've seen it all. I have a personal interest in the completion of the work at the manor house, mainly paying the bills that's for sure, but also I want to be around this time and see the house return to its splendour. It is my home, what the hell, be some influence here and there. I know I'm not a plumber, just a simple musician but I can help and now is the time to get cracking and find another firm whilst the good lady is on holiday. So there you are Albert, you know it all. No gossip please, had I realised the wife was such a problem things may have been different."

"Well, I can understand your resolve to finish the work Bentley but what I don't understand is your difficulty in securing another building firm, I can't believe it. God almighty, this place is buzzing with seasoned builders, car parks full of posh pickups, all stopping off for a drink then heading for home. Good God, they would sell their souls to work for a show business legend such as yourself, Bentley. Let me ask around, leave it to me, I'll find someone."

Bentley raised his arms in slight agitation. "Er no, I'm talking quality workforce Albert not bobajob lads. I need the best and I am prepared to pay whatever it costs, well within reason. I spent much of the morning phoning around only to be disappointed. Many did not have a large enough workforce and those that did were interested but fully booked for months ahead, so there are you, I'm stuck in forever land."

Albert rose to his feet. "I'm sorry to hear you're in such difficulties Bentley I really am. Let me get you a drink, cheer you up, what's it to be, whiskey?"

"Good God, no thanks, I shan't be stopping long Albert, I need to return home before the young gardener floods the cellars."

"Sorry, don't get it, cellars where, here? Flooding in this weather, what are you on about Bentley?"

"Oh, just private thoughts Albert, take no notice. A coffee will be fine, thanks."

"Right, remain seated Bentley, I shall pop into the restaurant and order a coffee. Drop of brandy in it?" Albert teased.

"No thank you Albert. Look, I'll get it Albert you stay here, enjoy your break."

An impervious Albert Judd stood his ground. "Bentley, I'm going, stay seated," within a minute returning to the table. "On its way Bentley, on its way, I shall be having one with you."

"With or without brandy Albert?"

"Without Bentley, of course."

"I believe you Albert, without question."

Relaxing for a moment, the pair gazed out upon the green.

"Do you know something Bentley?"

"Probably not, Albert, no."

"Well, we are very lucky in Barton, don't you agree?"

"If you say so Albert."

The landlord gestured out upon the village green. "Look at that view. Acres of natural beauty, outstanding village life set out before us. Old church, village pond, wonderful cricket pitch, first class team as we all witnessed yesterday. English village life at its very best, don't you agree Bentley?"

"I do, Albert, I do, it's a wonderful view and it is the reason I pay a visit to The Mariners from time to time, it's certainly not for the best bitter."

"Well, for whatever reason you visit Bentley, I am always pleased to see you."

"Thank you Albert, most kind. Now, you are aware are you that the land we look out upon with such pleasure, some eight acres or so of open landscape once belonged to Barton Manor, are you?"

"That rings a bell Bentley, tell me a little more."

"Well, local resident Alice Coates compiled a history of Barton-on-the-Green some years ago. She has passed away now unfortunately but it is a very intriguing read if you're into that kind of thing, which of course you are Albert, so I am rather surprised you haven't read it. The land was bequeathed to the village folk in 1913 by local MP William Wiggins, owner of Barton Manor. Once again, I must say Albert I am rather surprised at your lack of knowledge what with your delight in associating The Mariners with the Royal Navy. There's enough memorabilia hanging from the walls and ceiling to fill a junk shop," Bentley laughed.

"Oh well, perhaps I'll borrow it one day Bentley when I get the time to read it. Ooh look up, coffee arriving."

Recognising the approaching waitress Bentley rose to his feet. "Albert, what is your daughter doing waiting on tables. Hardly the job of a TV celebrity chef," he teased.

"Sshhh Bentley, keep your voice down, she's not in a particularly good mood this morning." Albert replied in a whisper. "She's worn out poor girl."

Reaching the table, Alice Jugg stood before them, tray in hand, pale faced and expressionless.

"Hello Alice, how are you young lady?" Bentley greeted her.

"Bloody knackered if you must know Bentley." Placing the two coffees upon the table, she turned and returned to the restaurant without further comment.

"Mmm, as you say Albert, in need of a good break I would say. Pass the sugar please old chap."

"Yes, she's tired, worn out poor girl, needs a break. This past week has been chaotic, never been so busy, well, ever since your stint on the piano my friend, I blame you Bentley," he laughed. "It's getting to her at the present. I must promote someone to stand in for her capable of running the restaurant for a few days so she can get some sun on her face, a bit of relaxation. I can't ask the wife to take over the responsibility of the restaurant on top of everything else she does. Still, never mind, life goes on. Business is thriving that's the good thing and if it carries on like this I will have to get a manager in, perhaps retire to Palm Springs, what do you say Bentley, good move?"

Bentley nodded somewhat ruefully. "Yes, spot on Albert, I'll come and visit you, wonderful golf courses."

"Erm Bentley, I know this is a change of direction but tell me, that chap yesterday looking for you, scruffy man, I told him to go and put a shirt on, remember?"

"How could I forget Albert?"

"Well last night in the bar the main conversation was centred on that chap selling ice cream cones on the green, many recognised him as your old band mate, guitarist, erm?

"Syd Mitchell."

"That's it Bentley, Syd Mitchell. According to the many that recognised him he was a bit of a lad during your golden years I believe."

Bentley nodded in agreement. "Still is Albert, I wouldn't be surprised, despite losing his hair and looks. He was a little excitable in the early days. Fame and fortune Albert, everything comes at a cost my friend."

Albert moved a little closer, tone of voice dropping, interest growing. "Tell me Bentley, do you miss performing?"

"I do, without a doubt, but not as much as I thought I would have to be honest, why do you ask? Hey listen, don't you ask me to perform here again and certainly not tonight anyway."

Albert laughed. "No, no. The reason I ask Bentley is how did you cope with the excitement after a show with all the adrenaline flowing, it must have been hard to come back down to earth surely? One often reads of partying going on all night, sometimes for days with endless drinking, groupies, a life of over indulgence. Tell me what, was it like?"

"What you are asking Albert is what were the ladies like, am I right?

"Well, naturally I'm a man of passion Bentley and it is always hinted at in the press." Albert persisted.

"Yes Albert, temptations of course everywhere but as you age a little common sense and restraint comes into force and in my case, I calmed down a bit. In truth there was a period of my life when I found show business a bit of a sham, full of B celebrities, attention seekers, much like today Albert if truth be told but please don't quote me. Are you aware that much of the music business consists of folk with little talent where many cannot sing or play a note without help from the recording studios who with a twist of a knob and the turn of a switch, electronic interference enhances the recording. The amount of so-called artists I have run into in my lifetime are endless who, during a live performance, cannot reproduce a studio sound for love nor money. As for today's lot, I would go for Last Night of the Proms for an authentic sound if I were you."

"Ah, but what about you Bentley, your very popular recordings, all hits or thereabouts. Did they receive a little help in the recording studio?" Albert retorted.

"Of course Albert," Bentley laughed, "but keep it to yourself please, old boy."

"Ah, so you are no different from the rest eh, Bentley, a bit of a con artist?"

"Of course Albert, but I can put together three or four chords if pushed."

"I know Bentley, you are a master of your arts and I'm pulling your leg. Did you ever tire of playing?"

"Yes, I did for a while as it happens, always travelling, never at home, a job to muster up enthusiasm at times, probably an age thing in the end, mind you, during my heyday it had its upsides, periods of extravagance, top record sales, plenty of money. I invested in property in the early days, offshore investments and the cash rolled in, I did well. Mind you, three divorce settlements in the intervening years stripped me of a little of my savings to say the least, but we won't go there but if a further catastrophic divorce ever happens I probably will end up living in a semi in Uxbridge. Life can take many paths as you know Albert, but this may be of interest to you as you are in the mood for conversation."

Bentley continued. "A few years ago the band's drummer Angus Pertwee got married, something he soon regretted as it happens but that's another story. The wedding reception was held in a hotel in Eastbourne, her hometown, the name of the hotel being The Grange, privately owned of high status situated away from the beachfront on high ground. The view from the penthouse, which I was fortunate enough to occupy for the night, was awesome, a different world, I loved it, the view and peace and quiet was as good as anything I had ever experienced. At the time I was heading for a divorce from my second wife so without her in tow, or as it happens a regular lady friend, I was alone but I awoke around midday slightly under the weather to say the least with company. No Albert, not what you're thinking. It was a Siamese cat, very affectionate and it stayed with me all afternoon as I sat on the balcony recovering from the previous night. I enjoyed the view and company so much I booked in for a further night. Then that evening in the bar, I was introduced to the owner and engaged him in conversation. Business was good he told me, much as yours Albert is at the moment," Bentley laughed, "and he was in mind to purchase some available adjoining land to increase the size of the hotel. One thing led to another and a further drink or two, I take out my chequebook, place it on the counter and write a cheque for £2,500,000.00. Yes, I can see what you are thinking but I secured a 25% share in the hotel on the provision, two of them actually, one being I would have access to the penthouse whenever in the area without cost of course if available, one has to be fair, secondly, a cat flap discreetly placed at the bottom of the door so that should the cat, by the way I discovered was named Barney, wish to join me at any time I was present, entry and departure would be easy for him. They agreed and all was confirmed and signed within weeks. I stopped many times over the following years whenever in need of a little piece and quiet and the company of Barney. I never told any of my future wives that I had access to such a hideaway implying work commitments for any of my sudden and increasing departures when I was in need of peace and quiet. I don't blame them for thinking I was up to no good, the reason given for all subsequent divorces of course, but despite my past lifestyle, I was not up to anything, I just loved the view, solitude and the cat's company. He always seemed to know when I was there. I loved that cat." Bentley signed.

"So what happened Bentley? The hotel, the cat, do you still go there?"

"No, I haven't been back ever since I retired in 2003.

I can't keep disappearing for days on end without explanation any longer, but my holiday home is still flourishing I believe."

"What about the cat?"

"Ahh dead I would imagine Albert. I really must make the effort to visit sometime; it would do me good, fine memories."

Bentley struggled to his feet. "Right Albert, I'm getting stiff sitting here, that's me, I'm done, off home. I've told you more than I should, I could be open to blackmail here if I'm not careful."

"Oh don't go Bentley, have another coffee, better still let's have a drink together, small whiskey or something. Oops, funny I should say that, look behind you, we have a visitor."

An ever-alert landlord rose to his feet pointing towards the bar. "Your pal Chuffer Rudd, Bentley. Chuffer, over here."

"Oh God, time I was off, not my day for Chuffer, Albert."

"Hang on Bentley, don't go yet," a restraining hand upon his shoulder, Bentley remained seated.

"I must say Albert that it comes to mind that you are very generous with your invitations these days, two invites in one day, unheard of from you."

"Well, why not Bentley, life is too short and I'm having an hour off you might remember, anyway he is good company, Chuffer; he might even put his hand in his pocket and buy us a drink, tight old sod."

"That's a little unlikely Albert as you well know, anyway once again I've already told you, I don't want a drink this lunchtime, no happy hour today thank you sir."

"Oh don't be such a misery Bentley, a small one won't hurt you. Ah, here comes the old boy. Welcome, Chuffer."

Standing before them rotund as a beer barrel without a tap, Chuffer greeted the two with a broad grin. "Good to see you lads, not often I'm invited to join two VIPs at the table, what's the occasion, one of you won the lottery have you?" he teased.

"No, not quite Chuffer but our friend Bentley is a little unsettled today, be kind to him," Albert teased. "He can't find a group of good tradesmen to continue work at the manor house, can you Bentley."

A somewhat irate Bentley looked across the table at the landlord. "Please Albert, Chuffer is not interested in my problems, he has better things to do."

Albert raised his hands in apology. "Sorry Bentley, it just occurred to me that his lads could have been some help to you as you are so desperate."

"I'm not that desperate, Albert, never have been and never will, if I wanted their help I would have asked him weeks ago."

Standing at the corner of the table overlooking the two a deep frown upon his forehead, Chuffer tapped upon an eardrum with a forefinger several times in annoyance. "Sorry chaps, I can't hear a word you're saying, give me a moment or two I'll sort it out." Removing his hearing aid, he blew upon it whilst checking the battery. After several minutes and returning the aid to its place of rest, normality was embraced with a welcome sigh of relief. "Ah sorry lads, thanks for your patience, now then, where were we, what did you say earlier Albert?"

Albert shook his head vaguely. "Nothing important Chuffer, was it Bentley?"

"No, not that I'm aware of Albert." Chuffer joined them at the table looking at the pair in amusement. "Right, I'll be off for a drink then, is there anything you two require."

Pointing towards the empty coffee cups that was placed at the end of the table, Chuffer offered a refill. "Coffee my friends?"

"Well that's very kind of you to offer Chuffer but a brandy would go down rather well at the moment, what say you Bentley?"

Bentley nodded in somewhat reluctant agreement. "Yes I say so, good idea, while you're at it why not make it doubles, eh Albert."

"Yes, why not Bentley, good idea."

Chuffer rose to his feet, once again fiddling with his earpiece. "Sorry chaps, bloody thing, can't hear a word you're saying, must be a fading battery, two coffees was it? Sugar?"

Within several minutes, Chuffer returned to the table, tray in hand. "Here you are gentlemen, two coffees as requested. Great victory yesterday eh chaps?" He raised his glass in the air. "Here's to us, Barton-on-the-Green first eleven, cheers lads!"

Albert viewed his coffee with some dismay. "If I may say so Chuffer it's a little off the beam to celebrate such a momentous occasion with a mug of coffee, don't you agree Bentley?"

Bentley nodded in mock agreement "Oh without a doubt Albert, now a drop of brandy, that's a different matter."

Chuffer joined the two of them at the table. "I suggest you try it gentlemen, you may be pleasantly surprised." A quick toast of appreciation, a rueful Albert returned his mug to the table, nudging his friend. "Brandy Bentley, drink up."

Gazing out upon the green the three embraced several moments of quiet appreciation lost in their own world, finally disturbed in their moment of peace and quiet by the arrival at the table of a waitress with a few words in the ear of the landlord, rather concerned that the bar was under siege and in need of some assistance. "Give me a moment Sarah please, I'm on holiday," a slightly irritated Albert ushering the girl away. Raising his glass, "Cheers chaps, another few minutes I shall have to leave, good to see you both, I've enjoyed it."

"Chuffer addressed the landlord. "Albert, what was it you were saying earlier concerning our friend here, Bentley. Some difficulty in securing suitable builder lads I believe, is that so? Yes, before you ask, I heard you both. Don't look so surprised Bentley, it's amazing what you can hear if you pretend to have hearing difficulties," Chuffer giggled. "Old trick of mine. When I was in the army stationed in Aldershot, I used to drive the regimental sergeant major potty. I was only eighteen, first time away from home," he laughed "good old days but I must be truthful Bentley, I was a little put out when you implied that you would only use my lads as a last resort. I do recall not so long ago a considerable amount of stonework laid and completed in just a few weeks right in the middle of winter. I must add, the work absolutely transformed the rear of Barton Manor, enhancing the garden. You were well satisfied at the time I recall, even your good wife was very impressed, her comments were most commendable, what say you Bentley my friend."

"True enough Chuffer," Bentley conceded "your lads did a cracking job, no complaints whatsoever, even from the matron of the manor. As you say, she was well pleased."

"Thank you Bentley. May I further add whilst I'm on my soapbox that my lads could have achieved a lot more at the manor had you stuck with us and not employed a fancy firm from Portsmouth, Messrs Musgrove & Co. They must have cost you a small fortune and then to top it all they walk out on you because Mrs Browne was a little too critical. I ask you, what sissies! Me and my boys have suffered more criticism over the years than anyone, but we don't pack it in."

"Well, that is reassuring Chuffer, I will definitely put you on my list if ever I'm in need of someone to change the light bulbs in The Mariners, always a job I've found rather tricky." Keeping a straight face Albert rose to his feet. "Right gentlemen, who's for another without the coffee. Brandy Bentley?"

"Good idea Albert, why not."

"Chuffer, same again?"

"Of course, old chap."

Watching the landlord depart towards the bar, Chuffer tapped upon the table in slight irritation. "Bentley, let me tell you, I have known for months the reason they left, although you never mentioned it to me personally. I am a businessman, I keep everything close to my chest, that's my way. I knew sooner or later you would come to me and the lads for help so here I am Bentley, take advantage of my forgiving nature and tell me what you want doing my friend."

Bentley sighed inwardly sensing a tricky few moments in store. "It's not as easy as that Chuffer, it's a lot of work, some of it a little difficult shall we say."

"Bentley, Bentley," Chuffer interrupted, "listen to me. My lads are as capable as any and turn their hands to anything. Shall I tell you something?"

"I fear you're going to Chuffer."

"Indeed I am Bentley. A few years ago, I received a call at home and my boys and I were offered a job on the Isle of Wight. Guess where Bentley?"

"I'm sure you're going to tell me in a moment Chuffer."

"I am for sure. Queen Victoria's summer residence, Osborne House. We did a lot of renovation and repair and we were there for months, it's on our working portfolio, I must show you it sometime."

"Mmm sounds interesting Chuffer. Did you ever meet her?"

"Meet who?"

"Well, Her Majesty, Queen Victoria."

Chuffer paused for a moment. "No, not personally Bentley but I met an old boy, bit of a gardener who knew her well."

"Really?"

"Oh yes, yes. What with the passing of time and so forth she was a little forgetful you know and when it came to settling our account he helped enormously, popping in to see her personally and had her sign the cheque, good of him eh."

Re-joining the two at the table, Albert was greeted with much laughter. "You seem happy chaps, what's the joke?"

"Life and times of Queen Victoria, Albert."

"Oh, well I'll give it a miss Bentley, before my time, cheers lads. Have you settled your differences Bentley?"

"Differences, what differences Albert? I have been explaining to Chuffer my thoughts for the future. Foremost the gates wired up and in working order controlled from within a renovated lodge house and occupied by a good natured 24 hour security chap, perhaps with a family, all to prevent the theft of lawnmowers."

"Lawnmowers?"

Bentley burst into laughter. "Sorry lads, another thought, I'm losing it, must be the brandy. What I was about to say was that after the gates and lodge there is the question of the Victorian glasshouses that I…"

Bentley was interrupted by an excited Chuffer. "Ah Bentley, the greenhouses. I was speaking to, you know, the man, the entrepreneur, pork sausage magnate, well I was talking to him this morning, he asked if …"

"Chuffer, please don't go there, the greenhouses are not up for discussion, not for sale under any circumstances, nor the land they sit upon so please tell our sausage magnate next time you see him, end of subject. As for you and the boys, I would consider future assistance to help with the lodge house and gates, providing you can begin work within days. Failing that I shall look elsewhere, it's up to you Chuffer."

"Yes, yes, I'm up for that Bentley." Chuffer extended a hand. "Shake on it. Strangely enough my lads have had a little difficulty securing payment for a roofing job in Lower Barton, couldn't come at a better time."

Chuffer rose to his feet. "Well, time I was off, it's approaching 1 o'clock and the daughter-in-law's cooking homemade steak and kidney pudding and if I'm late my lads would have eaten it all. Must go, good to see you both. I will bring the lads to the manor sometime tomorrow Bentley so you can tell us what you want doing and I'll give you a price somewhat, see what we can do ok? Thanks Bentley, be seeing you Albert."

Watching Chuffer depart Albert turned to Bentley. "Do you know Bentley, I've only just discovered this several weeks ago. Chuffer owns 300 acres of farmland in Lower Barton, been in the family over 200 years, can you believe that. Five sons, strapping lads all of them, use the bar a lot they do. As for farming, that's not all they can do, they turn their hands to anything, so I was told anyway."

Bentley nodded. "True Albert, true. I visited their farm once a while ago. Farm shop full of their own produce. All the lads are married and living there in converted barns, outhouses etc, almost a village within itself and several of the lads wives run a donkey sanctuary and believe it or not the farmyard is used for coach alterations and car repairs, you wouldn't believe it, one hell of a hive of activity. The comings and goings are unbelievable, makes you wonder if it's always above board if I'm honest, a lot of dodgy looking characters hanging around in groups, still one thing is for sure Albert, if our constable gets wind of any wrong doing he will be on them quicker than a case of measles." Bentley started to laugh. "I can just picture him standing out in the field overlooking the farmyard, up to his knees in broccoli disguised as a scarecrow on surveillance duty, Barton's answer to Worzel Gummidge."

"Just doing his duty though," Albert added. The pair roared with laughter. Finally, Albert rose to his feet. "Ah, what a laugh eh Bentley but I must go and return to work, I'm getting some dirty looks from the bar staff, they are a little busy. But before I depart, tell me, how old is Chuffer?"

Bentley thought for a moment. "No idea, but if he was in the army on National Service as he hinted at I would say he was early 80's somewhat."

"Good grief really, doesn't look it does he? A little overweight perhaps but looks well, must be country living Bentley."

"Must be Albert, there's hope for all of us."

A cry for assistance from behind the bar hastened Albert's departure. "Have to go Bentley otherwise I'll have a strike on my hands. Another drink?"

"No thanks, I'm fine Albert."

Lost in engaging thoughts of Constable Willoughby

dressed as Worzel Gummidge, Bentley was slow to notice the appearance of Maurice Gibbins dressed in flamboyant attire crossing the room headed in his direction, his mode of dress causing much amusement and comment by the many alert to his arrival.

"Ah Bentley, found you at last, thank God, I've lost valuable time looking for you. I've spent the last hour outside your place. Tried phoning you with no answer naturally and the gates are padlocked with no entry. I finally spotted a lad watering the garden and asked him as to your whereabouts and he said nothing, just pointed towards the village then turned his back on me so I climbed back into the Rolls, circled the village, spotted the pub and put two and two together regarding your fondness for a little recreational drink etc and found you, clever aren't I?"

Maurice looked around him. "What a splendid watering hole Bentley, no wonder it's your second home, may I join you old chap?"

"Be my guest Maurice but let me tell you, you're wasting your time. I know why you're here. I am not returning to the road, my time in the limelight is over."

Maurice glanced down upon his watch. "Oh good God, is that the time, I've got to be in London in an hour. Look, hear me out Bentley please, one word to set that blood racing."

"One word?"

"Yes, one word Bentley."

"Go on."

"Vinyl. Vinyl, Bentley."

"Vinyl? Yes, so?"

"A resurgence of vinyl recordings." Maurice moved closer. "Its popularity is growing." Bentley looked at his agent in puzzlement.

"So, I am aware of it, what's your point Maurice?"

"Bentley, Bentley, think. The return of popularity of vinyl recordings and your re-emergence in local news etc on the television and radio. You must take advantage of it. Let's get you on TV, interviews, back on song, big money. I have spoken to our recording company and they are up for it. Think Bentley, Moonrock Rumble on vinyl with your greatest hits? Think of it. A gravy train, public consciousness, a return of Bentley mania. Don't tell me that doesn't excite you Bentley? Come on, a show business legend such as yourself, you wouldn't be human."

"Well, convince me Maurice; tell me exactly what you have in mind for my re-emergence into the limelight."

Aware of many overhearing their conversation, Maurice lowered his tone. "Well first of all, a hot spell of publicity with appearances on TV and radio as I've said coupled with live appearances in big venues by you and the boys, speaking of which, should you agree, would be overjoyed by your decision Bentley."

Once again, Maurice looked at his watch with dismay. "Oh God, I've got to go, spent too much time sitting outside your place Bentley. I've got an appointment in London at 3pm, business, possible clients, girl band, not my cup of tea but…" he shrugged, "it's business. So you'll leave it all to me to see what I can come up with, yes? I'll get in touch in the next few days and outline a future direction. If we can agree on the path to follow we will be up and running. What do you say, rebirth in vinyl, come on Bentley, what can be better?"

"You do what you have to Maurice and I'll give it some thought, but you do know my wife will have the final say in this don't you?"

"Don't they all Bentley, right I'll be off."

"Maurice, before you go, one question."

"Yes, what would that be Bentley?"

"Why do you dress like a circus clown?"

"To invite attention Bentley, good for business my

friend. I will be in touch, so long."

Standing at the window to witness Maurice Gibbins departing from The Mariners car park with an extravagant double hoot on the horn and a wave of the hand, the yellow Rolls Royce convertible headed towards Guildford, final destination, London.

Already suffering many misgivings concerning his abject surrender to his agent's proposal, Bentley returned to his seat, closed his eyes, head in hands seeking a few moments quiet reflection before a return to the manor house. "May I join you?" Bentley raised his head, opening his eyes to a delightful picture of grace, beauty and mischief.

"Good Lord, Melody, what are you doing here?"

"Same as you Mr Browne, in need of a little relaxation and good company, time to forget the world's problems for a spell. Well Bentley, who was he?"

"He, who?"

"Bentley, don't be difficult, the chap who has just left you, the dedicated follower of fashion," she giggled.

"Oh him." Bentley sighed.

"Yes, him."

Engaging the closest seat possible, she reached for his arm. "Well, who was he, a former band member?"

"Well yes, you would think so young lady to look at him but as a matter of fact he was my agent, Maurice Gibbins, down from London for a brief visit, wants me to return to the world of show business."

"Oh, a return to Butlins on the cards is it Bentley?"

Bentley laughed. "Yes, you may take the mickey young woman but I can assure you I will not be returning to Bognor, always raining when I was there if I remember," he paused in reflection. "Yes, always raining, never stopped. Tell me, how did you know I was once a redcoat?"

"I was teasing you Bentley, I had no idea." Melody let go of his arm. "Bentley, a drink is on its way, you are stopping I hope."

"No, not for me Melody, I must be off; I've been here far too long as it is, things to do."

Melody held on to his arm again. "No way Mr Browne, I insist you stay, join myself and my good husband for a drink, I am told you like brandy Bentley."

"Who told you that?"

"Albert Jugg of course, the landlord. Now tell me Bentley, what's it to be if it's not a return to Butlins. What has your agent in mind for your future? Could it be Hyde Park or Glastonbury?"

"Huh, I should be so lucky. Depends on many things Melody. What he wants really is for me to return to public consciousness at the same time as a compilation of all my old best sellers are recorded freshly on vinyl and released with the maximum publicity."

"Ah Bentley, sounds a good idea to me, I'm a great fan of Fleetwood Mac and I've heard it on vinyl, it's great, the tone is so different, earthy and honest."

Bentley nodded in agreement. "That's the true attraction but there are many pitfalls should I go ahead, my wife is not keen on my return to show business so I don't know."

"Oh Bentley, I can understand your misgivings," Melody shrugged "but we women are, you know, a little bit apprehensive at times but all relationships are full of uncertainties Bentley. I am married to a man of the cloth for a start," she laughed. "But on a serious note, 'scuse the pun, I'd buy your recording on vinyl. It's nostalgia Bentley to us of a certain age. It could sell like hot cakes, especially at Christmas. Remember Cliff Richard? He made a fortune from Christmas sales. A few months back in business could provide you with enough funds to enhance the manor house in wild extravagance. Just think Bentley, indoor Olympic size swimming pool, ballroom, countless servants, your cup could runneth over Mr Browne," she laughed.

"Enough, enough young lady, I appreciate your humour but my head is in a mess as it is without you adding to it. Please, a change of subject if you want my companionship for a further 5 minutes. Tell me, how is your husband, I hope he is recovering from his wounds?"

"Yes, getting there Bentley thank you. We visited the hospital this morning and they changed the plaster. A couple more weeks and he'll be back on the cricket pitch as good as new. That is why we are here, we thought we'd pop into The Mariners for a minor celebration with a pint or two of Mr Jugg's favourite bitter."

"Bitter Melody, you drink bitter? I'm surprised, I thought you would be one for a glass of rosé."

"No, I'm not as rosé as I may look Bentley. Don't be fooled by one's Doris Days appearance, I'm quite a rough diamond as it happens."

"Such as Calamity Jane?"

Melody roared with laughter. "Yes, not quite, but heading that way. Well, and here we are Wild Bill Hickock. Bentley, meet my husband Sean." Standing beside the table, a man of large stature placed a tray containing several pints and one large brandy before them.

"Pleased to meet you mate, heard a lot about you

Bentley and that's only in gossip columns in the papers." He laughed and extended a hand in greeting. "Just a joke mate, no offence."

Bentley rose to his feet accepting his handshake. "Pleased to meet you vicar."

"Less talk of vicar if you don't mind Bentley, my name's Sean, don't stand on ceremony mate."

Melody laughed. "Come on, drink up you two, no punch up. Here's to the glorious weather, long may it last." The pair raised their glasses. "A fine English pint and wonderful weather, cheers."

The following hour was an introduction into modern Christian philosophy with Bentley warming to the eccentric couple with every increasing minute spent in their company. While naturally strong in their religious leanings, their good-humoured beliefs expressed in overriding good humour, their solutions to the world's problems expressed in strong but somehow inoffensive language and many anecdotes relating to their years in Australia were a source of much amusement for Bentley.

Finally all drink consumed and citing an early evening WI meeting in the village hall as a reason for their early departure, the pair rose to leave insisting upon Bentley that an evening or two at a church service on perhaps a regular basis would help Bentley in God given time of course to reduce his dependency on brandy and perhaps console him and reduce his feelings of isolation and loneliness until his wife's return to Barton. Wishing them well and thanking them for their well-meaning concern for his mental wellbeing, Bentley watched them depart in quiet amusement. Embracing many within the lounge with their cries of 'praise the Lord brothers', the pair left the premises.

Finally, out upon the village green and with some difficulty walking a straight line the couple were very much a cause of amusement to the few out and about on the green who were witness to their laboured progress towards St Michael's Church.

In the hope of finding further agreeable company after the early departure of the engaging religious couple, Bentley left the comfort of the bay window to join the familiar gathering at the bar, welcomed by all, there to remain for several hours until finally calling it a day late afternoon.

Returning to the outside world, he was to be greeted by an unwelcome change in the weather and a noticeable change in temperature, bringing with it low cloud and drizzle and putting an end to all wishful thoughts of an evening spent on the terrace. Crossing an empty green and reaching the manor, he was greeted by a large sack of Royal Mail dropped off close to the gates. Affixed to the neck of the sack was a small note written in pencil, brief and to the point. *"To the lord of the manor – could not enter the premises due to padlocked gates. With love, Postman Pat xx."*

Removing the mailbag out of the rain to leave within the protective deep recess of the lodge porch and with the rainfall increasing by the minute, Bentley walked the meandering driveway with much haste. Entering the courtyard and approaching the cold, unwelcome façade of the building, Bentley was struck by a feeling of uneasy isolation already missing the comfort and companionship of The Mariners. Confined to the inner sanctum of the manor due to the further declining weather, Bentley sought the pleasure of the piano but to little avail finding concentration a little difficult and calling it to a halt within the hour. The possibilities of a return to the limelight with all the additional problems uppermost in his mind. Brandy in hand, he turned to the questionable comfort of the television, there to remain for the rest of the evening, vague witness to much that passed him by without thought or question. Finally retiring to his bed around 10.30pm, there to lay awake much of the night, his mind working overtime, finally drifting off as daybreak approached.

Around 8.45am the following morning a very irate Chuffer Rudd, accompanied by two of his sons, stood outside the impenetrable gates to Barton Manor with growing impatience. Reduced to ringing the house several times that morning without response, Chuffer was in a mind to call it a day but, finally persuaded by his lads to try one more time, he was greeted with welcome success. "Hello?"   "Ah Bentley, at last. Would you be kind enough to open the gates old chap?"

"Er, who exactly am I talking to?"

"For God's sake Bentley, stop messing around, who do you think it is, Father Christmas, it's me Chuffer, we arranged to meet this morning, remember?"

"Oh God, sorry Chuffer, had a bad night, little sleep, give me a moment. What time is it, oh never mind."

Some forty minutes later, a contrite Bentley appeared at the gates still in his dressing gown. "Sorry Chuffer, my sincere apologies."

"Enough apologies Bentley, just let us in, at least thank God the rain has stopped." Once inside the gates the relieved businessman and his team approached the lodge house expressing much verbal relief. "Thank you Bentley, at last. There you are lads. As I told you, much to be done but well within out scope. We start by stripping the ivy from the walls to expose the wonderful Victorian brickwork. Come on Bentley, open up the lodge, let's have a peep inside, ooh what's this?" Chuffer stood to examine the sack of Royal Mail in the corner of the porch. Bentley moved forward to retrieve the sack.

"One of the main reasons you're here Chuffer, to return the gates to full working order and transform the lodge."

Chuffer radiated harmony. "No problem my friend, eh lads, leave it to us Bentley, we'll have that in working order within days, eh lads?" The two brothers looked at one another with some foreboding. After a little further hesitation, the pair finally nodded in agreement.

"No problem Dad, jobs done."

"There you see Bentley, my lads can't wait to begin, straining at the leash. Come on then, open up and let's get inside. I'll get back to you tomorrow with some clarification and idea of cost, ok?"

Bentley nodded in agreement. "Fine by me Chuffer, one thing to remember though this is Grade 2 listed with certain restrictions." Chuffer raised his arms in protest. "Bentley please, no sermon, have you forgotten, me and my lads have a rich pedigree, Queen Victoria's country home, Isle of Wight, remember? We're craftsmen, eh lads?" Dismissing their father's remark with deep sighs and offering no comment, the two lads disappeared within the lodge. Chuffer, quick to follow, paused at the doorway.

"Bentley, I'd leave it to us now if I were you, go back to bed, you look worn out." The grateful musician nodded his head wearily. "Thanks Chuffer I will, but before I depart, any sign of a gardener or two today?"

"Yes, a young lad, we asked him to let us in but he said he didn't have a key and anyway, if he did, it would cost him his job and just turned and went away. Surly little sod, just like his grandad."

"No sign of him either?"

"No Bentley, no."

"Alright, thank you Chuffer, I'm off. When you leave close the gates and I'll pop up later and lock up, ok?"

"Fine Bentley, fine."

Early afternoon, refreshed in body and mind, a return of fine weather a bonus and intent upon a rare visit to his local golf club situated in the village of Liphook, heading towards the barn Bentley's attention was captured by the sound of music omitting from the open doorway of the potting shed. Leaving golf trolley and bag close by, Bentley approached the large wooden structure with mounting interest. Within the cluttered interior, garden apprentice Nigel Rawlings, his back to the entrance, was making use of a large workbench intent on returning many garden implements back to their original splendour. Entering the doorway with a little stealth Bentley stood behind the lad for several seconds. A response unforthcoming, he tapped the lad upon the shoulder. "Hello, anyone there?" Dropping a wire brush amongst a collection of flowerpots the startled lad turned to face Bentley, finally omitting a heavy sigh of relief.

"Phew, it's you governor, I thought it was Grandad for a moment, he don't like me to polish garden tools, says that job's for farm labourers not for trained horticulturers like us; a bit strange at times is Grandad," the lad shrugged ruefully. "Me, I don't like using mucky tools, makes digging harder, hard enough as it is eh gov?"

"If you say so lad. Er, any chance of you turning the music down a little." A compliant lad turned to the radio, "There you are gov, now, how can I help you."

"Well for a start, I thought we'd agreed to address each other by our Christian names, me being Bentley, you being Nigel."

"Ah sorry Mr Browne, I forgot, I'll try and remember in future."

"Good lad, do your best."

Wishing to keep the conversation light and airy Bentley sought the change of subject. "Cosy retreat for you two horticulturers when the need arises eh lad, well what I mean is whenever the weather is unsympathetic of course," Bentley teased.

The lad looked around him with little enthusiasm. "S'pose so. Grandad calls it our head office."

Bentley managed a wry smile. "Yes I'm sure Nigel. Is he in today?"

"No skipper, still on paid sick leave, three days up to today, be back tomorrow."

"Oh good, look forward to it." Bentley turned to go. "Right I'm off lad."

Looking around his gloomy surroundings, he noted a heavily laden wheelbarrow covered by a check tablecloth close to the doorway. "Hello, what's this?"

Across the room, an anxious lad looked up from his task at the bench with some alarm. "Don't go there governor, it's out of bounds."

Much to the lad's dismay Bentley lifted the corner of the cloth to reveal a large amount of fresh fruit and vegetables. "Good God, where did this lot come from? Don't tell me, the veg garden. Wonderful, well done lad, I'll have some of that. In the words of Hot Chocolate, one of my many contemporaries, everyone's a winner, baby, that's the truth." A delighted musician addressed the lad. "What did you say earlier Nigel, I didn't catch it, something about out of bounds, what do you mean?"

With a heavy sigh, the lad left his workbench and taking the tablecloth from Bentley's hand, he covered the produce without hesitation. "Sorry gov, I must warn you not to touch any of that stuff. It looks OK I know, but looks are misleading. Grandad said it was the bad spring, so much rain and the potatoes got scurvy, broad beans covered in midges and so on, then we had the curse of the visiting South African killer bees killing our native bees so very little pollination anywhere, so if I were you gov, I wouldn't touch any of it but it's up to you."

Bentley looked at the lad with amusement. "You're having a laugh surely boy?"

"No I'm not skipper, ask Grandad."

"Well he's not here is he."

"No, but he will be tomorrow."

"Well to my mind it would take pride of place on the top shelf of Harrods; you are having a joke Nigel?"

The lad stood his ground. "No joke gov," he insisted, "you have to know what to look for, it's part of horticultural knowledge. Grandad said hopefully things will improve in a few weeks time if the good weather carries on you never know, the runner beans are doing well, still, if you want to take the chance governor then it's up to you." He shrugged his shoulders and returned to his bench.

Unsure whether to laugh or cry, Bentley accepted defeat. "Alright lad, you're the expert, you and your grandad, I'll take your word for it and I've no wish to suffer stomach problems at my age let alone a virus. Looks like I'll be heading for a supermarket this afternoon, doesn't it?"

"Sorry gov."

"Right, I'll get on my way."

Leaving the hut Bentley headed back towards the barn followed closely by the lad. Spotting the bag and trolley outside the barn the youth raced ahead to probe among the many golf clubs, finally withdrawing a club from the bag. Addressing a bunch of thistles, he adopted the appropriate stance for a seven iron producing several swings of an impressive nature before handing the club back to an approaching Bentley.

"Well done lad, natural swing, mind you the idea is to hit a golf ball, not a bunch of wild…"

"Thistles gov."

"Yes, yes thistles."

"Any time you're indeed of a caddy gov, I'm your man."

"Yep, I'll bear it in mind lad, most times I use a buggy, it's an age thing, but you never know. Right, I must get away before the afternoon is over; I'm in a little need of relaxation. Ah Nigel, while you're here, the mowers, are the keys back in place ready for work?"

"Yes, I got them off Grandad last night Mr Browne."

"Good lad, right I'm off."

Entering the barn Bentley was accompanied further by the lad. "What is it lad, you following me, nothing to do?"

"I'm concerned gov."

"Concerned, about what?"

"Your trip to the golf club governor. Even if you use the B127 it's still a busy route, takes time, particularly at this time of day, but to take the A3 driving a grass mower would be asking for trouble, besides which it will take ages, I'm not happy about it."

"Bentley viewed the boy with some concern. "You gone potty lad? Good grief, I've done many silly things in my time, some unrepeatable but from my recollection I have never ever sat upon a motorised lawn mower driving on a motorway or a minor route for that matter to enjoy a spell of golf and I certainly do not intend to start now. I shall be taking the wife's soft-top, give it a buzz, enjoy today's weather. Open the barn doors for me would you lad please."

"Sorry gov. When you asked for the keys I thought you were using the mower to go to golf."

"I value your kind concern lad I really do, but no, I shan't be going on a mower."

Out upon the driveway, hood down, engine purring, all ready to go and barn door closed behind him. "Have a good time Mr Browne, sorry about the fruit and veg."

"Not to worry lad, see you tomorrow."

"No no, not tomorrow governor it's my day at college."

"College?"

"Yes gov."

"Good lord, I didn't know you went to college?"

"Yes, Guildford Horticultural College, I go once a week."

"Well done Nigel. Higher education eh, good stuff, how long you been going?"

The lad thought long and hard. "Mmm, over a year now skipper."

"Oh well done, never had a clue. Right, time to move on lad." About to engage first gear Bentley had a sudden thought." "Er, one minute lad, don't I pay you for a five day week?"

The boy pursed his lips. "Hope so gov, yes," he nodded.

"So, for the past year during your time at the manor house I have been paying you towards your horticultural education?"

"Well I suppose so gov, looks like it," the boy laughed. "Grandad arranged it with your Mrs."

"Er, well thanks for putting me in the picture Nigel, I learn something every day, although in your case once a week eh. See you sometime lad."

"Ta ta gov."

Returning to village life late afternoon, a mentally recharged Bentley pulled into The Mariners car park in an optimistic frame of mind determined that day to banish all further pessimistic thoughts from his mind and embrace the future with full on optimism. Most importantly, accept that moving to the manor house was a mistake and openly admit so to his long-suffering wife. Determined to complete all renovations post haste and subsequently put the manor up for sale as soon as feasible and perhaps returning to Hampstead Heath in the near future, hopefully purchase a summer retreat in Florida or perhaps a similar destination, say Italy. Any agreeable options to save him from a costly divorce no matter what.

Entering the saloon bar in pragmatic mode greeting all he encountered with a broad smile and warm acknowledgement he approached the bar to be greeted as per normal by an effervescent landlord.

"My my Bentley, you're in fine fettle, won the lottery have you old chap?"

"Less of the old if you don't mind landlord. No, no lottery Albert, I'm embracing positive thoughts for a change. I have just returned from Nipook, our golf club you may recall. There I played 9 holes followed up by a swift pint in the bar and had a chat with a few acquaintances before returning to my favourite watering hole in my most favourite village, Barton-on-the-Green. So here I am Albert, buzzing like a bee."

"Mmm, sounds good Bentley, I could do with a little of what you are having myself. Well, what's it to be Bentley, tea, coffee, brandy, whiskey, best bitter, glass of water perhaps?"

"No, I'll stay on a pint of bitter if I may Albert, that'll do for me."

Albert reached beneath the counter producing a newspaper placing it in front of Bentley. "Have a look at this Bentley, this week's Barton Gazette, it should enhance your positive frame of mind even more."

Turning to the centre pages, he placed it in front of him. "There you are Bentley, centre spread, the Sunday cricket match. Focal point naturally with the victorious team all standing proudly upon the majestic steps leading to the entrance of this fine establishment surrounded you will note by local dignitaries of much repute, but who overshines them all, the tall figure standing on the topmost step has the spotlight, village resident Bentley Browne."

Bentley raised his arms in mild apology. "Sorry Albert, I couldn't get down the steps. I had just left the bar you may remember and I was trapped on the topmost step my friend, that's showbusiness."

Bentley allowed himself a little chuckle. "Do I detect a little irritation in your manner Albert? What's your point; do you want me to leave my friend?"

"No, no good God, I have no problem with you or any of the others centre stage, it's just an exasperated landlord leant upon the counter. What I find so annoying is the fact that little attention is paid to The Mariners in either photo or print. I must admit I feel let down. Here am I the owner of one of the most successful public houses and restaurants in the South of England, a bastion of village life, providing comfort, fine food, broad entertainment, well not all the time of course, a variation of best bitters second to none, a public house spanning 200 years of rich English history and we don't get a mention. I find it annoying to say the least. Uh oh, sorry Bentley, customer."

Returning within the minute, an apologetic Albert returned the paper beneath the counter. "Sorry Bentley, still I've made my case now, I'll put it to rest. Hey, I'm so busy complaining I forgot your drink oh, and by the way, there was a footnote in the paper hinting that you and your team, meaning obviously your lads, could be appearing at the forthcoming fete, a joke surely Bentley?"

"Really? Oh God, I hope so Albert but I wouldn't be surprised, my agent works in mysterious ways, a master of the dark arts. As a matter of interest Albert, who organises the damn fete?"

"Parish council old chap."

"Oh God yes of course, what's up with me? Run by?"

"Mr Patel, corner shop, chairman, council chairman old chap."

"Of course, oh Mr Patel. Do you know he approached me a week ago with a request to appear at the do? I will have to have a word with my agent Maurice Biggins when I return home. You remember Maurice Albert, popped in here to speak to me last weekend."

"It's hard to forget him really Bentley, centre of

attention. Oops, talking of centre of attention Bentley, over the way, PC Willoughby. Sit down Bentley, he's heading over here."

Across the way, entering the saloon and pausing at the doorway, a sharp eyed on duty Constable Willoughby spotted Bentley and immediately headed his way without hesitation. Ordering a small lemonade from an ever-attentive Albert, the young constable turned to address the musician.

"Mr Browne, I thought you'd be here, good to see you, just a brief word with you if I may sir. Your car in the car park, a posh red soft top, a Mercedes, very impressive."

"Yes, sounds like mine constable, very observant of you, what's your point?"

"Well the point is sir, you have a flat tyre. I thought I best inform you in case you are unaware of it. I feel it's my duty as a local constable to ensure village life and protect it."

"Are you sure it's my vehicle constable?"

"Oh yes sir, I am, but in truth it's not your car sir, it's your wife's. I am aware of that sir because I have noticed her many times driving within the village. I am also aware at this moment in time your good wife is away on a cruise so unless the vehicle has been sold sir, you are the driver today, am I correct?"

"You are once again constable correct, yes."

"In which case sir, I presume you have a joint insurance on the vehicle?"

"Yes, true constable, it applies also to four other vehicles safely locked away in our barn up at the manor. Unfortunately it doesn't apply to our lawn mowers."

"Oh, great shame about the mowers sir but I trust you are following the path of truth Mr Browne. I have been trained at Hendon to note deception sir, but in this case Mr Browne, you have my trust. My main point of interest lies in the fact that you are familiar with today's high technology in wheel replacement Mr Browne. You are familiar with the difficulties?"

Suppressing a laugh Bentley kept a straight face. "Erm yes. In my younger days, I drove an Austin A40 constable. Forever in trouble with wheel problems, before your time of course, but it could be very tricky; nevertheless I am confident I shall manage constable, thank you."

"Very well sir, I shall leave you to it, only I don't wish the pre-passage of village motorists brought to a sudden halt through an inept wheel replacement leading to a blocked road sir preventing movement throughout the village this evening."

"No problem constable, leave it to me, I can assure you I am a top man at wheel replacements."

Constable Willoughby turned to go. "One more thing sir." The constable pointed at the counter, "Er, that pint sir, is it yours, only I trust you are aware of drink and drive limitations sir. I very much hope this is your only drink during this afternoon sir otherwise, I suggest strongly you leave the vehicle here overnight and walk home. You are familiar with the pathway of course, it should be no problem."

"I accept your concern constable but no, I shall return home by car thank you, I know my limitations."

The constable looked down upon his watch. "I'm off duty from this moment onwards sir and as I have no wish to prolong my working day any longer I shall say goodbye sir and trust your compliance with the law sir."

"Indeed constable, thank you for your concern, I shan't forget it for some time."

"Just doing my duties."

Noting the constable's departure, Albert returned to address his friend. "What was that all about Bentley?"

"Well at a guess Albert I'd say he was sent by the good Lord from above to test my new found optimism in life and he certainly succeeded. Why on earth would an on duty police constable point out a flat tyre on a stationary car in a pub car park, you would think he had better things to do. He certainly is an odd ball. He came in to inform me that the wife's car, which is the one he is referring to, I gave it a spin this morning to keep the battery charged, had a flat tyre. He appeared concerned as to whether I had the necessary qualifications to change the wheel then gave a lecture on drink driving."

"Oh, no need to change the wheel today Bentley, leave it overnight, do it tomorrow, get someone to do it for you."

"Leave it overnight, the wife's pride and joy, no chance Albert. With all due respect Albert it's a soft top Mercedes worth a small fortune and spotted by a chancer it would disappear overnight, shipped abroad in a container to make a few bob and should that happen the wife would ensure I was hung, drawn and quartered out there on the village green I assure you. No sir, I'll fix it and get it home Albert, thanks all the same."

"Er Bentley, what about your drink, you haven't touched it."

"Albert, that wouldn't be a very wise move would it. The constable is out there in the smoking area enjoying a cigarette. No doubt he will be keeping an eye on me. Right, I don't know if I'll be in tomorrow, Chuffer's lads are starting work on the lodge, it's all go. Remain optimistic Albert, that's my word, bye."

Safely home and with the Mercedes secured within the barn, Bentley entered the manor to be greeted by a continuous irritating bleep of a message recorded on the landline by Chuffer Rudd. "Ah Bentley my friend, brief word concerning tomorrow. The lads should be awaiting entry outside the manor gates tomorrow at approximately 7.45am. With them will be two large skips and equipment to begin work on the lodge as arranged. Please, no repeat of this morning's fiasco, a two hour wait for entry, not again please."

"May I make a suggestion Bentley to secure free movement for all of us until the gates are in working order? I'll give one of my lads a key and he will get some duplicates made, what do you think? That will enable all of us entry when necessary. I trust you get the message, I would pray so anyway, but I must go now, my granddaughter Sally is having a celebrity tenth birthday barbecue at the farm and I'm cooking the sausages so see you tomorrow my friend, 7.45am outside the gates, well I hope so anyway, sleep well."

With the continuation of fine weather confirmed by the early evening news, Bentley made himself comfortable upon the terrace with a small whiskey in hand and the PO mailbag close by. There, he set about a search of discovery. Much to his pleasure, the majority of letters were of a similar tone and nature to those of the previous week, many hopeful of his return to the world of entertainment. Lost within his task, a phone call from within the manor drew him once again to the library.

"Hello?"

"Bentley?"

"Christina, my love, so good to hear from you, how are things? Where are you now?"

"Madagascar Bentley, just arrived, it's wonderful here, I do so wish you were here as well, it would do you the world of good my love, far better than driving my precious car around the dangerous country lanes of your beloved England."

"Sorry, didn't catch that Christina, the line faded my love?"

"Don't fool with me Bentley, I know all about your trip, you even had a puncture I believe."

"Really Christina, I am dumbfounded, where did all this nonsense come from, where did you get this information, MI5?"

"Ah that would be telling my sweet. I've also been informed that pickle of a man, something Rudd whatever and his family are to do further work at the lodge house, is that a fact Bentley?"

A disjointed Bentley was lost for words.

"Bentley, Bentley are you there?"

"Yes, Christina, still here, just about. Er, I employed them because I need a little help to push things on here before you return home my sweet, a little surprise for you, that was my wish, still, never mind. Who keeps you so informed Christina? It's all, well to put it mildly, unsettling if I'm honest."

A broad laugh came from the line. "Have no fear Bentley, I have many sources of information from friends of both of us my love, no malicious intent I assure you, all looking out for your well-being and mine of course. Oops, must go, a group of us are leaving the ship for an evening of enjoyment and they are calling for me. Must go. Love you, bye."

In mind to wonder if he was being tracked by satellite, Bentley returned to the terrace. Barely seated for five minutes, he was again called to the phone.

"Bentley, my friend."

"Maurice?"

"It is indeed Bentley, your agent Maurice, just a chat to keep you up to date as promised."

"Go on then, tell me the worst."

"Worst my friend, far from it, cause for much

celebration my dear chap."

"Go on."

"Well to begin with, vinyl is a certainty. The recording studio can't wait to get started and hope it to be on sale accompanied by much publicity by the end of the month. Top billing at Glastonbury which will be confirmed in a week or two which will lead to press releases and TV interviews rest assured, so things are on the march, Bentley."

"Mmm, you have been busy, Maurice, well done."

"Yes, but now what we need is a period of rehearsing hopefully at your place Bentley, starting this weekend if you agree, the lads can't wait."

"Oh, you been in touch with them then?"

"Well of course I have. What do you say?"

"My place, rehearsing?"

"Yes, the lads would love to meet up with you, Friday night."

"Hardly lads Maurice."

"Well true Bentley, the old boys would love to meet you on Friday. If all goes according to plan, stay overnight. You live in a palace, big enough to house an army. We'll rehearse Saturday and Sunday and by lunchtime Sunday afternoon, everything should be tickety-boo, all ready to go. So what do you say?"

"Yes, why not, could do with the company Maurice, would be great to see everybody again. Mind you, I may live in a palace with plenty of bedrooms but unfortunately very few beds. If they are willing to sleep in a chair, fine, failing that perhaps each should bring a sleeping bag, accompanied with a flask," Bentley laughed.

"Steady on Bentley, at their age, sleeping bags? Oh, we'll think of something, a hotel somewhere ... or God knows what. Er, well what about your fine pub?"

"Ooh no chance Maurice, it's a fine place for a visit but it is a pub, not a hotel. As you say, we'll come up with something."

"Well there you are Bentley, we're on the move my friend, right must go, got a date at the Dorchester in half an hour my boy, charming young lady too."

"Well, it's alright for some Maurice."

"Oh yes, make hay while the sun shines Bentley. Oh before I go, you may recall I visited you last Sunday at The Mariners."

"Course I do Maurice, a couple of days ago, the reason for your phone call today, I'm not as senile as you think."

"No, no of course not, don't take it that way. Well, prior to finding you in The Mariners I popped into the shop on the green for a packet of cigarettes, I'd run out you see, standing at your gates for a couple of hours trying to get in.."

"I get your point Maurice, carry on."

"Well, in the shop I got chatting to the owner Mr Patel, nice chap and your name came up. He expressed a great interest in your career. During out conversation, I expanded on what I had in mind for your future, if you were in agreement of course. He suggested an appearance at the council local fete on the green in a couple of weeks' time, which I thought it was a great idea, quirky I admit, but…"

"Maurice, it's a village show, all over in a couple of hours, barely more than several hundred people turn up. It's more for the local children, slides and roundabouts and so on and ice cream, hardly appropriate for the re-emergence of a super group such as ours, surely. You are joking Maurice I hope?"

"Bentley, Bentley, you are missing the point. The re-emergence of one of the country's most favoured band set in an English country fete, however small, is quirky in my view, unpretentious. It's in its presentation. A small stage set up on the village green.

That should draw attention, everyone welcome, it's a winner Bentley, trust me. Once it has got the media interested it will go ballistic, believe me. With my contacts, this time next week we will be the talk of the nation, you'll see."

"Ok Maurice, I'll leave it all in your hands, you're the governor."

"I am indeed Bentley, publicity is what I do best my friend, now time to call it a day, I have a date as I said at the Dorchester so I can't be late, quite a little cracker she is. Come on Bentley, don't be so glum, life's too short. Chin up old son. In a few weeks' time you will be making regular appearances on TV and be back at Claridges as in the good old days. Right must go, I'll keep in touch."

Retiring to his bed that night without a further nightcap, Bentley slept a very welcome seven hours without disturbance.

The following morning as planned and on time as promised, the gates were thrown open to welcome a group of eager workmen. Bentley handed the key to a delighted Chuffer Rudd. Determined to keep a keen but relaxed eye on all future progress, Bentley left them to it.

With the time approaching 9.00am and with no sign as yet of his senior horticulturist, Bentley returned to the manor house, there to prepare a fried breakfast, the first sign of normality returning to the household since his wife's departure on holiday.

CHAPTER 24

Dem Bones – Dem Bones – Dem Dry Bones

After a hearty breakfast, Bentley left the manor house, certain in mind to allow the Rudd dynasty a little time to follow their own agenda for a day or two at least before intervening to play a leading role in all future renovations. Making his way to the far edge of his estate intent upon a visit to his prize Victorian glasshouses set down close to neighbour businessman Nigel Smethurst, whose desire to purchase the classic structures and land was a source of much irritation and puzzlement to Bentley. Approaching the four dilapidated structures, he was greeted by piles of broken glass restricting easy pass. Forced to reconsider his point of entry Bentley's attention was caught by the sight of a familiar figure emerging from behind the desolate stable block carrying with him a large wicker basket. Cautiously awaiting Rawling's approach with mixed feelings, Bentley sprung from the shadows to confront his startled gardener.

"Huh, back are you Rawlings? Good show, nice of you to get in touch, all going well is it?"

Taken by complete surprise the gardener dropped the basket upon his feet, its contents out on the floor plain to see. "Oh it's you Mr Browne, I should have known, you're making quite the habit of jumping out on unsuspected folk these days, nearly gave me a heart attack. I'm surprised to see you down here, thought you'd be with the local mafia up at the gates."

"Local mafia Rawlings, what are you on about?"

"The Rudd family. I see they've started work on the lodge. The village mafia I call them, they got their fingers in every pie them buggers." An irritated Rawlings kicked out at the bucket before quickly regaining his composure. "Mind you, if they make a good job of turning the lodge into a modern home and it's up to my Mrs liking and all, we would consider moving in, ideal location for your head gardener governor."

"No no Rawlings, forget it, no chance, sorry. If it's occupied at all it will be by a commanding figure of firm resolve, security a must."

Rawlings sniffed disapprovingly. "Well cometh the man cometh the day, I can turn my hand to anything."

"Yes, so I noticed Rawlings. That bucket, you going to leave it there are you? What's in it?"

"Nothing governor, it's empty, I dropped it thanks to you."

"Alright Rawlings, let me rephrase my question, what

was in it?"

"Fruit gov, plums, Victoria plums."

"Where from?"

"Windfalls governor, a tree behind the stables, I've been doing some pruning. It's been a wet spring skipper, reduced growth everywhere. I was taking them to the workshop, leaving them there overnight to see if there is any sign of ......" A hesitant Rawlings struggled for words.

"Blight."

"That's it governor yes, blight, got to give them a thorough examination, don't what no scurvy or such like, do we governor?"

"No certainly not, if anyone knows what to look for Rawlings, it's you."

Rawlings nodded in agreement. "True gov true, me and the lad are top end gov, top end, take my word for it."

"Oh I do Rawlings, I do. Glad to see you've got your mojo back, plenty to do have you?"

Rawlings reached for his tobacco pouch. "Oh yes, plenty to do gov, you know me."

Bentley turned to go. "Yes I do Rawlings, I do."

"Oh governor, hang on a minute."

"What is it now Rawlings?"

"You on television gov, the other day, been a while since you've been on the box governor. It's the first time I've seen you on TV but it was you alright, I couldn't believe it."

A curious Bentley delayed his departure returning to his employee's side. "Go on."

"Well it's funny. I was recovering from my serious bout of summer flu you know and I was laid up in bed one afternoon, too weak to venture out, the Mrs caring for my wellbeing, quite worried she was, in fact I............"

"For God's sake Rawlings, get on with it, there are things I want to do."

"Alright gov, don't lose your rag, thought you were supposed to be Johnny Cool, still, if you let me I will continue. As I was saying, I was watching TV one afternoon, some far off station it was, I don't know what they call it, very popular now I know but most films are in black and white, good though, old stars I remember like Dirk Bogarde and Kenneth Moore, I remember growing up with them and going to see them at the good old Odeon in Petersfield."

"Rawlings, please."

"Alright gov. Well there you were who come on, Detective Inspector Dawkins, you, in your heyday."

Bentley turned to go. "Sorry, couldn't have been, I'm not that old, Jack Dawkins was filmed over a good few years in colour, not in black and white I can assure you, colour Rawlings."

"I never suggested your series was filmed in black and white gov but that many of the films on that channel are a look back in time gov, I mean your series was filmed, aw I don't know, how long do you reckon?"

Bentley thought long and hard. "Er, a little under 40 years I suppose."

"Ah well there you are then governor, 40 years ago. If I'm honest you were a good-looking lad, had a good presence on film. You played the part well, mind you in them days coppers were rough and ready, you wouldn't get away with it today governor."

"Rawlings, it was fiction, set in the 50's."

"Yeah I know but it mirrored the times didn't it gov. I must admit I wouldn't have crossed swords with you, you were a tough looking bugger."

"Thank you Rawlings, most kind."

"No offence, governor." Rawlings flicked his cigarette end into an empty water butt. "Mind you…." Rawlings produced a long weary sigh. "In them days I was a handsome man myself, you ask many of the women in the village. I was quite a catch I was, still am to many, you know what I mean gov? Very fit, very physical horticulturist, it keeps you active, I mean, when I asked my good wife to marry me, going back in time of course, she burst into tears, very emotional she was, mind you." Rawlings reflected. "She was two months pregnant at the time."

"Oh right, well, nice of you to tell me that Rawlings, time to go I think."

Rawlings reached out upon Bentley's shoulder. "Just one more thing governor."

"Go on."

"I've been thinking. Do you know what gov?"

"No Rawlings."

"Well, we are very alike."

"We are?"

"We are gov. Same generation, both blessed with good looks. If I hadn't chosen the horticultural path to follow we could have ended up on telly together." Rawlings laughed with delight. "Just think of that, I could have been cast as your detective sergeant or even better, your chief inspector, keep you in check I would have done. I would have suited that role, perfect casting in my mind."

Wishing to close all discussions on his TV days, Bentley reached down to recover the Victoria plums returning the fruit and basket to Rawlings.

"Here you are Rawlings, I really must go."

"One more thing gov."

"Ahh, I don't believe this, what now?"

"My wages gov, this week, no problem I hope? Friday tomorrow."

"None whatsoever Rawlings, I shall manage."

"You know what gov, like I was saying; if I'd starred alongside you in the TV series I would have been entitled to royalties eh, what with repeats an' all, just like you I imagine. You getting some from your programme?"

Bentley nodded his head. "Yes yes, I shall benefit a little I suspect, not a lot though."

"Ah well, such is life, I shouldn't get bitter about it governor. Right I'll get off, leave you to it."

"Hang on a minute."

"Gov?"

"Those Victoria plums, they won't end up for sale at some local market will they?"

Momentarily lost for words Rawlings expressed concern at such a suggestion. "Gov, please. What kind of bloke do you think I am?"

"Well that's it Rawlings, nobody knows, so I certainly don't but I shall find out one day after all, I am a hardnosed copper aren't I, don't forget that."

As if I could inspector. One more thing before you go Mr Browne."

"Go on, I knew you would have to have the last word."

"Well gov, I would suggest you gave a little more thought to me and the wife moving into the lodge, think on it Mr Browne, the Mrs would welcome all visitors to the manor house with a promise of a cup of tea and a scone, all would be welcome."

"For God's sake Rawlings are you losing it? What am I, part of English heritage? This is a private home Rawlings."

"Ah yes gov, but what about turning the manor into a posh hotel eh for the very wealthy, think of the cash flow."

"Look Rawlings, please go away, you're driving me crazy."

Finally accepting his presence no longer welcome a sombre faced Rawlings departed, taking with him the large basket of plums under his arm. Heading towards the potting shed and closing the door behind him without a backward glance leaving a very much-relieved Bentley to spend several hours of honest toil as was his intention relieving each greenhouse of much broken glass. Finally calling it a day mid-afternoon he returned to the house, there to spend a relaxing half hour upon the terrace. With the time approaching 4.15pm, a recharged musician headed up the main driveway, hopeful of much meaningful progress made that day upon the lodge house.

Approaching the main gate, Bentley acknowledged many of the workforce about to call it a day with a farewell wave of the hand. Across the way and leaving the lodge house securing the door behind him, Chuffer Rudd's eldest son Tom, a familiar figure throughout the village and well liked and respected by all. Spotting Bentley's arrival, he approached him offering a warm handshake.

"Good to meet you Mr Browne, my name's Tom or Thomas if you prefer. I'm glad you're here; you've saved me a trip to the manor house. I have two keys to offer you, one for the lodge house and the other for the padlocked gates both cut today sir. Dad instructed I handed them to you as soon as possible."

Bentley looked around him in admiration. "You've done well Tom. Where did all this come from?" Bentley pointed at four large skips filled to the brim.

"Unbelievable. What's happened, the village been dumping their rubbish here do you think?"

The clearly amused eldest son rested his arms upon the nearest container. "No, can't blame the village folk Mr Browne, all this rubbish came from up there." He pointed to the higher reaches of the lodge house. "I couldn't have picked a worst day to work in the lodge, the temperature was unbelievable. As I am sure you are aware Mr Browne, during the First World War, before my time thank God, the manor house, your home sir, was commandeered by the War Office for use as a hospital for frontline troops injured and the many who lost a limb or two God help them. Well I had the misfortune to enter the loft on the hottest day of the year, more out of interest than expectation. I found it full to the brim with old bed sheets, blankets, mattresses, single beds, endless crockery, you name it, I found it. All of it had to be dumped in the skip sir as you can see but there is more to come. Follow me Mr Browne."

Re-entering the lodge house, the pair entered the main social room. There stacked in several piles almost as high as the ceilings were artificial limbs of many variations.

"There you are Mr Browne, what do you make of all that? Let me introduce you to the world of orthopaedics."

"Good God, not much one can say Tom, perhaps I should get in touch with the War Office, what say you?"

"Well, bit late now Mr Browne, the First World War is over and I think they'd be a little bit dated for any of our lads injured in say Afghanistan etc, wouldn't you Mr Brown? Still, one is never sure. I'll leave them for you to sort out sir if you don't mind."

Leaving the gatehouse, Bentley stood back and admired the lodge frontage stripped of all its overhanging ivy.

"You've done well Tom, brickwork looks terrific."

"Well, there was a slight problem with the pressure hose cleaning the brickwork but it exposed the loose pointing Mr Browne but we'll get over that, look on the bright side." He pointed at a round plaque set high upon the front fascia depicting a stone-faced Victorian citizen.

"Sir William Wiggings Mr Browne, restored to Victorian splendour."

"Well, I am amazed Tom. I give up, you've done really well. What's up for tomorrow then?"

"Well, tomorrow Mr Browne we have it in mind to strip the lodge of all Victorian furniture and such like, dig a channel across the front of the entrance here, lay cables in preparation for the electrification of the main gates, one of your main objectives I believe Mr Browne. Can't say I blame you sir, a lot of visitors yesterday showed up outside displaying an awful lot of interest. I would say a few were from the press, social media and such like, all taking snapshots of this that and everything. A few were rather disappointed they couldn't enter the driveway hoping to see you I think, mind you, they couldn't get in, we were all parked up blocking the entrance. So if you want me to let them in tomorrow Mr Browne just say the word sir."

"No, good God no thank you. Mind you, having said that, tomorrow afternoon my old band mates are paying a visit. Will they be able to enter what with a trench and cable on the agenda?"

"No problem Mr Browne, it should be done by mid-morning, I'll see to that. Your old band mates you say, ooh I'll bring my autograph book."

Bentley laughed. "I wouldn't bother; most of them have forgotten their own names let alone anything else. Right, I'll get off and leave you in peace. Thanks for everything today, leave you to lock up can I?"

"You can sir, part of the job."

"Right, so see you tomorrow Tom."

"You never know sir. I've enjoyed today but given a

choice I'd sooner be on the farm running things however, Dad insisted he needed my leadership so I'll do my best for a day or two then return to nature hopefully."

Bentley offered his hand in friendship. "Goodbye Tommy and thanks a lot."

"Not Tommy Mr Browne please. Tom or Thomas, no offence."

A wry Bentley smiled in acknowledgement. "I understand Thomas, see you tomorrow."

"You will Mr Browne, bye bye."

Bentley returned to the manor in good spirits, finding the significant progress made upon the long neglected gatehouse in such a short period of time a cause for celebration. Within minutes of entering Sir William Wiggin's former home and in mind of an early evening gin and tonic upon the terrace, he received a phone call.

"Hello, Barton Manor, home of the establishment."

"Is that you Bentley or perhaps the butler, who knows in this mad world? Er, this is your agent Maurice as I am sure you are aware. I need a quick word Bentley."

"Hello Maurice."

"Ah Bentley my old chap, sorry, have I disturbed you?"

"No more than usual Maurice, I was heading for the outside world to enjoy a little evening sunshine but never mind, how can I help you?"

"Oh yes Bentley, the weather, it's wonderful, even here in London, let's hope it lasts until next week eh, the fete."

"Yes, that would be nice Maurice, now, what do you want? My coffee's getting cold."

"Well, I'm phoning to keep you up to date."

"Go on then, report."

"Well, I'm pleased to say everything is sorted Bentley with accommodation provided for the chaps by way of a 40 foot length, 5 berth luxury American motorhome. I've hired it for the weekend. I shall pick it up tomorrow. It has everything you could wish for, wonderful sleeping arrangements, cooker, TV, the lot. So we rehearse in the manor and sleep and relax in the motorhome, what do you think?"

"Yes, sounds ideal, good thinking Maurice but one thing though, who is paying for it?"

"Bentley Bentley, live for today my friend, we'll sort it all out tomorrow at our leisure. I have had further thoughts though Bentley, essentials, food and drink.

Are you well stocked up at the manor to provide sustenance for five guests over the weekend my friend?"

"Good point Maurice, er no, not at this moment, no woman in the house you see. Tomorrow I'll nip out first thing and stock up."

"No no, leave it to me Bentley," came the firm response. "You get the less essentials, milk, coffee, sugar etc and I'll get the drinks and nibbles. I'll keep it simple, no need for roast potatoes and beef and all that sort of thing, mind you, I shall be handing you the bill my friend," Maurice laughed.

"Many thanks Maurice."

"My pleasure Bentley, now listen further. I hope to be at your place at around 4.15pm tomorrow afternoon, the lads are planning to arrive a little later, about 5ish, is that ok?"

"Sounds good Maurice, yes. Looking forward to seeing you all. One thing before you go old chap, you're a knowledgeable fella, what do you know about artificial limbs?"

"What sort of question is that? Nothing, I've never needed one, why don't you ask your local doctor. You can get it on the National Health if you need one, cost you a fortune privately Bentley."

"Not quite the answer I was expecting or wished for Maurice. See you tomorrow, bye."

Inwardly delighted at the impending get together, Bentley took to the piano that evening running through many of the group's favourites for several hours, finally retiring to bed a satisfied musician.

Awaking later than planned the following day, Bentley had four major objectives in mind to follow that morning. First, a trip across the green to Patel's corner shop for the minor items. Second, a quick necessary tidy up of the great hall and library. Third, locate further garden furniture to place upon the terrace just in case of the need. Fourth, there to be seated himself with a drink in hand to greet his team upon their arrival.

First objective top of the list, Bentley left the manor house. Approaching the gatehouse, he was greeted by a rather smug Chuffer Rudd. Raising his arms in triumph, he pointed towards the lodge.

"Told you so Bentley, me and my team, look at that, what an improvement eh?"

"Yes, very good Chuffer," Bentley conceded willingly.

"Very good, excellent I would say my friend."

Bentley looked around him. "On your own Chuffer, where are they?"

"Who? The lads?"

"The workforce, I see their pickups but no sign of them."

"Tea time Bentley, time for a break, they're seated in the Lodge."

"Why not Chuffer, we all need a break at times."

"Indeed Bentley, indeed."

Bentley pointed upon the drive. "Oh, I see the cables are laid, excellent, well done."

"Yes Bentley, it shall be filled in before lunch have no fear allowing easy entry for your band of shipmate's arrival."

"Oh, you're aware of our reunion are you?"

"Of course Bentley, everybody within the village knows, I wouldn't be a bit surprised to find many gathered outside in a few hours to greet them either."

"Good grief, I never thought of that Chuffer, it never occurred to me."

"Social media Bentley, you should catch up with international technology, you're front page news at the moment my friend."

"Well, if you're right Chuffer, let's hope they contain themselves and don't try to overrun the manor,"

Bentley laughed.

"Have no worries Bentley, my boys will manage the gates until 5.00pm then they'll be going home so it's up to you from then on in, ok?"

Ah, thanks Chuffer, I appreciate that. Now if you'll forgive me, I must cut across the green, I need some provisions for my visitors and before you ask Chuffer no, it's not whiskey, it's tea, coffee and a few biscuits."

Chuffer approached the ornate ironwork. "I never said a word Bentley, never said a word. Here, let me open up for you. Now to repeat myself, my lads shall ensure security is maintained at the gates for the rest of the day until 5.00pm then my friend, as I say, it's down to you; we shan't see you again until Monday."

"Thank you Chuffer, I'll catch you later?"

"Well you'll have to be back within a couple of hours, my working days end at midday these days; don't forget I'm an old aged pensioner Bentley."

Entering the corner shop, Bentley was greeted by a delighted Mr Patel emerging as if by magic from behind a shelf of breakfast cereals. "Mr Browne, my friend, so good to see you sir after all this time."

"After all this time Mr Patel? It's barely seven days since your visit to the manor house, you've lost me there."

Mr Patel pursed his lips in surprise. "Not possible. A week, is that all? It seems a lifetime ago Mr Browne, a lifetime, still, if that is what you say then I'm not one to question such a gentleman as yourself. You've changed your mind about appearing at our grand summer extravagance this year I'm given to understand?" With sudden doubts crossing the shopkeeper's mind, he addressed Bentley with serious concern. "Or unless I'm wrong and you are here to cause me further dismay with a change of direction once again perhaps? Tell me I'm mistaken Mr Browne, so many lives will be filled with sadness, you are a national treasure."

"Am I indeed, a national treasure? I think I've heard that before today. Your compliments have no boundaries Mr Patel but let me reassure you I shall appear at the summer extravagance as you call it, somewhat reluctantly I might add, the reason being there is a bigger picture unfolding."

"Oh yes yes, I am aware Mr Browne, vinyl recording, future progress."

Momentarily speechless, Bentley reached for a bar of chocolate. "I'll take this if I may Mr Patel?"

"£1.20 Mr Browne."

"How do you know Mr Patel?"

"Well, I sell them Mr Browne, I'm a businessman."

Bentley reached for another chocolate bar in exasperation.

"That will be a further £1.20 my friend."

"Er Mr Patel, vinyl recordings, please tell me how do you know as it's a private matter?"

"Oh I know of your journey Mr Browne, your future pathway. I am in constant touch with our mutual friend and businessman Maurice, errm, at this moment in time I'm at a loss for his surname but I'm sure it will come back to me given time Mr Browne."

"Gibbins, Mr Patel."

"Oh yes yes, Gibbins, a fine man, we have many forthcoming discussions to be finalised, we must prepare for the big day on the green, a wonderful celebration of our English country life."

"Yes, quite so Mr Patel, English country life at its finest, also very good for business I imagine. I am given to understand your family and many of your cousins provide very much a large percentage of the fete's attractions, hog roast, a beer tent, children's slide, a roundabout, even splat the rat, all good earners I would imagine Mr Patel," adding cheekily "also very noisy and smelly according to my wife."

"Yes yes, your good wife does have a point Mr

Browne, but you are well informed, they do provide a good return if the weather is favourable of course but importantly, a large percentage goes to Barton Green Council to finance any future events."

"On which I am sure you provide future assistance."

"Yes, it is my duty Mr Browne, I am a council chairman."

"Yes, so I am aware Mr Patel, quite a challenge I imagine."

"Indeed it is sir, indeed it is."

"Of that I'm sure Mr Patel. Right, I must be on my way soon before I forget the reason for my presence. I need two quarts of full cream milk, coffee and teabags. Where do I find such items?"

Mr Patel raised his hand in protest. "Stay as you are, stay as you are, I shall get them for you, it is my privilege to assist you." Soon returning with all three items, he placed them beside the till. "Will that be all Mr Browne, no added delights for your important visitors this very day; I have many items on special offer sir." He reached upon a shelf for a litre of whiskey. Brandishing the bottle in the air, he pointed at the label. "Single malt sir, the finest, yours with a discount price of 10%."

"Well very generous of you Mr Patel, fine offer but all

major items are being purchased by your good friend Maurice from his local Tesco store I believe."

The shopkeeper returned the bottle to its place of rest without comment. "So be it Mr Browne, nothing I can interest you in?"

"Well Mr Patel, I must admit I was rather taken by your fine display of fruit and veg outside the store, very, very inviting."

A beaming Mr Patel nodded his head in agreement. "Oh yes, my pride and joy sir, I supply much of the village including Lower Barton with fresh outdoor produce of high quality. Waitrose and Tesco have no such quality sir, nowhere near approaching mine Mr Browne."

"Well, I must say it looks very inviting, I am rather taken by the plums, rather tempted to buy some I must say."

"Oh yes, they are one of my best sellers sir, a wonderful example of English Victoria plums."

"Yes. May I ask you Mr Patel, who supplies you with all this wonderful produce?"

A slightly uneasy Mr Patel turned his back on Bentley to address several shelves close by heavily laden with weekly magazines, straightening many and replacing a few with later editions, finally stepping back satisfied with the results to address Bentley's point of interest.

"Mr Browne, we have many suppliers of home grown produce from many living within the village sir. I have a further four first class shops in the surrounding area, all successful, staffed by many of the Patel family I am proud to say. I am a major player Mr Browne, always on the march seeking to enlarge my empire. I am an entrepreneur, company director and parish council leader; I have much to be proud off in my lifetime."

"Yes yes, indeed Mr Patel, I agree, you have." Bentley reached for his wallet "Well, I must make a move, have much to attend to, now how much do I owe you sir?"

Mr Patel weighed up the costs with slow deliberation. "The sum of money outstanding Mr Browne is £8.30 with a further sum of £2.40 for the chocolate wafers protruding from your shirt pocket sir. Total sum, £10.70 sir. You have a bag Mr Browne, I have plenty here?"

Bentley produced a Waitrose carrier bag from his back pocket. "I do. Now payment Mr Patel. I trust you accept Euros sir?" Bentley teased displaying a straight face.

A slightly indignant council chairman declined the offer with a shake of the head. "No thank you Mr

Browne, the Patel's only deal with coins of the realm sir, foreign currency brings with it many problems."

"Card payment accepted Mr Patel?"

"Yes, that will be fine Mr Browne."

Payment completed, Bentley turned to go.

"Here, let me sir." Mr Patel reached for the door and once outside Bentley addressed the large array of fruit and veg.

"Forgive me Mr Patel." Reaching down, several plums despatched within the inner sanctum of a Waitrose carrier bag and quickly continuing on his way without a pause, Bentley raised an arm in appeasement to a protesting shopkeeper.

"Have no fear Mr Patel, I shall return within a day or two with payment, trust me sir, trust me."

With the village green behind him approaching the B2019 running close by his esteemed residence Bentley's pathway was obstructed by a line of cars parked up tight upon the roadside edge. Outside the manor a gathering of predominantly middle-aged women standing in close contact were engaged in excited conversation. Close by, camped upon the roadside grass verge, a smaller group of four ladies. Quick to recognise the approaching figure crossing the road before them and soon up upon their toes without hesitation, the four excited ladies surrounded the musician with cries of delight bringing him to a sudden halt. The team leader wearing sunglasses and a bright red sunhat grabbed his arm.

"Bentley Browne, it is you isn't it? Yes, I know it is, I recognise you, you've barely changed at all, a little heavier perhaps, eh girls. Tell me Bentley, is it true that you and the band are playing here next Saturday?"

"Yes yes, it's true sweetheart, but not here." He turned to point behind him. "We're playing down there upon the green." The redhead removed her sunglasses poking him playfully in the stomach. "We know that silly, but you are playing next Saturday, confirm it, it's true, is it Bentley?"

"Well, so I'm led to believe madam, yes." Bentley conceded.

"Oh madam! Get him girls, one minute sweetheart, now madam. Come on Bentley, you are the band leader you should know, is it yes or no?"

"Yes darling."

"That's better. Oh that's smashing. Hear that girls? Bentley said yes, they are playing." Cheering in unison the four women hugged one another in delight. "And Syd Mitchell, tell me he'll be performing won't he Bentley?" the redhead pleaded. "We love Syd don't we girls, it wouldn't be the same without him and he's coming here this very day I believe with the group to rehearse, is that true?"

"Yes, he is ladies."

"Is he still hot stuff Bentley?"

"Well, not for me to say but he looks OK to me but tell me, I'm slightly concerned as to your knowledge, how do you know the band is visiting my house this afternoon, it's rather a private matter?"

"Oh many know Bentley, village gossip," the redhead snorted. "My sister told me days ago, she lives in Lower Barton." She pointed at her friends. "We live in Guildford us lot but when we heard we had to come today in the hope of seeing Syd and we shall definitely be back next Saturday without a doubt won't we girls?" Her companions nodded in complete agreement.

"Well, if you forgive me ladies, it's been good to meet you but I must be off." Reaching into the carrier bag, he produced a litre of full cream milk giving it a little shake. "Before this milk comes to the boil."

With his impending departure greeted with a little dismay by the women, he was once more subjected to further hugs and kisses amid cries of, "we love you too Bentley, as much as Syd my darling."

Finally extracting himself from the tight clutches of the group from Guildford, Bentley approached the gathering at the gates, the majority standing to one side to allow unrestricted entry, a few with smartphone in hand intent upon a shared snapshot. Granting their wishes with good grace, Bentley was cornered outside the gates for a further ten minutes. Finally, patience running short, he bade farewell escaping the excited crowd to enter the manor, there to be greeted by an amused Chuffer Rudd.

"Glad to be home old chap, the price of fame eh?"

"I know Chuffer. Where the hell did they come from and how do they know of the lad's visit? I'm told it's village gossip, do you believe that is so?"

"I do Bentley yes and further bad news for you Bentley. A BBC TV crew were outside a little while ago and asked where you were. I said I had no idea so they shot off to a pub I wouldn't wonder but they'll be back this afternoon, you wait and see. You're hot news Bentley my boy. Also, a further report concerning your head gardener."

"Not Rawlings, surely?" Bentley replied wearily, looking upon his friend in apprehension.

"Yes, Rawlings. Well he turned up half an hour or so ago, entered the lodge house and offered unwelcome advice to my lads which didn't go down too well and he was told to sod off in no uncertain terms. He didn't like it at all."

Bentley offered a hand in gratitude. "Good, well done Chuffer, that'll teach him to keep his long nose out of things in future I hope."

Chuffer pointed at the gathering outside. "The crowd seems to be growing Bentley. Look, as I'll say once again, my boys will ensure the gates are locked and secure for the remainder of today. They will let your visitors enter and close up behind them but their day ends at 5.00pm my friend so following their departure, all security is back in your hands, as for me," he glanced upon his watch, "I'm off. Half a day to earn my pay as they say, huh," he laughed with pleasure. "I just thought of that Bentley, good eh, the brain still functioning, not bad for an old boy eh?"

"Yes, very good Chuffer, very poetic, worthy of a Wordsworth, must be catching Chuffer."

"Always good to see you Bentley. If you're wondering where the workforce is at present they are in the lodge stripping old pipe work and fittings, redundant boiler, bath and such like, in readiness for future replacement."

"Sounds good Chuffer."

"And Bentley, sorry I'm a bore but one more thing before I retire to The Three Mariners for a welcome drink. A firm of very high repute based in Portsmouth will begin work on the gates on Monday working with the smartest technology available in gate management so I'm told, so we are well on the move and that said, so am I. Will you be joining me at The Mariners Bentley, my shout?"

"No no, another day Chuffer, as you know, I have visitors to welcome remember?"

"Oh yes, sorry of course you have, sorry old chap, perhaps the mind is going after all." he laughed. "Right, I'll pop into the lodge and tell the lads of their responsibilities concerning all occurring this afternoon, remind them once again of the incoming visitors. What time Bentley, remind me?"

"4ish Chuffer."

"That's right, 4ish. Right, job done. Now, let's see if I can emerge from your excited crowd of admirers without a fatal injury eh? Bye Bentley."

"Bye Chuffer, thank you."

With a wave to the crowd outside Bentley headed up the driveway. Reaching the courtyard he was confronted by a stone-faced Rawlings parked under a large chestnut tree, cigarette in hand, seated upon a silent motor mower. "Ah, there you are governor, I thought for a minute you'd gone to the pub and forgotten it's my pay day."

"No, Rawlings, not forgotten," Bentley sighed reaching for his back pocket. "Here you are, all there, no need to count it."

Rawlings shook his head in disagreement. "I shall check it gov, mistakes are made in life, not always intentional." Double-checked, satisfaction evident, Rawlings reached for the ignition.

"Er, before you go Rawlings."

"Gov?"

"Your lad, Nigel?"

"Yes gov, what's he been up to, not a problem I hope?"

"Yes, somewhat. I've been informed that I'm paying for his day at college every Thursday, is that correct?"

Rawlings shrugged his shoulders displaying little concern "Er, yes, in a roundabout way gov, yeah, your good missus put you in the picture has she?"

"No, she has not but let me inform you Rawlings, I may be fortunate enough to have deep pockets but the news that I am paying for a student's education is not on. How long will he be at college may I ask?"

"Couldn't say gov, I should think a couple more years at most, summat like that."

"And I'm to pay for it am I?"

"Well, it was your Mrs's wishes gov when I first come here," the gardener replied dismissively.

"Well, we'll leave it at that for now Rawlings, there's something I want you to do as soon as possible. Stop what you're doing, not that you're doing anything at present Rawlings."

"Well I was waiting for you governor, it's pay day," he insisted.

"Yes alright, we'll leave it there for now. Forget what you have planned, I want you to go to the barn now."

"You may remember the weather at this time last year Rawlings, or you may not of course, but as I recall it was pretty dismal, so the terrace was stripped of its finer less resilient garden furniture and stored in the barn. Now what with this fine spell of weather, it's time for its return. I have visitors this week as I'm sure you're aware so if you don't mind pick it up within the hour before their arrival and lay it out upon the terrace please."

"Ah right, so one minute I'm taking the furniture in for storage next I'm bringing it out. What a farce, I'm not a labourer," Rawlings snapped, "I'm a horticulturist."

"A gardener Rawlings."

"Yes, a gardener, what it says."

"Exactly Rawlings, there's the connection. A gardener and garden furniture, part of your horticultural responsibilities so unless you wish to offer your immediate resignation Rawlings, which I shall very sadly accept immediately of course, I should get on with it please."

A response to his arrival unforthcoming and the hope of a warm greeting dashed and with his patience exhausted, a slightly irritated agent left the courtyard behind him in hope of human contact. He was quick to embrace the enchanting view unfolding before him, the English country life at its finest, a rich jigsaw of manicured grassland and mature flowerbeds stretching as far as the eye could see. Captivated by his surroundings he gazed upon the imposing structure of the grand house, transfixed by its tall ornate chimneys, numerous stone gargoyles set upon many aspects of engaging brickwork all gazing down upon a high stone terrace. A final brushstroke completed a magnificent picture of Victorian splendour. Although a man of substantial wealth himself, Sir William Wiggin's legacy of mid-19th century achievement invoked no small degree of envy. Lost in appreciation of all that lay before him he was momentarily unaware of the threatening behaviour of an approaching figure brandishing a garden spade.

"Oy you, get off my lawn, what you up to?"

Suddenly reconnecting with the modern world with a jolt, Maurice Gibbins raised his arms in appeasement and stepped backwards momentarily speechless.

"I said who are you, what you doing here?"

"I'm looking for Bentley Browne."

"Do you know him then?"

"Yes of course I do, I'm his agent, Maurice Gibbins."

"Ah, one of his mates are you, a few of you coming to party this weekend so I'm told."

"Well, I don't know about partying, more like a weekend's rehearsal I hope. Er, would you mind lowering the spade my friend, you're making me rather nervous."

A compliant Rawlings lowered his arms. "Sorry, one can't be too careful these days Mr Gibbins what with one thing or another."

"Oh quite so, I understand. Have you seen him today, your boss?"

"I have yes, unfortunately." Rawlings replied with a scowl. "He's gone to seed ever since his wife shot off on holiday, lost all signs of perspective in life he has." He pointed upon the terrace. "He's up there sunning himself, lazy bugger."

"Oh right, I'll get up there, thanks for your help, Mr er?"

"Rawlings, head horticulturist. My old man was head man at the Duke of Cumberland's place for many years, top man in his day."

Maurice looked around him. "Well, it runs in the family I would imagine, you do your father proud. May I know your first name my good sir?"

"Why?"

Well, so we can end our meeting in a gracious manner."

"It's Ernest," came the somewhat reluctant reply.

"Ah well, pleased to meet you Ernest, you've done a grand job on the manor grounds to my mind, very good indeed."

"Well, very kind of you to say so Mr Gibbins. Could I ask a favour?" He gestured towards the terrace. "When you meet up with your friend up there, sing this song to him would you, you being part of a pop group, should be easy for you, here it goes… ready…..

Dem bones, dem bones, dem dry bones, dem bones dem bones dem dry bones, dem bones dem bones dem dry bones, see the way of the Lord….That's it," Rawlings giggled. "He'll know where I'm coming from."

An amused Maurice nodded his head in acceptance of Rawling's request. "Well yes, I'll give it a go, mind you, I haven't got much of a voice but we'll see. I'll say goodbye to you Ernest."

"Alright then Mr Gibbins, thanks a lot."

With a wave of the hand to the departing gardener, Maurice climbed the nearest assemble of steps leading to the pinnacle of the terrace. Upon the top, he was greeted by a colourful array of garden furniture set out on the far-reaching stonework. Within its midst of many colours dressed in vest and shorts, a drink in hand seated beneath the parasol, Bentley waved his agent forward. "Maurice, my friend."

Approaching the musician Maurice greeted him with a mild rebuke. "Ah Bentley you old villain. Now tell me, why weren't you at the courtyard to greet me? No fanfare, no bunting, very disappointing and now once again I've had to come searching for you."

An apologetic Bentley raised an arm. "Sorry Maurice, the delights of an afternoon in the sunshine with a drink in hand was too hard to resist I'm afraid." Bentley rose to his feet. "Here my friend, let me get you a drink."

"A bit early for me Bentley, perhaps later." Shielding his eyes, he looked out upon his surroundings with much appreciation. "Wonderful, what a view, are the surrounding fields beyond the walls yours old chap?"

"Mostly Maurice yes but some belong to my neighbour of course."

"Well, very impressive Bentley."

Maurice looked up upon a clear blue sky. "Phew, another humid day Bentley. Er, would you mind if we went indoors for a while, it's far too hot for me."

"What! Maurice, please! A few days of sunshine and you're complaining? Tut tut, some people. Grab yourself a recliner and join me under the parasol. Are you sure you won't have a drink?"

"Oh go on then, a small one."

Joining Bentley under the parasol, he breathed a sigh of relief. "Phew, that's better."

"Go on then, tell me where it is." Bentley insisted.

"Tell you where what is?"

"The luxurious mode of transport of course."

"Bentley I told you. I parked in the courtyard expecting you to welcome me there not to find you encamped on the terrace. As I have remarked, it was very disappointing for me."

"Oh well, I do apologise Maurice. Didn't the lads at the gate tell you I was to be found on the terrace?"

"No, they did not, mind you; I didn't have time for a chat as they were too eager to shut the gates behind me. Outside there's a gathering the size of a football crowd," Maurice remarked smugly. "An award for good publicity eh Bentley?"

"Your doing no doubt Maurice?"

"Who else Bentley, who else?

"So, where are Syd and the others, any sign of them?"

"Ha, listen to this Bentley, you'll love it. When I pulled up outside the gates I was behind Syd funny enough, he was driving his ice cream van, can you believe it, no Rolls Royce to be seen."

"What, you're saying…"

"Let me finish Bentley please. Yes, he arrived in his ice cream van. Anyway, he looked out of his window, saw me behind him, raised a thumb and waved me by, parked up onto the grass verge near the gates with the crowd moving aside and clapping their hands. He raised his hatch, rang the bell, and started selling ice creams to an excited crowd. You wouldn't believe it, they couldn't wait to get a cornet, he must be making a fortune, well hopefully not as much as our vinyl sales, eh Bentley," he laughed.

"Well Maurice, at £3.50 a cornet he won't be far short."

"Don't you dare Bentley, we're onto a winner with vinyl, trust me, trust me."

Drawing his chair closer he addressed Bentley in rather serious mode. "Your gardener Bentley, I just ran into him, odd sort, somewhat aggressive isn't he?"

Bentley nodded in agreement. "Yes, yes he can be. What did he say then?"

"Well nothing much, more grumpy than anything, implied you were losing it Bentley, mind you, if I'm honest, living in a place like this on your own with wife away must be very challenging, very lonely and all, I don't think I could cope myself."

Bentley shifted in his seat somewhat uneasily, "Well, no problem for me Maurice, I'm a bit of a loner. We do have a full time housekeeper but unfortunately she's away recovering from surgery, back soon I hope."

"Well, if it were me Bentley I'd have a permanent staff looking after my every need."

"Yes, many have said the same Maurice but I have it in mind for changes in the coming months. I shall look into it. Any other comment to make my friend?"

"Oh yes, as you ask." Maurice laughed. "Your gardener insisted I sang part of a song to you."

"Oh yes," Bentley sighed, "and what would that be

pray?"

"Right, here we go Bentley. *Dem Bones, dem bones, dem dry bones, dem bones dem bones dem dry bones, dem bones dem bones…"*

"Yes, right oh Maurice, I get the point, I know what he's up to thank you very much."

"So it connects does it Bentley?"

"Yes, he's trying to wind me up Maurice. Now can we move on, perhaps enjoy an hour's sunshine?"

"Ah yes, before that Bentley and before Syd sells out of cornets and turns up with the lads, let's engage in serious discussion. Do you mind?"

"Must we?"

"Well, yes, before the chaps arrive. Let me outlay my plans for the next few days Bentley, see what you think."

"Does it make a difference what I think Maurice? Have another drink."

Maurice shook his head in slight annoyance. "No thanks. Now listen Bentley, this is what I hope to do."

"Go on then, tell me all Maurice."

"Right, first of all Bentley, this evening, we shall run

through a few of our songs, see how we stand together after all this time apart." Maurice pointed at the half-consumed bottle of wine. "Today is not the day for a booze-up Bentley so take it easy please, tomorrow night perhaps after a day of full rehearsal, agreed?"

"If you say so Maurice."

"I do say so Bentley. Of course, as you are well aware, we will not be accompanied by other musicians and amplification will be very limited this weekend, also the day we perform at the fete we will all appear very humble, offering entertainment in its simplicity with no unseen background accompaniment, sound or amplification that you might hear miles away. No fireworks on stage either." Maurice paused in thought. "Mmm, if I can find one that is," he mused. "Oh well, our music will be a lot quieter, Moonrock Rumble with no studio enhancement of sound so you might struggle a little."

Bentley nodded in agreement. "So be it, we'll get by Maurice, we'll get by."

"And," Maurice continued, "you shall be performing for a limited period, no more than an hour in my opinion, then enough, away. What we need is full publicity this coming weekend because what we are after is not a long-term return to show business. You don't want it and the lads don't want it. It's about as much publicity as we can muster leading to the nationwide sale of our new vinyl recording, hopefully encouraging worldwide sales, I hope so anyway, then a return to retirement for you and the boys with full pockets. I myself," Maurice looked around him in further admiration of his surroundings, "shall buy such a place as this I think, although larger of course with much more staff, or perhaps purchase a further residential home in Monte Carlo, I'm not sure at this moment in my life but I shall continue with my business, I'm still comparatively young unlike others," he sniggered.

"Yes, thank you Maurice, thank you."

"Just a joke Bentley, just a joke. If I may continue old chap, I have spoken with a few influential associates within the entertainment business, so the coming few days should produce a wave of publicity so be prepared Bentley, keep a smiling face in public, OK my friend?" Maurice beamed in satisfaction. "I have done all I can at the moment to promote the little white lie that we are appearing at the fete without payment, which indeed we are, but I am also saying it's a one off in support of Barton Village life. Should the emergence of our vinyl release come into conversation at any time, I shall deny all knowledge of its birth and so should you Bentley and the boys if ever questioned."

"A bit deceitful Maurice, not so sure I like it." A

disapproving musician reached for his glass.

"Bentley, Bentley, all show business is based on deception my friend. How many so-called top star celebrities, A listers, whatever you call them are worth a fag packet? One in ten Bentley, believe me, one in ten, mind you, you of course are top drawer, worth at least a packet of twenty cigarettes my friend, only count that with Syd and the boys of course," the pair laughed knowingly in unison.

"Yes, yes." Bentley looked at his watch. "Good God, it's 4.15pm, shouldn't they be here by now Maurice? I'll have to get up at the lodge; the workforce will be away soon, I'll have to get up there now."

"Remain seated Bentley, I'm on my way. Hang on, someone's ringing." Maurice reached for his phone. "Hello?"

"Hello Maurice, it's me, Angus. Stormy Norman is with me. Just to let you know, we shall be there within fifteen minutes, ok? Hopefully to be greeted by an open bottle. See you soon."

Maurice raised his phone in triumph. "There you are Bentley, modern technology, instant communication, you should embrace it, it is 2019 you know, not 1860. Right, I'll get up there now to greet them, hopefully Syd will be ready to come inside having sold enough ice creams to afford a holiday on the Isle of Wight.

All we need is bass guitarist Nobby Funnell who I'm hoping will be along soon and then we'll be up to a full house again, meantime Bentley, give the drink a miss my friend and return to the manor to give the lads a greeting when they arrive, ok?"

Bentley rose to his feet somewhat unsteadily. Standing to military attention, he offered a salute of obedience to his agent. "Yes skipper, whatever you say skipper, I'm on my way."

CHAPTER 25

A Return to the Limelight

With a hectic weekend finally reaching closure and normality returning to the manor house following the departure of all visitors late Sunday evening, Bentley awoke the following day to a change in the weather with many days of continuous sunshine replaced by heavy clouds and drizzle. With no need or reason to embrace the dismal outside world in any fashion whatsoever he returned to the comfort of his bed, biscuits and a mug of tea in hand. Although the memory a little blurred he engaged many thoughts of the past 48 hours, a weekend of surprising pleasure, most memorable to mind, Sydney, entering the manor house triumphantly waving a large collection of bank notes in the air, confirmation of his business acumen selling ice cream cones to the many excitable fans gathered outside the gates that afternoon. Further warm thoughts uppermost in mind was the impromptu rehearsal set up that evening within the imposing great hall overseen by a buoyant Maurice seated high up upon the opulent grand staircase witness to an immediate reconnection between five aging musicians of immense talent back together again in a familiar world of their own.

After several hours of intense rehearsal, bringing

much satisfaction to all concerned, the musical reunion was brought to a close by a delighted Maurice. "Well done boys, or should I say old chaps. Wonderful stuff, a few cock ups but swiftly recognised by you all and put to right. A magical few hours but we don't want to overdo it tonight do we? We shall return tomorrow with the promise of even better to follow I'm sure, so gentlemen, I suggest we retire to the luxurious motor home stationed within the courtyard for a little relaxation and a drink perhaps, in moderation of course. We shall have a full day's rehearsal tomorrow chaps so don't forget, a good night's sleep is essential but tonight we shall conclude a fine evening gathered around the TV set. No, no, before you protest, not a cooking programme but to observe the 10 o'clock news in which I promise you we shall feature highly, trust me now, come."

Retiring to the motor home and its many comforts his promises were confirmed. Both ITV and BBC ending their worldwide news items with coverage of several features concerning the band's return to the limelight with much emphasis centred upon the group's arrival at Barton Manor for the weekend's rehearsal, there to be greeted at the gates by an effervescent Maurice Gibbins, also, Syd Mitchell receiving much attention filmed at some length. The top attraction for many, waving from the open hatch of an ice cream van, offering ice cream cornets to the many onlookers at a 10% reduction in price. Maurice Gibbins, standing within the dense crowd, was approached by Lily Barnfield, a young feisty left wing reporter from the BBC.

"May I ask you Mr Gibbins, as manager of one of the world's most famous groups, a few pertinent questions?"

Always quick to respond to any form of publicity, a buoyant Maurice waved her forward. "Of course my darling. Ah, I see it's you Miss Barnfield. Yes well, ask what you want if it isn't of a personal nature my dear."

"As if I would Maurice, as if I would. No, what puzzles me my sweet is that you are the manager of one of the world's most famous musical groups about to perform after many years in hideaway and chosen retirement yet you choose to make a comeback and perform in Barton Village of all places instead of a major venue such as let's say, Hyde Park, Glastonbury or the Albert Hall. It just doesn't make much sense to me and why may I ask come back at all. Short of money are we Maurice? Also, I'm given to understand there will be just the five within the group so I'm somewhat mystified as to how you hope to reproduce your most famous recordings live without sufficient backup, meaning further musicians etc, huge amounts of amplification and you will be stuck in the middle of a field surrounded by a crowd of noisy country bumpkins," she laughed. "Excuse my sense of humour but I am driven by honesty for the truth in life."

Her choice of words, invoking a little hostility from the many village locals present, an ever relaxed and assured Maurice stepped forward quietening the uneasy crowd with calm assurance, his reply to the searching probe receiving much applause.

"Hopefully on the day my dear we will be received with an abundance of goodwill and appreciation by all present upon the green. You speak of lack of presentation, glamour, sound effects, lighting, further supportive musicians. My dear lady, we are going back to basics, raw simple honest music played by a group of first-rate musicians. We are reforming this coming weekend for a one-off support of quintessential English village life and all it offers. That is my word on it. Now forgive me but I must move on, time is of the essence, we must press forward with a little rehearsal this evening so please forgive me. In the words of Vera Lynn who reached her 100 years of age not long ago, we'll meet again, don't know where, don't know when."

With a wave to the crowd, Maurice slipped behind the manor gates. Following close behind him was Syd, receiving a roar of approval from the crowd. Joining their band mates, the two headed up the drive towards the manor house accompanied in sound by a rendition of Moonrock Rumble. Finally the news item came to a close to be followed by a weather report, a time reached where all retired to bed.

With a sigh of immense pleasure at all recollections that morning and with the time approaching 9.00am, as there was no change in the weather, Bentley, intent upon a further half hour upon the bed received a phone call.

"Hello, Friar Tuck's fish and chip shop, how can I help you?"

"Bentley please, I have little time to suffer your idea of humour my man, it's me, Alice. I'm ringing to inform you that I shall be popping into the manor house this morning within the hour so be prepared."

"Oh, why so my precious, why would you pay a visit so early in the day, if indeed at all?"

"Well, let's say I am very much aware that you have had visitors at the manor, as indeed does the whole world I imagine after all the TV coverage this weekend. God only knows what your good wife will make of it all; still, we shall put that to one side for the moment at least. My instincts tell me that the manor house will be in need of care and attention following the departure of your fellow band members. I will be accompanied by my dear friend Melody; we shall conduct a survey and respond accordingly to what we find."

"Please Alice, no need," Bentley protested, "all is fine here, everything in pristine order I assure you."

"Bentley please, I am a woman and you are a man. Over the weekend, you received a visit from a noisy group of men to stay there a couple of nights. Experience tells me it will be in one hell of a pickle. I promised your dear wife I would keep an eye on you until she returns; it is my duty to fulfil. We shall be there within the hour my dear."

"Oh well, if that's the case I shall await your arrival and the delightful Melody of course with ill-concealed delight Alice."

"And so you should Mr Browne, so you should."

Somewhat aggrieved at the rapid change in events compelling him to leave his bed without delay, Bentley left the manor house behind him within 30 minutes. Approaching the main gates with little sign of activity to greet him apart from two men dressed in white overalls seated within the confines of a large white van emblazoned with the words, "The Sharp Brothers, Worldwide Electronic Communication at its Finest." Across the driveway, an open ditch displayed many cables prohibiting easy entry or departure. Engaging two men in the van in conversation, Tom Rudd, spotting the arrival of Bentley, left them to continue their coffee break in peace greeting his employer with a warm welcome.

"Morning Mr Browne, good to see you sir, bit of a miserable start to the day unfortunately."

"Yes it is Tom, bit of a change eh." Bentley gazed upon the damaged driveway. "What's this, preparation for a third world war invasion from Putin's Russian Empire?"

Tom laughed. "No, not quite Mr Browne. A slight problem with modern technology. It's all set up for the final tests on the gates but there's no response so we've had to dig down again, no problem though, should be filled in so I'm told within the hour hopefully," he gestured towards the lodge house, "when the boys have finished their tea break that is but it's not a problem for you Mr Browne is it? I hope not."

"No, no problem as such Thomas but I was hoping for a drive in the countryside and perhaps finish with a short spell of golf to help me clear my head after a very hectic weekend, but however, I shall take a stroll across the green, weather permitting. Between you and I Thomas, I must disappear for a few hours so should you be approached by two females asking any questions regarding my whereabouts you have not seen me, ok?"

Tom tapped upon his nose displaying a knowing grin. "Your word is my command major; trust me, not a word sir. Oh by the way sir, that rubbish outside from your many fans, we shall clear the lot of it up within the hour. Trust me, when you return it shall be a pleasure to the eye sir."

"Not really your responsibility Tom, I'll get Rawlings to do it."

"No, me and the lads will do it, leave it to us sir."

Bentley approached the gates peering through with some hesitation. "No-one approaching is there Tom?"

"Not that I can see, no."

"Right, I'll get off. Do they still open manually?"

"Yes, let me help you."

Making his way through the discarded cartons, plastic cups and bottles then crossing the B2019, he approached the open green keeping to the tree lined outer edges out of sight of the many council workmen working close to the parish church. Avoiding the wider reaches surrounding the village pond and thankful of no sign of two formidable females crossing the village green, Bentley emerged from behind the cricket pavilion opposite The Three Mariners.

Across the way, Albert, sporting a colourful apron with brush and pan in hand was determined to return the outside area set aside for smokers to pristine order. Catching sight of his friend's approach, he raised his arms in dismay at all that lay before him. "Look at this Bentley."

"Don't blame me Albert, I wasn't here last night."

"Ha ha, of that I'm well aware my friend. Here Bentley, take this would you?"

"Yes of course." The landlord handed over two ashtrays to his friend laden with butt ends.

"If I had my way I would command many to take their rubbish home with them, cigarette butts, crisp packets, paper plates, you name it they leave it and it's a bloody disgrace. But, as I'm told by my dear wife, it would not be in the interest of sensible business acumen to push it too far." The landlord shook his head in dismay. "She is probably right." Carrying a further two ashtrays he joined Bentley outside the marquee holding one of them close to his nose. "Here, smell that Bentley."

"You are kidding me?" Bentley protested.

"Marijuana my friend."

"So, what's new?"

"True, but guess who was sitting here last night?"

"No idea, I was in a world of my own elsewhere but you're about to tell me Albert."

"Your gardener Bentley, Rawlings, he was seated here last night."

Bentley laughed. "Are you suggesting there's a connection Albert?"

"I am yes, I had to book a taxi and send him back to Lower Barton, the man was a pain."

Completing his task, Albert headed inside The Mariners. "Come on Bentley, time for a coffee on the house my friend."

Once seated in their most favoured spot overlooking the green, coffee close by, Albert rested his head in his hands. "Phew, I'm warn out Bentley, also are some of the staff. We were packed out last night; the restaurant even ran out of French fries," he laughed, "the first time ever. The daughter nearly had a seizure; there so many customers in you couldn't move, all in hope of seeing you and your fellow musicians celebrating your reunion seated at the bar. It was manic, I didn't get to bed until 2.00am this morning so I'm glad there's a change in the weather today if I'm honest. It's a blessing, a chance to relax, perhaps we won't be so busy," the weary landlord raised his head, "still, that's enough of me complaining my friend, what about you, how did your weekend go? I heard you mentioned on TV yesterday several times, never actually saw you being interviewed, always seems to be your agent, not you, why is that?

Slightly irritated Bentley reached for his coffee. "It's more to his liking, what he's paid for; I prefer to do my talking on stage Albert."

"Tell me Bentley, that reporter on TV last night, the young woman, she had a point when she asked why you are to appear at an obscure village fete and not Glastonbury or such like, er it is a little strange."

A somewhat evasive Bentley gazed out upon the village green offering no explanation. "Ah, weather's improving Albert."

"Is it, yes. Well?"

"Well what?"

"Why the village green and not Glastonbury?"

A further irritated musician viewed Albert with dismay. "Oh you'd have to ask Maurice, he's the brains behind the outfit, now can we move on please?"

"Sorry old chap, to be honest Bentley, if it all goes ahead on Saturday and the weather remains pleasant, I honestly don't know how we will cope with expectations and that is PC Willoughby's prediction as well. He was in last night, spent half his time chatting up my daughter, wasting his time thank God. He offered his opinion on the forthcoming gathering, expressing in no uncertain terms how he would enforce the law regarding parking and traffic movement should it prove necessary," Albert shrugged. "Whatever that could be, what with the publicity on TV, press and local radio, the village will be swarming, still," Albert raised a smile, "business will be good, Council Chairman Patel will be delighted, I bet he's rubbing his hands in glee at the prospect. Also, I've just remembered something that may amuse you. That so called musician and comedian Art Nouveau popped in last night and had a few words, you do remember him?" Albert laughed.

"Who could forget him, what did he want?"

Albert looked around him before answering with slight hesitation. "Well, he threatened me with court proceedings. Keep it to yourself though Bentley, I haven't even told the wife. He wants his money for that night of, well, disarray. Can you imagine? What a cheek eh? He said the girls deserved payment, they did no wrong and neither did he. He protested over and over again saying his entertainment was well valued and if payment was not received by next weekend he would start court proceedings. In the end I walked away and said I was far too busy to listen and told him to put it in writing."

"Well, best thing Albert is to keep it to yourself for

the time being." Bentley gazed out upon the bar area. "If I may say so, it appears to me there's a shortage of staff on duty, summer flu perhaps?"

"No Bentley, I've given a few the day off, with pay I might add. They deserve it, we've had a very busy few weeks and they needed a break."

"Well, I'm impressed Albert, that's very generous of you."

"Not really, it's down to you Bentley. People arriving in The Mariners night after night hopeful of seeing you somewhere within the bar. You are partly responsible for our good fortune as I've said before, many times my friend, although we do happen to provide damn good food, hospitability, real ale and we are fast approaching top ten recognition as one of the most of successful country inns and restaurants in England, that is a fact Bentley, take my word for it," Albert concluded smugly.

"Yes, yes I'm sure Albert, I'm in total agreement, you have a lovely place. Also may I say, as I glance across at the clock on the cricket pavilion, time is approaching midday. What about a whiskey, on the house?"

"My pleasure Bentley, my pleasure and when I return I have further news that may interest you, hold on my friend."

Returning to his seat of comfort within a minute, two large whiskies in hand, Albert displayed much eagerness to resume the conversation. Drawing closer to Bentley, he pulled upon his arm. "This my friend will interest you, I have further news concerning your gardener."

"Oh God, not more surely Albert?"

"Ah, there is much you should know Bentley."

"Go on."

"Well, you ask anyone who was in last night who came into unfortunate contact with Rawlings and they will agree with me that the man was off his trolley. He was in early evening, grabbed a seat at the bar and informed anyone prepared to listen about the discovery of a pile of human bones dating back to the 18th century discovered, guess where?"

A weary Bentley took a sip of his whiskey. "No idea Albert, where?"

"In Barton Manor, your home, suggesting a massacre of sorts he wouldn't stop talking, then, listen to this, he implied that you had it in your mind to turn the manor house into a first class hotel, a spa and retreat for the wealthy only, suggesting you were in mind to install him in the lodge house, the one being renovated by our friend Chuffer Rudd where there he would be confirmed as head of security, now what do you say to that Bentley?"

Bentley gazed up to the ceiling somewhat speechless."

"Well, there's not much I can say Albert, so any more to come to give me grief?"

"Yes there is, plenty. After a couple of pints, he left the bar to sit outside in the smoking area, there to cause mayhem. I was called out several times to calm him down. He was potty, would not stop laughing, giggling, hugging and kissing everyone, well all within touching distance, men and women alike I must add, though that didn't go down too well I can tell you, particularly with the women," he laughed, "kept bursting into song, repeating, what was it, *"roll out the barrel,"* yes, roll out the barrel and such like, in the end I had so many complaints I sent for a taxi, as I think I told you but here is my main point Bentley, what I was referring to earlier on, cigarettes. As I helped him into the taxi the smell on his jacket was undeniably weed Bentley, then this morning, when you arrived as it happened, I was picking up butt ends where he was sitting and I think, without a doubt, this proves a connection, don't you agree?"

"Yes Albert, without question, I've picked up on his behaviour several times myself."

"You have?" Albert addressed Bentley with some concern.

"Of course. I've spent a lifetime in show business Albert. Part of life for many, an unmissable aroma."

"But he's not in show business Bentley, plus he's rather an old chap to be a junky, surely?"

"No, not really Albert, in my time I've seen it fortify many of all ages, an escape from everyday reality."

"Have you used it Bentley, you must have been tempted at some point, showbiz and all?"

Bentley shook his head in solemn denial. "No my friend, never smoked, never wanted to, my weakness is an occasional scotch as you're well aware."

"Occasional Bentley?"

"Well, perhaps a little more at times I concede. We all have a weakness or two Albert, what would be yours?"

Albert thought long and hard. Finally leaning forward he addressed his friend in close confidence. "Pork scratchings Bentley."

"Oh my dear friend, a terrible addiction, you have my sincere sympathy."

"Thank you Bentley, your concern is most welcome."

"Think nothing of it Albert. Any other interesting tittle tattle for my concern?"

"Er yes, I suppose this would interest you. Your friend, the freelance reporter from The Portsmouth Echo was in last night hoping to find you and the band like many others within my welcoming establishment. She was very disappointed of course not to find you, mind you; she was soon jotting down a lot of Rawling's garble. I would not be surprised to find it a main feature in The Portsmouth Echo at some point mid-week my friend."

"Oh terrific, that's all I need, thank you very much Albert, I'm feeling a lot better."

"Doing my duty as a landlord Bentley, village gossip. Now, how about a further whiskey to soften the blow?"

"Er no, make it a pint please Albert, it will last longer and so will I, I think, it's going to be a long afternoon."

Re-joining Bentley at the table after some delay, two pints of the very best ale in hand, Albert offered an apology. "Sorry Bentley, somewhat caught up in things, we appear to be getting busy again." He gazed out upon the green. "Also, the weather seems to be on the change, the sun is breaking through somewhat and," Albert pointed at the bar, "the place is filling up unfortunately. I need a break but we are a little short staffed due to my generous nature so," Albert raised to his feet again somewhat reluctantly. "I must be off

Bentley. Oh by the way, I've just spoken to Catherine, she would welcome you to the restaurant with open arms, your presence would be more than welcome my friend but if you want to make it happen make it snappy, she is getting very busy."

"French fries on the menu I trust?"

"Most certainly Bentley, yes."

"Good, count me in then. I'll finish off this pint of best bitter and head for the restaurant, many thanks Albert, I've enjoyed your company, part of it anyway."

"You're welcome Bentley, cheers my friend."

"Cheers Albert."

Time fast moving forward, a well-cared for, content, slightly inebriated musician rose to his feet bidding farewell to those seated close by, his departure once more unfortunately subject to many requests for a selfie, a cause of a some delay. Finally, with a wave goodbye, leaving by the back entrance, he was greeted by a further change in the weather that day, a return to cloudless skies and warm sunshine, as predicted by Albert. Following the familiar pathway to the manor and noting much progress made in preparation for the forthcoming village celebration. Large swathes of grassland manicured and many acres of village green cordoned off awaiting forthcoming occupation by quintessential modes of outdoor entertainment. Approaching the manor gates, he found much to please him. The unwelcome rubbish had been removed from the perimeter and all returned to pristine order. To his further delight, the open trench was refilled and gravel re-laid accordingly. After a few brief words with the workforce, Bentley continued on his way. A somewhat theatrical free-spirited musician followed the long winding driveway, his rather unsteady preamble a cause of much amusement to Thomas Rudd and his departing workforce. Entering the manor house with caution, immediately conscious of the overwhelming aroma of freshly cut flowers positioned in many corners of the imposing hallway, encouraged by the silence with no sign of activity and the possibility of an undetected arrival growing by the second, Bentley removed his footwear, crossing the recently polished oak flooring on tiptoe. Entering the library and locking the door behind him, he raised his arms in triumph. His wishes of escaping an encounter with his formidable housekeeper growing by the second, the musician gazed upon all the familiar surroundings with much relief. Intent upon remaining in silent solitude tucked away in the library for the remainder of the day, crossing the room intent upon locking a further point of entry from the adjoining billiard room, all hopes were dashed coming with the triumphant call from the open doorway.

"Ahh, got you Bentley, made it home at last have

you?"

Entering the library and taking to the nearest armchair, lack of patience evident, arms folded tightly, her features a picture of cold disapproval, she addressed Bentley.

"So, it is you is it, you made it back then?"

Having little choice but to accept he had reached his point of surrender, Bentley adopted a conciliatory pose with a heavy heart.

"Er yes, I think so Alice, good to see you, how are you old fruit?"

"Old fruit, please Mr Browne, a little more respect, I am your guardian angel."

"Yes, yes of course, my apologies my angel."

"That's better Bentley. Now, sit yourself down and please keep quiet if you can, your good wife would like a few words with you."

"My wife? Really? Returned home has she? Nowhere to be seen my lovely, not a sign of Melody either, where is she, making me a welcome cup of tea I hope?"

Alice reached within her shoulder bag for her phone. "I would say you've had enough to drink for the moment Bentley, now please, I was about to call your wife, as for Melody, she has returned to the vicarage, her husband has a christening to attend to in Lower Barton and he cannot drive for a further few days. You may recall he was involved in a fracas at The Mariners a few weeks ago, you were there I recall. If you were ever to attend a church service Bentley at St Michaels, you would notice his difficulty in climbing the pulpit. He has to address the congregation seated on a canvas camper chair, poor man. You have no idea Bentley how us Christians suffer. Now please, some silence."

Rising to her feet, she handed Bentley the phone. "Your wife Bentley."

"Hello, is that you Bentley?"

"Mmm yes, could be."

"Don't tell me, you've been drinking," adding with a heavy sigh, "what's new?"

"Well just a little my love, just a little social gathering, you know how it is."

"Yes I do Bentley. Now listen if you can. I have concerns relating to many things and the answers I receive will influence my decision concerning whether to return home within the week or prolong my holiday and file for divorce, the ball is in your court Bentley, you hear me? Bentley, do you hear me?"

"Er yes, yes I do indeed my cherub, yes, I didn't quite catch all you said, I'm putting my socks back on."

"What? Putting your socks back on, what is that meant to imply, what are you up to Bentley?"

"Changing my socks my love, that's all, now what did you say earlier?"

"Good God Bentley, you're getting worse. Let me get straight to the point. I am given to understand that you intend to disregard my profound wishes and return to show business. Is that to be yes or no?"

"Er, neither my love, neither."

"How can that be so please Bentley, yes or no?"

"If you will let me explain Christine please. I am responding to the wishes of my agent for a limited period only. You remember him, Maurice, you recall the name I trust, having met him on many social occasions in the past my dear."

"Of course I do Bentley, who could forget him, overdressed, pompous….I shan't say it."

"Yes, well many would agree with you no doubt, but please let me continue. What the pompous old so-and-so has in mind is to reform the group for six months at the most, hopefully to receive monumental publicity during this period of time whilst releasing unto the world a compilation of our most favoured recordings on vinyl, hopefully leading to worldwide sales that will enhance our bank balance by a substantial sum my sweet, thus enabling us to join the super, super rich. I am sure you would love a bolthole in Monte Carlo, a yacht in the harbour at your command my sweetness, also what would you say to perhaps a place of rest in the Bahamas perhaps?"

"Yes yes, all sounds very, well, acceptable Bentley but the manor house, what would you do with that?"

"Sell up my love, sell up when all the renovation is completed of course, then we get a good return. So there must be a compromise, it won't be right at this moment, must plan ahead you understand but..." Bentley trailed off into silence, loss of words evident. Finally, much to his relief, Bentley received a warm response.

"Well, I'm lost for words if I'm honest Bentley, the promise of a move from that Victorian monstrosity fills me with delight, I'll not deny it and the prospect of a move to Monte Carlo with my own yacht captain and crew, well, wonderful, Monte Carlo here I come. What can I say? However, I want you to bear this in mind Bentley, should you change your course, digress in the slightest, you know where we will end up, don't you?"

"Oh yes, undoubtedly my sweet, on the rocks."

"Yes Bentley, on the rocks. Right, on that high note I shall leave you my love, six months then we sell up and head for Monte Carlo. Oh Bentley, wonderful. I do miss you so much Bentley, mind you, I must have it in writing. Oh, I've just been told I must go my darling, the captain requires my presence at his table. Take care, bye, bye, I'll keep in touch."

A relieved Bentley returned the phone to Alice. "Well there you are Alice, who'd expect that, I've won the lottery."

"Oh really, how much have you won?"

"Well, not sure of the exact sum Alice but I'll let you know. Now my dear, join me in a drink?" A buoyant Bentley reached within the drinks cabinet.

"No thank you Bentley, not at the moment. Are you going to tell me or not? What did your good wife have to say, I'm intrigued?"

"Yes, I'm sure you are Alice but it's a private matter between my wife and I and it's not for others to know, even your good self my love but I'm sure you got the gist of our conversation, the look on your face says it all, however, there is no imminent divorce I shall say on the cards at the moment at least, thank God." Drink in hand, Bentley returned to his housekeeper's side, reaching out to her in consolatory fashion. "I'm sure my good lady will tell you all when you next phone her no doubt, to keep her well informed of my latest misdemeanours for which I offer no apology. Right, a spell on the piano I think."

Turning abruptly, Bentley's passage was halted by a forceful poke in the stomach. A little sensitive to his comments the housekeeper adopted a rather well rehearsed familiar aggressive expression. "I follow your words Bentley with great interest, however, I make no sense of them. I speak to your wife on many occasions for which I make no apology. I am fond of you both and have some concern for your future relationship but I have no wish to be the cause of any underlying discord between the two of you, I am certainly not a gossip, I have no reason to defend myself. When I last spoke to your good lady, last night as it happens, I made no reference to the latest tale circulating village life relating to a pile of human remains discovered recently in the manor grounds, your manor grounds, your home Bentley for which of course you must be aware but say nothing."

Bentley turned to the piano. "I say nothing of this because I know nothing," shrugging his arms in dismissal "all news to me Alice, I have not been informed of such a discovery I can assure you."

"What? Nonsense Bentley, you must be aware of the discovery on your property?" An incredulous housekeeper struggled to her feet. "Human remains discovered by your head gardener and you're unaware of it?" Alice shook her head in a further display of disbelief. "Your gardener was in The Mariners Sunday night so I believe, concerned about bones he had come upon buried in the garden, he was in quite a state by all accounts, could have been the shock of his discovery I suppose," she nodded thoughtfully "and you had no idea, I just can't believe it."

With a further dismissive shrug of the shoulders and barely containing his amusement, Bentley returned to the drinks cabinet. "Well in all honestly I have had a lot on my mind these last few days. Perhaps, as you say, I have been informed of the grim reality but with the recent rehearsals and work on the gates and lodge house I've put it all to one side, my memory lets me down from time to time. Rest assured I shall seek Rawlings out tomorrow and have a word. As a matter of interest Alice, have you seen either of my gardeners this day?"

"Yes I have as it happens Bentley, caught sight of them lunchtime heading for their work hut I suppose for a wholesome cup of tea perhaps, unlike your good self eh Bentley?"

"Quite true Alice, quite true." Bentley nodded in acceptance of her words. "Now what about you. Fancy a small gin and tonic my dear?"

"No thank you Bentley, I must get home, my Bunny will be waiting for his tea, likes it on time my man does." Alice reached for her shoulder bag. "If I'm honest Bentley I must confess the manor was not as bad as I had anticipated, your visitors must have behaved themselves."

"Although we found plenty to do I must admit, dusting etc. I changed your bed sheets by the way, all nice and fresh up there. Right, take care, must go, can't keep my Bunny waiting any longer. One other point Bentley before I leave, what is this talk circulating that you intend to spend a small fortune to transform the manor house into a five star hotel for the rich and famous? Do you know what, for once I agree with you Bentley, you may have a point, this house is far too large for the two of you, I know it's a stately home, not quite as large as many I've seen, but still in need of a full-time staff to care for you. There are areas of this building I have never even set eyes on and never will thank God. Perhaps your wish is not such a bad idea after all. Right, I really must go, my Bunny awaits, would you unlock the door for me Bentley please?"

"Of course Alice." Once out within the grand hallway, Bentley escorted his housekeeper to the porchway. "Many thanks Alice, good to see you but may I proclaim in all honestly my dear I have no intention of turning Barton Manor into a first class hotel for anybody, it's a fallacy perpetrated by my head gardener, all down to wacky baccy Alice."

"Wacky baccy, what are you talking about now Bentley? You defeat me. Take care my good man, the Lord takes notice of all our comments and inner most thoughts releasing them to us all on judgment day, be warned my dear."

Nodding his head in weary acceptance of her departing few words, Bentley returned to the library, there to receive a phone call from Maurice.

"Bentley my friend, just to let you know I'm on TV tonight, BBC2, 7 o'clock. They wanted you, they were very insistent, but I was adamant that it was me they have, not you, not your scene, they could take it or leave it and they gave in, wonderful eh, 7pm, BBC2 tonight. Right, to business Bentley. You do recall us all getting together a few days ago and discussing our big day out this coming Saturday, do you? No misgivings I hope?"

"No no, I'm fine with it I think. Look, go through it once again Maurice will you, just to be on the safe side, remind me Maurice."

"Good God Bentley, you are a pain, now listen my friend, I have to be out this evening, I have an engagement with a rather lovely young filly, so listen please, this is what we are going to do. We, the group, shall all arrive at the manor house Friday night. Once again, I shall be bringing the mobile home for all to sleep in and of course, that does not include your good self Bentley. The following day mid-afternoon we shall load up with our somewhat limited musical equipment, in your case not a grand piano Bentley, I'm afraid you'll have to bring one of your smaller versions. Right, once all aboard we shall leave the gates behind us and head for Barton Green, you follow?"

"Yes, so far Maurice, thank you."

"Right. Reaching the cricket pavilion, we shall park up alongside. A large area of course will be cordoned off. Naturally, there we shall unload, carry it all to the pavilion, set up ourselves on the veranda, very humble of us really don't you agree? I mean in days gone by we had lots of assistance of course, done by roadies eh Bentley. As you know, I am in constant touch with Council Chairman Patel. Several of his sons and many associates will be there to greet us, help us unload, security so on and so on. Just think Bentley, you will be performing on the decking of a First World War army barracks, now a cricket pavilion of course but, what a rich history old boy, what say you?"

"Er well, really Maurice, don't you think it's a little degrading us setting up ourselves after all these years of much acclaim and roadies etc? And here we are, good God unloading and setting up. I'm not really happy with it."

"Bentley, Bentley, it's back to basics old chap. We are displaying a little humility, good for business, future vinyl sales you know, that's what it's all about Bentley. Come on, wake up old chap, we must sustain the illusion that we are reforming for a one off in support of English village life and of course, one shall also still deny any knowledge of the release of any vinyl compilations of our previous chart hits, you know the drill."

"Yes, but once again Maurice, why?"

"Why? Well it's in our best interest to sell records; it's a way of living old chap."

"Yes, I don't deny that Maurice, but we are musicians, why deny our knowledge of the vinyl production?"

An exasperated agent raised his voice in frustration. "Bentley, it's a sales pitch old chum, that's all. The very nature of our performance is unusual for such a well-known group. Hopefully it will bring us to the mind of many out there, not normally our fans, resulting in gigantic rewards over the sales counter, that's what it's all about, don't you understand, pure and simple, image Bentley, image, we are bringing it back to the people Bentley, we are humble royalty Bentley."

"Well, let's hope you've got it right Maurice and we're following the right path."

CHAPTER 26

A Day's Delight

The following day with the time approaching 7.40am, a restless and rather unsettled Bentley left the comfort of his bed earlier than usual that morning. Curtains withdrawn and standing at the open bedroom windows the musician was greeted by the certainty of yet another glorious day, much as promised by the BBC Southern news early hour broadcast that morning. Eager to embrace the outside world and determined to make the most of the day's promise, the musician was driven by an urgent need to visit the many far corners of the manor grounds, long neglected since his purchase of the property some three years since he was much aware that his life was approaching a critical stage and that the coming days could well be the final opportunity to pay such a visit. Showered, shaved and with breakfast behind him, he crossed the great hallway attired in suitable outdoor clothing of a straw hat, shorts, walking boots, a supporting walking stick and completed with a shoulder bag containing a flask of coffee and pen and paper. Halted in his tracks by a phone call from within the library, slightly impatient, irritation evident in his tone, the musician answered the call.

"Hello?"

"Hello, is that you Bentley?"

"Yes it is."

"Ah good, can I have a word or two?"

"Who is it?"

"Nigel Smethurst, entrepreneur, sausage magnet, your neighbour. Have you a minute sir?"

"Well, that is all the time I have at the moment Mr Smethurst, I'm on my way out."

"Oh Nigel please Bentley, we have met."

"Mmm yes, so I recall. Could you make it quick Nigel, perhaps a minute as promised?"

"I shall, I shall Bentley. I assure you, I will get straight to the point. I've heard much over the past few days suggesting the future of Barton Manor is in question. May I be so bold as to ask if that is so Bentley?"

"First I've heard of it," came a guarded reply.

"Oh right, perhaps I've got it wrong but rumours circulating the village imply you are in mind to turn the manor house into a five star hotel for the hoi polloi and super rich."

"Really? Well I repeat once again Nigel, that's the first I've heard of it."

"Oh right, in which case I apologise for wasting your time Bentley, however, whilst I'm on to you I trust you do recall our previous conversation we had a few weeks ago outside the garden centre? At the time, you were in no mood to consider selling me the Victorian greenhouses and adjoining land. My desire to own them is still very strong so my friend, should you ever change your mind, get in touch, money's no object," Smethurst laughed, "well within reason old chap. So what do you think Bentley, will you give it some consideration?"

Returning the phone to its place of rest without further comment the musician embraced the morning sunshine with gusto. Quickly into his stride, he was soon way beyond the barn and outlying buildings. Bentley explored many areas of rural landscape, much new to him. Most impressive was a dense overgrown apple orchard, the ground beneath each tree laden with countless yearly windfalls many the size of coconuts. Close by, a small but lush area of ancient woodland and there within its confines, a sizeable fishing lake, a legacy of Sir William Wiggins an avid fishing enthusiast at the time, finding it a necessary escape from the pressures of Victorian politics. According to village historian Alice Coates, the lake was conceived by Sir William. The tree felling, ground clearance and shape due to the willingness of many Barton Green villagers, the ambitious project taking a total of four years to complete. In return for their hard labour, a lifelong accessibility to fishing rights from Monday to Thursday, somewhat limited however during Friday and the weekend due to its popularity among friends and government officials close to the politician. In a gesture of goodwill however, Sir William released 7 acres of outlying manor ground to the village for recreational purposes and grazing rights. Confirmed in writing legally bound, the land was subsequently used for the purpose of village cricket, a delight for many village folk at the time and indeed to this present day. A long lasting gesture of good intent by the lord of the manor.

Coming to a halt at the water's edge, he was transfixed by his idyllic surroundings, an oasis of peace and tranquillity and was soon seated in comfort upon the edge of a reasonably secure corner of half submerged landing stage. With coffee in hand, Bentley reached for his pad and paper, intent upon writing down a brief outline of the present difficulties facing him in the hope somehow of clarifying his position and finding a solution.

At the top of the list, his major concern was the sales of the vinyl recordings should they fail to hit top mark, sales disappointingly low and not enough revenue to move to Monte Carlo and join the super-super-rich. It would be a source of such concern for his dear wife that the possibility of an expensive divorce would be high on the menu.

The second major concern. Would a divorce leave him destitute? No, far from it he decided, he could manage a divorce and still keep the manor house and his lifestyle. Did he in all honestly wish for a return to show business? After much consideration, he decided yes, perhaps the occasional gig, large or small, no problem. A little acclaim is always good for the soul, very much like the occasional scotch he mused, so maybe now and again, yes. Did he personally wish to go to Monte Carlo and join the super-super-rich? A gut feeling no thanks. He'd had enough of such a lifestyle years ago, so the answer would definitely be no, which in itself led to further questions that morning. Did he wish to leave the manor house behind him at all? Again, no. He had come to love village life and the general acceptance of his presence at the manor by the village population apart from, to be expected, a few oddballs. Wherever he went he was generally greeted with warmth and friendship by all, so no, he did not wish to move.

Many thoughts were also given to Smethurst's comments on the phone that morning concerning rumours circulating the village about the possibility of the manor house being turned into an exclusive hotel. Without a doubt, Bentley conceded that it was worth much consideration. The manor had plenty to offer and the transformation into a world-class hotel would re-open its doors to life and laughter. The renovation of the top floor, previously the servants' quarters, would be ideal living accommodation for the hotel staff and management, the middle floor with 18 en-suite bedrooms more than acceptable to remain as they were. The great hall, with some little alterations would provide much seating for evening entertainment. Billiard room, library, lounge and countless spacious rooms would provide relaxation for the many. An acre of enclosed vegetable gardens would be enough to provide many provisions. The stables done up and re-engaged with horses would be a delight to many and the fishing lake, admittedly in need of a little dredging, had much to offer. All that was needed was a little enterprise and hard work. The possibilities of turning Barton Manor into a world-class hotel was there for the taking, but only for the bold and brave. Could that be him he wondered?

Rising to his feet, his 4 hour adventure at a close and retracing his steps, every pace confirming without doubt his good fortune in the ownership of Barton Manor. Once again with the barn within sight and approaching the vegetable garden, the prospect of a gin and tonic seated upon the veranda the driving force, the musician almost collided with Rawling's grandson emerging from one of Smethurst's most desired fixations carrying a large bucket of freshly picked strawberries. Both caught unaware and both eager to continue upon their way without the wish or need to engage, the pair eyed one another with a little dismay. Suppressing a weary sigh, Bentley addressed the lad with good grace.

"Hello young fella, off to Wimbledon?"

The lad responded with a blank expression. "Wimbledon, why should I be going to Wimbledon?"

"Tennis lad, tennis, you're carrying strawberries."

"So?"

"Ugh, never mind boy, just having a joke." Bentley looked around him "No grandad?"

"Not here gov."

"No, I can see that lad. Is he around, I would like a word with him."

The lad pursed his lips, eyes focussed firmly on the ground. "No, he's not well."

"Oh, what's wrong?"

The boy raised his head to address Bentley somewhat reluctantly. "Er dunno gov, Grandma says he's been overworked lately, the hot spell and all that and he needs a break so they've gone off to Bournemouth to stay with my mum's sister, Aunty Faye. That's all I know Mr Browne." Avoiding further eye contact the boy bent down to address his boots, cleaning his toecaps. "Is that all gov, can I get off?"

A sympathetic Bentley nodded in agreement. "Yes course you can, that's alright. So, when do we expect your grandad back at work then lad?"

"Can't say gov, who knows with Grandad, he's been a bit odd lately," the boy muttered, "mind you, he's always been a little bit odd, Grandad, in my view."

"I couldn't possibly comment young fella. When do you think he will return, if ever, hopefully a little less odd as you say, any idea?"

The lad shrugged his shoulders dismissively. "No idea gov, when Grandma says so I should think, mind you, he is entitled to sick pay. Should it happen to me, come to think of it, I might fall sick and join him, a spell at the seaside would do me good, what say you governor?" the boy replied with a self-satisfied smirk.

An unphased Bentley retained his composure. "You're testing my patience to the limit young fella, that's all I have to say, now can we depart from discussing holidays in the sunshine and focus on the present. For a start, will you need help to cope in the future? Shall I get someone in to assist you, perhaps on a permanent basis to replace your grandad?"

The boy looked at Bentley in horror. "No, no I'm fine Mr Browne thank you, I can cope and Grandad will be back soon I'm sure. Oh before I go, I forgot to say gov, that chap Rudd doing the work up at the lodge, he was looking for you earlier, he said the village copper wanted a word with you."

"What?"

"That's what he said."

"How long ago was this?"

"Ooh, a couple of hours, possibly three, I dunno."

"Oh well done lad, thanks for telling me, why didn't you say so earlier?"

"Well, what does it matter, I'm saying so now aren't I?"

"Oh well, better late than never I suppose. Thank you, I'll get up there."

"Er, gov, before you go."

"Mr Browne please lad, what is it now?"

"Any chance of an increase in my wages. I'm in a sort of responsible position, well until the return of Grandad that is?"

Lost for words, Bentley addressed the youth firmly. "Sorry, you will have to speak to the lady of the house I'm afraid, she's the one in charge of finances my boy."

"Ah, but she's away on a cruise Mr Browne."

"Yes, the curse of holidays eh lad?" Approaching the manor gates Bentley was welcomed by a delighted Chuffer and his band of merry men.

"Bentley my friend, where have you been, we've been worried about you?"

"Here and there, here and there, exploring my surroundings Chuffer, taking note of my assets. Now then, what's the problem, what did you want?"

"No problem old chap, we're all finished. Gates are completed and in fine working order. The lodge stripped and updated, new boiler, radiators, heating, everything you can imagine and as required, all up to English heritage commands, demands, whatever you wish to call it. We need further guidance of course on re-decoration etc, but for the moment, we're there. Let me show you the gates in operation Bentley."

The next half hour was spent in the endless appreciation of the silent effortless gate movement at the press of a button. "There we are Bentley, all yours," Chuffer pointed towards the lodge "within the lodge, awaiting your security team and control boards. All set up and ready to go."

"Yes, many, many thanks Chuffer, now then what about constable Willoughby, I believe he's been here this morning, what did he want?"

Chuffer and his lads burst into laughter at the mention of the constable's name "Ha-ha, what a.... I won't say it Bentley." Chuffer put a finger to his lips. "The constable said he had received information regarding the findings of human remains at the manor house so we showed him the pile of orthopaedic limbs in the lodge and it left him rather speechless, eh lads? He left the premises without a further word about them. You should have seen his face Bentley, a picture of dismay."

"Yes I have Chuffer, many times unfortunately."

Overcome by a brief fit of laughter, Chuffer turned away. Finally, merriment under control, he returned to Bentley's side. "Sorry Bentley, forgive me, what I was about to say was Constable Willoughby touched upon the forthcoming fete expressing concern regarding traffic movement on the day, health and safety being a top priority of his. He said he was in mind to enforce a one-way traffic system throughout the village, adding the point that further additions to his problems that day were a group of old age pensioners brought in to provide afternoon entertainment upon the village green that would make further movement very, very difficult." Chuffer looked at Bentley with a little amusement "Sorry for the disclosure Bentley, his words, not mine, isn't that right lads?"

Displaying much amusement and nodding in

agreement, with a final wave goodbye the workmen climbed aboard their respective vehicles preparing to leave the premises. With many theatrical gestures, Chuffer addressed the gates with pod in hand. All departures complete within a minute followed by immediate closure of the gates, the businessman returned to Bentley's side.

"There you are Bentley, job done. I'm sorry once again about Willoughby's comments, he's such a pillock."

"No problem Chuffer, if I'm honest I have some sympathy for him, he's spot on about the pensioners that's for sure," the musician conceded with a smile.

Bentley looked around him expressing much appreciation. "Thank you very much for everything, Chuffer, you've done very well, it's great. As for the pile of orthopaedics within the lodge, I shall get in touch with the National Health governing body and see if the limbs are of any use to them, if not, I shall request Rawlings to bury them in the garden, rather ironic eh Chuffer considering the rumours he has spread concerning them, that he could end up disposing of them."

"True enough Bentley. How you put up with the man I shall never know. I've heard him many, many times standing at the bar, a little merry one could say, telling many untruths, a few of them to your detriment my friend. I would have kicked him out long ago if he had worked for me."

"Yes I know what you're saying Chuffer, but despite his failings he's a good worker, reliable, knows what he's up to, most of the time anyway and for reasons unknown to myself, I tolerate his delight at causing mayhem and disarray wherever he goes, it's in his bloodstream, his spirit of life I suppose. I have no major problems with him, I can live with it. He thinks I don't know what he's up to but I do, from selling manor house garden produce to Patel at the corner shop, spouting many untruths concerning the manor house and mis-information that he was going to move into the lodge house as head of security. He keeps my mind active Chuffer just trying to keep one step ahead of him."

Chuffer looked upon the musician with some bewilderment. "Ah, he wouldn't last a day with me, but we are all different my friend. Ah, here Bentley, take the pod before I forget to give it to you."

Handing over the gate control unit Chuffer pointed at the lodge. "As I have said, it's all set up inside for you should and when the security team move in but until then you have complete control of entry and exit my friend. Oh, I forgot to say, you have a further sack full of mail delivered today within the lodge, you must be a very popular person Bentley. Also, a further point of interest, your housekeeper delivered many bags of groceries, toilet rolls, washing up liquid and God knows what and said she will be fit enough to return to work starting from Monday. Hopefully she'll see you before but she's not going to bet on it, not with the busy weekend that you have in front of you. Right. So that's it, I shall get off. Oh, one more thing, I've got a mind like a sieve." Chuffer reached within his pocket to produce a further key. "Key to the lodge house Bentley, take it before I forget. It's all locked up and secure and the windows boarded up, take a bulldozer to get in."

Bentley dismissed the offer without question. "No Chuffer, you keep it, I want you back Monday morning first thing so we can discuss a further work schedule for you and the lads. I have a hectic weekend in front of me as you can imagine so shall we say 10ish Monday morning, here at the gates?"

"Yes, fine by me." Chuffer agreed.

"Meanwhile Chuffer, I'll see you at the village show on Saturday I hope?"

"No, not me Bentley, I'm afraid not, far too old, it's going to be mayhem in the village on Saturday, at my age who needs it. I shall take a trip to Bletchley Park, I'm a keen fan of English heritage and I always have been. I'm fascinated by that place and its war effort and association, so hopefully I shall return to find the village life back to normal, almost anyway. Another further point before I go Bentley, this week's Portsmouth Echo, have you read it?"

"No, should I?"

"You should old chap, there's an article about you, I'll drop it through the gates tomorrow." Chuffer teased. "It mentions you and your many marriages and seven children which was complete news to me, I've never head you speak of them at all."

"Well I've had no reason to Chuffer," came a firm reply.

"True Bentley, true. Do you see much of them old chap?"

"Only when they're short of cash Chuffer."

"Four boys, three girls, is that right?"

"It is yes."

Chuffer looked at the musician with some surprise. "You appear rather reluctant to discuss them Bentley?"

"Do I, uh, it's not a problem Chuffer, it's just that I was not the best father to them, always out and about or on tour most of the time. When each marriage collapsed as they did, the ex-wives had the children, as they should, that's life my friend, however, I do get to see them occasionally and now and again I get a birthday card and a phone call, all I deserve really."

"Well that's not quite how they put it in the paper Bentley, you come in with much praise old chap but right now, looking at you, I can see you're becoming slightly irritated. You give the impression of someone who's swallowed a tadpole my friend, I'll get off."

A slightly contrite Bentley offered an apology. "You may have a point Chuffer, past memories and all that, however, I will say that the tadpole was rather tasty."

"I believe you Bentley, others would not. Right that's it, time to go."

Chuffer climbed into a smart Range Rover pointing at the gates. "Bentley, I don't know if you've noticed it but there are several dozen of your keen admirers outside the gates eager to get in so make sure you lock the gates safely behind me with your new electronic magical fob, right I'm off. So long my friend."

Ready to collapse upon the nearest sun lounger after his trek into the wilderness having taken its toll, Bentley returned to the manor house. There, within the porchway, he was greeted by two large shopping bags laden with groceries and attached to the double doorway, a note tucked in place behind a large brass knocker.

"My dear Bentley, where would you be without me? You have run out of everything except whiskey of course. Please ensure all

foodstuffs is put away in the correct manner, I've had no time today to ensure so myself because my toyboy Bunny and I are away for a romantic weekend to celebrate our engagement, yes our engagement. I know what you're thinking Bentley. I shall return Sunday evening to resume work on a permanent basis at the manor house the following Monday, much to your good wife's relief I must add. Please ensure all is neat and tidy within the manor following the weekend visit from your associates, God help us. I have a bill in hand Bentley to present to you for the sum of £47.10 for which I shall expect payment in cash, no Euros please. I shall enter the door on Monday at 9.00am. Make sure you're up and about. Goodbye. With love, your saviour."

Much relieved at being spared a trip across the green to Patel's corner shop that afternoon and escaping the certainty of being inundated with demands for selfies by the many camped outside the gates, a tired Bentley spent the remainder of the afternoon upon the sun lounger with a gin and tonic close to hand.

Taking to the library early evening to embrace a spell of television, he retired to his bed early that night to sleep a solid eight hours.

Lunchtime the following day, Bentley received a phone call from Maurice to reaffirm that he and the musicians would be arriving that evening as previously arranged.

With the entire afternoon spent preparing for their

arrival, his housekeeper's purchase of many foodstuffs the previous day was a lifesaver. The musician was up at the gates late afternoon to receive his visitors, their passage through the gathering crowd no problem, the gates closing behind them at the touch of a magical button.

After a successful rehearsal within the great hall that evening followed by a short get together in the motor home, alcohol very much restricted, all group members took to their beds long before midnight as instructed by their agent Maurice.

CHAPTER 27

D Day

Saturday, another day and a cause for celebration perhaps with a return to public acclaim hopefully in sight. Hopes running high with excitement rising and a tight rehearsal coming to a close approaching midday and a small luncheon to follow finished, the group of musicians split up, each mentally preparing for that afternoon's performance in their own individual way, meeting up later for a quick hand of poker and a small relaxing glass of comfort.

Finally, the clock approaching departure time and with all musical instruments aboard the group were urged to take a seat within the motor home by a fired up Maurice.

"Come on lads, the new world awaits us, destiny calls above and beyond."

Taking to the wheel and soon beyond the courtyard up the winding driveway and within a minute coming to a halt facing the manor gates, they were greeted upon their arrival with loud enthusiasm from the many gathered outside. Bentley, seated at the rear, was urged to the front of the vehicle by an impatient Maurice to implement the opening of the gates to no immediate response. He was urged to try again by an amused Syd but once again to no avail. Witness to all failure, an irate agent rose from the driver's seat to urge Bentley out of the side door.

"Stop messing about Bentley, there must be an electrical blind spot somewhere, go to the gates and confront them face to face my friend. Approaching the gates with pod in hand the leader of the band's woeful efforts were greeted with much amusement by the many standing at the gates. Across the way, watching with some disbelief, an impatient Constable Willoughby holding back traffic on the roadside outside the lodge house in hope of assisting an easy departure for the band of entertainers. Finally, irritation growing among many motorists at the holdup, he was obliged to step back urging all traffic upon their way to cause further confusion. With still no response forthcoming at the gates, Bentley was joined by an explosive Maurice.

"What the hell are you playing at Bentley? Look, give it here."

Reaching out, a furious agent grabbed the pod, pressing it many times but to no avail. Joined at the gates by the rest of the group, their appearance adding to further laughter and cheers from the crowd with unease and embarrassment felt by all, Syd approached Bentley, pointing at the gatehouse.

"There's a way out of this Bentley, no problem. Let's

get inside the lodge and sort it out. Once inside we'll find the power board and there's bound to be a key close by for manual use should the gate power fail, it's mandatory I'm sure, let's open up and find it, eh lads?"

Nodding in agreement, all present turned to face Bentley. "Is the lodge house locked up Bentley?"

"Yes Syd, it is."

"Right then, let's get in, job done, no problem, move on." Syd looked at Bentley with some urgency. "The key for the lodge must be on your key ring, surely Bentley. If you haven't got it with you, that's alright, we'll return to the manor house, get them and return and enter the lodge, yes?"

A rather downbeat Bentley looked upon the crowd outside the gates with some foreboding. "Er no, afraid not Syd, it's not that easy."

"Why not, where is it? C'mon Bentley, the key please."

"Bletchley Park, have you ever heard of it Syd?"

"Yes of course I have, wartime, National Trust, what has Bletchley to do with the bloody key?"

"Good point Syd."

The End

Printed in Great Britain
by Amazon